I0721327

Cover Design: Jay Aheer
Editing done by Jenny Sims Editing4Indies
Proofing Julie Deaton by Deaton Author Services
Interior Design by Christina Parker Smith

Titles by Natasha Madison

The Only One Series
Only One Kiss
Only One Chance
Only One Night
Only One Touch
Only One Regret
Only One Mistake
Only One Love
Only One Forever

Southern Series
Southern Chance
Southern Comfort
Southern Storm
Southern Sunrise
Southern Heart
Southern Heat
Southern Secrets
Southern Sunshine

This Is
This is Crazy
This Is Wild
This Is Love
This Is Forever

Hollywood Royalty
Hollywood Playboy
Hollywood Princess
Hollywood Prince

Something So Series
Something Series
Something So Right
Something So Perfect
Something So Irresistible
Something So Unscripted
Something So BOX SET

Tempt Series
Tempt The Boss
Tempt The Playboy
Tempt The Ex
Tempt The Hookup
Heaven & Hell Series
Hell And Back
Pieces Of Heaven

Love Series
Perfect Love Story
Unexpected Love Story
Broken Love Story

Faux Pas
Mixed Up Love
Until Brandon

Jan, Layla, Lori, Mary, Natasha M, Sandy, Saraha,
Teressa, Yamina, Yolanda
I can't do it without you guys!

ONLY ONE

Chance

THE ONLY ONE SERIES

ONE

Layla

"You look like fall," Brian, my producer and sidekick, says as I walk by his office door.

Shaking my head, I laugh as we both walk down the hallway. "You look tired."

"Well, I was up late editing the segment I aired this morning on women's hockey growth in the US." His dark hand runs through his hair. "You still look like fall, though."

"What does that even mean?" I ask him, then look down at my outfit. "It's blue jeans and a navy blue blazer."

He shrugs his shoulders like any man who has no idea why he said what he said, but he did it anyway. "I don't know. Maybe it's the brown purse." I stop walking once I get to my office door. "Don't forget we have the Oilers' Manning and Miller coming in today to discuss the charity auction this weekend," he says before walking off in the direction of the kitchen while I groan out loud.

"I hate Miller," I grumble. Every time he's mentioned, I automatically think back to the first time we met. It was my first week at the station, my afternoon sports radio show, *Lay it on You*, was on the air, and the radio station was having a fundraiser. He showed up to the event looking equally charming and arrogant clothed in dark jeans and a tight T-shirt. When we were introduced, he told me that he loved my show, especially my commentary on hockey as a sport, being as it was underrated in the South. I was super proud of those first few segments. He'd touched my arm gently and not at all creepy, and he actually made me laugh at a couple of jokes, which is hard to do. We were talking, he was flirting with me, and to be honest, I was flirting right back with him. I stepped away for a second to go to the bathroom, and I walked out to find him tongue fucking a blonde against the wall. Ever since then, I've taken him at exactly face value. 'Make out with anyone literally all the time because you're not special, Layla' value.

Grabbing the handle to my office door, I open it, mumbling, "How could I forget Manwhore Miller?" The sun shines on the signed Dallas Oilers jersey I have framed in my office. It was from the All-Star game last winter. Framed pictures of some of my sports idols that I've taken fill the wall. I never expected to be a sports commentator; it happened by luck. When I applied for a job at the local college radio station, I thought they would put me to work on the marketing front, but instead, they had me calling the hockey games because the last announcer had quit that afternoon. It just stuck, and I fell in love with it. Hockey, sports, commentating—all of it.

Brian sticks his head into my office on his way to our recording booth. "Ready?" he asks. I nod my head, grabbing my stuff and following him down to where we do the show. He walks into his producer booth while I push open the door to where I sit. Two windows give the room a bit of light. I put my coffee and notes down on the table right next to the bottles of water there for my guests. Sitting in the chair in front of the microphone, I grab the earphone and put them on.

"Check the mic," Brian tells me from where he's standing in front of the soundboard.

"Check one, two. The XYZ TEAM sucks," I say, looking at him. He nods his head, then laughs, pressing a couple of buttons on his side. I hear the commercials play as I get into the zone.

"Ten seconds," Brian says, and this time, I nod at him as I watch the on air sign light up.

"Hey there, welcome to *Lay it on You*, the Layla Paterson show." I smile every time I say those words.

When I started at the station, I was an intern, and then they gave me a shot, putting me on from midnight to four a.m. I thought it was going to be dead air, but I had assholes calling in all the time trying to one-up me, and I have to say I got their sports trivia questions right ninety-nine percent of the time. Well, more like ninety-five. Thank God for Google some nights.

The ratings had never been better for my slot. When the afternoon radio show host went away for vacation, they gave me his time slot for two weeks. It was like I was the queen of the castle. I went head-to-head with the men who called in. I went toe-to-toe with the other radio show hosts who didn't want me to leave by the end of two weeks. When they finally gave me the afternoon spot, I was with them for ten years at that point.

"For those of you tuning in for the first time, I'm your host, Layla. And I have Brian on the command with me." I look over and wait for Brian to chime in. "Brian, I believe you owe me ten bucks." He groans. "I'm not going to say I told you so, but I told you so. I told you that Montreal was going to win." I mention the game played last night when the team lost six to four.

"Yeah, yeah," he says, shaking his head. "Let's take a call, shall we?" he suggests, patching through a caller.

"Hey, Layla, longtime listener of your show," the guy on the phone says.

"Thank you." I lean back in my chair. "What did you think of the trio last night?" I ask, talking about the captain and his two assistants.

"The loss was a hard one to take," he says, huffing out.

"Nothing hurts more than having a team come into your building and leave with a win," I tell him.

"They made mistakes last night, for sure, but I think Weber is getting better and better," he says of Ralph. "Stevenson is perfect each time," he says of Manning, the captain on the team. "And Adams?" He whistles. "The guy is on fire. I think this is going to be his year." I inwardly groan and roll my eyes so hard that they might get stuck. "His stick is hot."

"Yeah," I say, agreeing with him as much as I hate to, "I'll give it to Adams. He's on a four-game scoring streak, and he's at a plus six." I throw out the stats that I looked up this morning, hating every single second of it. "I mean, if he stays out of the penalty box, he really does have a chance to beat his record last year."

The caller huffs out as they usually do when I try to prove them wrong. "Mark my words, this is his year."

"Listen, I wholeheartedly hope that you're right, but …" I roll my neck. "They didn't look like they were a team last night. Montreal came in and handed them their behinds on a platter. It was brutal out there. Justin Stone scored his first hat trick of the season, and we are only in October. Dallas needs to get it together, or there's no way they're going as far as they did last year."

We answer additional callers for thirty more minutes. When we get a commercial break, Brian pops back into my headset. "Just got word from Becca." I look over at him. "Manning is out today. It's only going to be Miller," he says, and another groan escapes my throat.

Somebody out there hates me. They have to hate me. Miller has been a thorn in my side ever since he set eyes on me one year into his contract during that dumb fundraiser. He came from Chicago, and every single time he sees me, he goes balls to the wall to convince me to sleep with him or at least have dinner with him. And it doesn't matter how many times I tell him no; it just pushes him to crack me harder.

I've been around these players for a long time. I've

seen the trail of women they leave behind season after season, and I vowed early on to never be that woman. My cold coffee tastes even worse when I see Miller fucking Adams, top centerman of the Dallas Oilers—and a walking sex god, according to himself—walking down the hall.

Brian gets up and shakes his hand. The manwhore is wearing jeans and a black Dallas Oilers shirt with a leather jacket on. His hair looks like either he just ran his hands through it or someone else did for him. He looks over at me and smirks like a fucking asshole. I ignore the way my stomach just rose and fell. Shit, is cold office coffee bad for you? Walking into the room with his motorcycle helmet, he places it in one of the two empty chairs.

"Hey, gorgeous," he says. I lean back and vomit in my mouth.

"Layla." I say my name, and he looks at me. "You know, in case you forgot."

"I can never forget you," he says, grabbing the empty chair and pulling it out to sit in it.

"Since when do you ride a death trap?" I ask as I grab my cup of cold, gross coffee and take a drink, my mouth suddenly dry.

"I usually take my bike out when I want to clear my head," he says. "It's not every day you feel like you got ass fucked by a cactus." He mentions last night's loss, and I want to laugh, but the coffee goes down the wrong pipe, and I end up choking.

Air struggles to find its way to my lungs as I cough.

Miller comes to save the day as though he's some kind of hero by rushing around the desk and slapping my back. "Jesus."

Pushing his hand away from my back, I say, "Get away," between coughs. He continues to rub my back, and I shoo him away with both hands.

He grabs a water bottle and opens it, handing it to me. "Here, take a sip." I can't even argue with him if I tried. I take the bottle and take a little sip.

"We are back in one minute," Brian says, and I look up at Miller, who just stands there over me.

Uncomfortable concern sits in Miller's eyes. "You can go sit down now." I push him away. "You know that when one is choking, the last thing you should do is slap them on the back. That's for trick shots and squat challenges in the locker room." Throwing his head back with a laugh, he sits in the chair in front of me, then grabs the headphones tucked off to the side.

"Welcome back," I say when I see the on air sign light up. "You guys are in for a real treat today. Miller Adams stopped by the studio today. He's not here to talk about last night's game, that's for sure." I smirk at him. "I think you still have whiplash from Evan Richards skating by you." He just looks at me with fire in his eyes. "Don't hate the player, hate the game." I hold up my hands.

His laughter fills my headset. "I'm definitely not here to talk about last night." He shakes his head. "It was a hard one, and we weren't ready for them. But we need to give credit where credit is due." He doesn't even try to make excuses. "The good news is that we are still early in the season. The bottom line … we need to play better. Not just for ourselves but also for our fans."

"I can agree with you there," I say. "So tell us why you're really here?" I look down at the notes that I made.

"To convince you to go out with me?" There's that stupid smirk again.

"Not going to happen. Tell us about the Dallas Oilers' charity auction coming up."

"It's a great event that we do every year, benefiting the children's hospital." His deep brown eyes go soft as he talks. "We raised a little over seven hundred thousand dollars last year, and this year, we are hoping to double that."

"Is that why you are auctioning yourself off?" Brian says, laughing.

I swear, my head almost shoots off my body at his comment.

"I'm not the only one," he says, humor coloring his words. "We have six or seven of us who are up for our bachelor auction. So if you want to come out this week-end," he says, "there are still tickets available. Plus, the Oilers owner, Nico, sent me with a couple of tickets to give away." He reaches into his inside pocket and takes out a white envelope. Dropping it on the desk, he says, "So, ladies, polish off that checkbook and come and support an amazing cause." I swallow down the stupid lump forming in my throat.

"Well, ladies, you heard him. Come one, come all," I say with fake enthusiasm. "That'll wrap us up for the day. On behalf of Brian and myself, we wish you the best rest of your day and hope you'll tune in for our show tomorrow." My headset is making me hot, so I slide that off and set it on the table.

When Brian enters the room, he approaches Miller, who pushes his chair back, and they shake hands. "This has to be the first time I've met you without a woman or two draped over you." He laughs and slaps him on the shoulder. "I'll never forget that one time in Vegas—" Brian starts to tell the story, but I put up my hand.

"What happens in Vegas should stay in Vegas," I remind him, and he laughs, shaking his head as he walks out of the room.

Miller grabs his helmet. "So what do you say? You wanna come ride the pony?" He smirks at me. Always fucking smirking.

"I don't ride motorcycles," I say, ignoring his look. "I don't trust you not to be reckless with my body."

"I can promise you I wasn't talking about the bike." He laughs, and I look up at him with my mouth open. "See you Saturday, gorgeous," he says, leaving me to pick up my mouth when he walks out of the room.

TWO

MILLER

THE THREE TRIPS to see the tailor were definitely worth it because my black suit jacket fits like a glove. As I straighten the sleeves of my shirt, I admire the shine of the black cuff links engraved with my initials. And just like that, with a run of my hand through my black hair, I'm ready.

Walking out of my massive walk-in closet and past the great room, I make my way to the garage where my black BMW is waiting for me. As I'm pulling away, I look back at my house. Is it big? Yes. Do I need all this space? Absolutely not. But I plan on staying here for a long time. I want to bring my wife here and have my kids here. And every time I walk through the doors, it's so easy to envision. I mean, why the fuck else would I buy a five-bedroom, two-story house for one person? Soon after, I'm pulling through the gates of my community.

Never in a million years did I think I would end up

playing in the NHL. Did I want it? Yes. Did I think it was possible? *Nope.* I played hockey like any other kid in Canada. I was good, but I wasn't great. I started my junior year in the low category, but something just clicked into place that year, and I moved up to the higher level.

The coach of that team took a liking to me, and he introduced me to one of the scouts he knew. I was drafted one hundred and twenty-ninth overall to Chicago. It was exciting, but I had to be realistic. The chances that I was actually going to play for them were slim to none. So I went hard at school and graduated with a degree in economics and mathematics. Something that only got mentioned when I was on the cover of *GQ* one year. I got called up one game and, let me tell you, playing your first game in the NHL is a feeling you will never ever forget. The fans on their feet, cheering for the team. The rush of the game is so much faster than you can ever imagine, and I made the best of it. I went on the ice and skated my fastest, passed smartly, and when the third period came around, I scored the game-winning goal.

From that day on, I was on the ice with them, but when the summer came around, they traded me to Dallas. I was shocked and confused, but I was excited for the start. Now I've been here for eight years, and I'm one of the oldest ones on the team. I shake my head, laughing. *Old my ass.*

Pulling up to the arena, I park in my designated spot. I climb out of my car and then grab my phone to text Becca, my agent, and tell her that I'm here. Then I take a picture for my Instagram.

The picture is of me smiling, and the caption is:

This could be all yours. *Going once, going twice.*

Putting my phone away, I walk into the arena and see all the changes they made in order to get us to party here. The arena has been transformed into a ballroom with a huge black stage at the back of the ice. Seeing all the round tables situated in front of it makes it feel weird that I played on this ice yesterday. The tables are covered in white tablecloths with crystal standing chandeliers. People mingle as waiters and waitresses pass out food and champagne. I spot the bar right away and start my way there when I'm stopped by a couple of fans who are attending. I smile and pose for a picture and then finally bump into Manning on my way to the bar.

"Look at you, Mr. GQ," Manning, my best friend and captain of the team, jokes as he slaps my shoulder. He's been calling me that ever since I was on the cover six years ago. "You look dapper." I shake my head. He's the only man who stands six feet six and is built like an ox who can use the word dapper.

"We are wearing the same fucking suit." I point at him, shaking my head. "Let's take a picture together and put it on Instagram so we can do a poll on who wears it better." I slide my phone out, and he pushes me away.

"I don't do that shit." He's the only one who refuses to take part in social media. However, he's the first to help out or donate his time. "It's enough I have to put up with the pictures tonight from the press. I don't need you adding to it."

"I'll take a club soda," I tell the bartender, "with

lime." Looking over at Manning, who puts his hands in his pockets, I see the vein in his head start to pulse. When I see what he's looking at, I laugh. His wife is the social butterfly. She is in the middle of everything, schmoozing and flirting. "Whatever, man. You get to take her home tonight."

Manning looks around before he talks. "Don't remind me." He brings his whiskey to his lips. To the outside world, they are a perfect couple, but those who know him, know he's living in hell. I don't know when it happened, but she might be the devil. "She threatened to post on Instagram and actually created an account for me."

"Did you tell Candace? She'd be so pissed if you didn't become one of her clients," I say to him. "Don't look now," I tell him, seeing Candace and her boyfriend, Ralph, walking toward us.

"Boys," Ralph says when he gets close enough. He is quieter than some of our other teammates. He's fierce on the ice, but no one would call him the life of the party.

"You," Candace says right away, pointing at me. "Are you insane?"

"Me?" I ask her, confused.

"Do you know how many DMs you got because of your Instagram picture?" I look at her as she glares. "My phone has been blowing up. One girl wants to suck your dick for a hundred dollars."

"What?" I ask her, taking out my phone to check my comments and seeing she's right. "What is with all these women? Also, only a hundred dollars?" I ask, looking up and seeing Layla walking in. I swear my cock springs to action the minute I catch a glimpse of her bare leg through the slit in her long strapless black dress. Her long brown hair curled and swaying, she stops a waiter and takes a glass of champagne, smiling at him.

"Earth to Miller," Candace says. "You need to edit that post," she tells me, and I just hand her the phone.

"Don't click on my photos," I warn with a wink, and Ralph pushes my shoulder.

"Is the ring on her finger not enough to tell you that you can't flirt with her?" He looks over at Manning. "Can you believe this guy?"

"Yes, I can." Manning nods. "Do you not remember when we all got his dick picture?"

"That was on Snapchat." I throw my head back and close my eyes, thinking about last year when I sent it by accident. "It was an accident." They all laugh.

"What is everyone laughing about?" Layla says once she comes closer to us, and I see her holding a glass of champagne.

"The time Miller sent his dick picture to everyone on Snapchat," Candace says and then looks at me, then back at Layla. "You look amazing, by the way." I'm about to tell her that she looks gorgeous when I hear someone talking.

"There you are." I look over to see Manning's wife coming over to us. She smiles at the guys and literally rolls her eyes when she sees Layla and Candace. "Nico would like a picture of us," she says, looping her hand through Manning's arm. "Shall we?" He takes his hands out of his pockets, and she grips his arm. He walks away from us without saying anything.

"Why is she like that?" Layla asks.

"At least she never poured a drink over your head," Candace says, and Layla laughs.

"I thought you were going to throat punch her," Layla says, taking a drink.

"Okay, let's go spend some money," Ralph says, pulling Candace away to the silent auction items.

"And just like that"—I smirk—"it's just you and me, gorgeous." I wink at her, and she rolls her eyes.

"You're so gross," she scoffs, finishing her drink and placing the glass on a passing tray. She smiles at the waiter as she grabs another glass and downs half of it in one shot. "Oh, look," she says, pointing at a group of women dressed to the nines who are all huddled together, all holding drinks, and all looking this way. "Well, there you have it. Your harem has arrived."

"You know green is not a good color on you." I push away from the bar and go up to her. She looks down at herself and then up again.

"Are you color blind?" she jokes, and I see her just eye me.

"You're green with jealousy." I get closer to her as she throws her head back and laughs.

"Jealous?" She finishes the drink in two gulps, then leans past me. Her hair brushes across my face, and her smell gets my cock going again. "Of you?" She pffts as she grabs another glass and finishes it, then swaps it out for a fresh one before the waiter can get away. "At every single party we've both attended, you've left with a different girl each time." She laughs now. "Once, you left with one girl, then came back two hours later, and left with another one. I'd watch myself if I were you," she says as she passes my ear and then comes back. She motions with her head toward them and then laughs again. "You'd best be careful of them." She looks at them. "Those girls look like they stab holes in the condoms." I shiver. "The blonde looks like she can be a baby momma." I look over at the blonde who winks and then sticks her tongue out and rolls it over her lips. "I think that is her mating call."

"That is horrible," I say, then put my hands in my pockets. "Are you ready?"

"For?" She looks at me and moves just a touch, and I can see her long smooth leg come out. A leg that I'm going to hook around my hip right before I slide my cock into her.

"I don't know about you, gorgeous." I get closer to her, and I can see her swallow. "But I know how this story ends." I've been chasing her for the past four fucking years. Everyone I meet falls for my charm, but not Layla. She's hated me since we first met, and it kills me that nothing I do changes her opinion of me.

"Really?" She crosses her arms over her chest, pushing up her tits.

"Really?" I nod.

"Is it with you catching chlamydia?" She laughs. "Don't worry, I heard all it takes is four pills, and you'll be back to normal." She turns then and starts to walk away.

"Is that so?" She halts. "In my story, it ends with you …" Walking closer to her, I look around to see if anyone is watching, then my voice goes low. "Naked under me."

"Don't hold your breath," she says. She storms away from me, and I can see that I almost got to her.

"Just a matter of time," I tell myself right before the blonde comes up to me. Her Southern accent hits me right away.

"Well, hey there," she says with a smile, and I swear my cock hides. "I'm Darla."

"Miller," I say although I know that she knows this. "Are you having a good time?"

"Not as good as I'm going to have tonight when I take you home," she says. I can already tell she's a stage five clinger. "So tell me, Miller …" She comes closer, trailing her manicured index finger down my suit jacket. "What do you like for breakfast?"

"Um," I say, and then I step back so her hand falls, "if you will excuse me, I think I see someone I have to say hello to." I smile as I lie, walking away from her. I turn to my right, and my eyes meet Layla's. She is shocked that I caught her staring, and she turns her head away so fast I'm surprised she doesn't have whiplash.

"It's game time," I tell myself. For the past four maybe even five years, I have tried and failed miserably to get her to date me. But I was never a quitter, so I'm not going to start now.

THREE

LAYLA

MY EYES LOCK with his, and the smirk on his face is making my blood boil. So what if I was caught looking at him? It's a big room, and my eyes were just wandering. *No one who is that arrogant should also be that good looking*, I think to myself as I finish off another glass of champagne. Besides, every time I look around the room, I find him flirting with another woman. Each of the women hangs on to his every word and then pretends what he is saying is so funny, making me roll my eyes. I can just imagine which one he's going to slide out of here with. Just the thought has me taking another glass of champagne.

"A penny for your thoughts." I hear from beside me and look over to see Candace holding a glass of champagne in her hands.

"I was just thinking that I hate dressing up and that half these people are fake." I look around the dimly lit room, I mean arena. I'm still always shocked when I attend functions here, and it's not hockey. The wooden floor put over the ice, and the tables scattered everywhere so people can sit. "Actually, more like seventy-five percent of the people are fake."

"I think more like ninety percent of the people are fake," Candace says to me, taking the last sip of her champagne, and just like any great event, there is always a waiter there to take your glass and offer you another one. I down the rest of the champagne and grab another glass. "Did you drive here?"

"Negative," I tell her, taking a sip. "You didn't think I would attend this thing and not drink?" I smile at her. Ignoring the flutters in my stomach, I look around the venue again and spot Miller talking to yet another woman. Why the fuck do they flock to him? Fine, he's good looking—I'll give him that—but he's an asshole. Okay, fine, he's also not that. I think it's just because he's cocky. It's as though he knows he's good looking with his perfect hair and brown eyes some women have called bedroom eyes. And then you have the scruff on his face that surrounds his perfect lips and his perfect fucking abs. God, he's the most annoying person I know. He's been on my ass to date him forever, and the more I deny him, the harder he pushes. I know his type. He's after the chase, and once he gets it, I'll be just another notch on his bedpost. From the way people talk, the bed frame already needs to be replaced.

Candace takes a sip of her drink. "I will say that your dress is fucking stunning." She looks me up and down, and I have to admit when I tried it on, I knew it was made for me. The black dress hugs my every single curve, and it's almost like a corset by the way it brings in my stomach and enhances my hips. But my favorite part is the slit that looks like it goes all the way up to my hip bone but only goes to my upper thigh.

"Isn't it?" I take a sip and roll my lips. "By the way, nice dress." I wink at her, looking down at the tight black dress she's wearing. "That isn't the one you bought." I point out. When we went shopping, she got a green off-the-shoulder dress that was short in the front and long in the back. It was perfect for her.

"I know that, asshole," she hisses at me, making me laugh. Candace and I met at an event for the hockey team, almost like this one, four years ago. Her brother, Evan, was playing for the Dallas team. The two of us struck up a conversation and just clicked. Ever since then, we've been best friends. There is nothing I wouldn't do for her, and I know that if I was arrested or stranded somewhere, I couldn't and wouldn't be able to call her because she'd most likely be with me. "Ralph 'accidentally'"—she uses her two fingers as quotations—"ripped it when he was zipping me up." She shakes her head.

"That's fucking gross." I look at her. "And hot AF." I wink at her. "I was going to say you had that glow."

She puts one of her palms on her cheek right when Ralph comes over and puts an arm around her waist. "What are you two talking about?" he asks before leaning forward and kissing Candace, then taking a sip of his drink in his hand.

"I was just telling Candace she has the 'I just got fucked' glow," I tell him. He coughs, and I roll my lips to keep from laughing. I hold up my glass to him as he tries to catch his breath. "Good job." Candace throws her head back and laughs while Ralph tries not to choke.

"She does not have the glow. It's all the glam she did," Ralph finally says. "I told you not to put all that stuff on yourself." He starts to rub her cheeks, and she pushes his hands away.

"There is no glam," she tells him. "Now, did you bid on anything?" she asks him of the silent auction, and he just nods.

"Oh, I haven't gone to bid yet," I tell them. "I'll catch you later. Save me a seat next to you," I tell them and turn to walk toward the tables set up at the back of the venue. I smile to a couple of people I know, and I stop to talk to Nico, the owner of the team.

"Hey there," he says, leaning forward to kiss my cheek. Nico screams sex machine, and he doesn't even have to try. His demeanor does it all for him. He takes no prisoners and apologizes to no one. He inherited the team when he turned thirty and became the youngest owner of any team in the league. It was a shitty team, to say the least, but he dug his heels in and went out there. He had a general manager, but everyone knew that Nico did his own bidding. If he wanted you, he made sure you knew he wanted you. There was no middleman with Nico. "So glad you can make it."

"Oh, you know me," I say with a shrug. "Always ready to play dress-up."

He laughs now. "I can spot that lie a mile away," he says. "But seriously, I wanted to thank you personally for all the publicity you gave this event on your show." He looks down and puts his hands in his suit pockets. "It was good to listen and not get my ass handed to me."

It's my turn now to laugh. "I'm not that bad." He just looks at me. "Listen, I say what everyone thinks. The only difference is mine is broadcasted live."

"Yeah, I'm not sure it's a good thing," he says. "Anyway, go and enjoy and save your money. The live bachelor auction starts in a bit."

I try not to groan as I walk away from him to the tables. I go through the prizes—a signed puck, a signed jersey, a game in the press box, and four tickets to the All-Star game—and I bid on the All-Star game package, thinking that I could give it away on the air. I'm about to turn around when I bump into a hard chest. Male hands automatically grab my upper arms. "Careful, gorgeous." I hear his voice and groan, then move my shoulders out of his touch. "What did you bid on?" he asks, walking to the table and going through the sheets. "Oh, look at this." He picks up a sheet and flashes it my way. "A weekend away in a hidden cabin." He winks at me. "What do you say? You, me?"

"How secluded is it?" I ask him, and he looks down at the paper. "Like, is there a chance they will find your dead body?" I laugh, and he just shakes his head. He's about to say something else when I see a blonde walk our way. Her hips swing, and her tits bounce. "Incoming." I motion with my head in the direction she's coming from.

It's his turn now to groan. "Don't lie, you love all this attention," I say, and I'm about to walk away when the blonde steps in front of me.

"Miller." She sings his name, walking to him and getting chest to chest with him. "I am so excited about the auction." I roll my eyes and turn to walk away, but not before hearing her beg him to take her home tonight.

I put my empty glass on a tray and grab another one when I hear Nico's voice fill the arena. "Testing one, two." I look up and see that a spotlight is on him now. "Testing one, two."

The chattering stops, and the room goes quiet. "If I can get everyone's attention." I look around now and spot Ralph and Candace sitting down at a table in front. I make my way through the crowd and find an empty chair beside Candace. I sit down and look over to see that Manning is sitting next to me, and his wife just glares at me. I smile at her and wave, but she turns her head, and I see Manning roll his lips. "Please help me welcome our captain Manning Stevenson." The applause starts, and he gets up, and so does his wife, kissing him on the lips as though he won an award or something. He walks up the stairs while he wipes off his lips, and I giggle, which earns me another glare from his wife.

"How drunk are you?" Candace says, leaning into me.

"Not drunk enough," I say, taking another glass of champagne. "Cheers." I hold up my glass, and she grabs her own, and we click glasses quietly. I listen half-heartedly to Manning's speech about why we are here, and my curiosity has me looking around the room to see who else is here that I haven't seen.

I spot the owner of the station sitting at a table with a couple of the players and their wives. I look around and spot Miller standing with five other men on the side. Our eyes meet again, and this time, he winks. I roll my eyes and look away. *What in the hell is wrong with you? This is the second time he's caught you looking at him. And why are you looking at him?* It must be the suit or the champagne. "I think this champagne is not good," I whisper to Candace, who looks at me and smiles. "Can champagne go bad? Like, can it poison you?"

"No." She takes a swallow from her glass. "Tastes fine to me." She puts it down, and a waiter comes over and grabs the two empty glasses and puts two more on the table.

"Am I going to have to carry you into the house?" Ralph asks Candace.

I lean over Candace to whisper to Ralph. "Don't pretend you don't like drunk sex."

"I like drunk sex," Candace says, not in a whisper, making Ralph just shake his head. I sit up now, looking at the stage as they bring the bachelors on stage. They introduce a couple of the rookies, and then they save Miller for last.

"And it is my greatest pleasure," Manning says with a smile. "Introducing my assistant captain, or what I like to call him, Mr. GQ," he says. The applause starts, and a couple of whistles are blown as he walks onto the stage and shakes Manning's hand and then looks out into the crowd.

"He's so gross," I say under my breath, and Candace laughs at me. The bidding starts with the rookie first. The highest bidder is five thousand dollars. The second one goes for the same price, and the third one goes for just a touch more. They all stay under five thousand dollars.

"Now," Nico says, "it's time for the last bachelor of the night." The girls all cheer, and I look over at Candace, who laughs. "We are going to start the bidding off at—"

"Fifty cents." I hold up my hand, and everyone laughs, even Miller.

"One thousand dollars," one of the women on the side says, and Candace looks at me.

"Not worth it," I say, drinking another sip. "So not worth it." I look into the glass.

"Twelve hundred!" another woman shouts, and I look over at the woman who sits there with a huge smile on her face.

"Fifteen hundred," another one says.

"Seventeen!" one woman shouts from the back.

"Ohh, this might be a hot ticket item," Nico says, laughing. Miller just looks down and shakes his head.

"Two thousand," the first one comes back with.

"Do I have twenty-one hundred?" Nico asks.

Now the girl who sang his name before shouts out, "Five thousand dollars!" The crowd gasps, and Miller just looks at her.

"Ten thousand dollars," Nico says, pointing at the one who just shout out the highest bid, "Going once, going twice."

"Twenty-five thousand dollars!" I shout. The words come out of my mouth before I can stop them, shocking everyone, especially me.

FOUR

MILLER

THE HOT LIGHT shining directly on me is making me sweat. I hear the bids coming in, and my hand tries to loosen the tightness of my shirt. Why the fuck did I think this was a good idea? I mean, the only time I felt okay about this was when Layla bid fifty cents for me. God, that made me laugh, and for one second, I forgot that I was in the spotlight. "Going once." I hear Nico, and I swallow down the lump in my throat. I'm trying to tell myself that it's not the end of the world. It's a date one night for a couple of hours. What's the worst that can happen? "Going twice." Fuck, here we go. The worst woman I've ever met.

"Twenty-five thousand!" I hear shouted, and gasps fill the room. My eyes look at the table right in the front. I spot Ralph and Candace, who are both looking over at Layla with their mouths hanging open. Layla isn't even sure what is going on as she realizes that the words came out of her mouth. The other women look over at her, and all she can do is stare at me. The room erupts in applause and cheers. The other guys who were on the stage with me are now clapping their hands and laughing hysterically.

"Sold," Nico says, pointing at Layla. "That has to be a record," he says, laughing, and then looks at me. "For that price, you better go get that woman a drink." Everyone laughs, and I walk down the step toward her. *What is going on here?* I think to myself. What did she just do, and why? Why would she just do this? She literally hates me. I mean, she tells me this all the time. She's pushed me away at every single advance for the last, I don't know, four years, and now this? My head spins with all the questions, but all I do is paste a smile on my face.

I can't help but smile, putting my hands to my chest. "Be still my heart," I say, joking, and she groans. "That was so romantic, gorgeous. I knew there was something between us. I just felt it." I pretend to make light of the situation, but my head swims with questions. Why would she do this? Can she even afford that? My heart starts to speed up, thinking that she just might have wasted all her savings on me, and I'm not okay with this. Do I want to date her? Damn straight I do, but not if it's going to put her into debt. I'm going to go to Nico and just pay it off.

"Oh my God." She puts her hand to her mouth and then looks over at Candace. "What did you just do?"

"What did I just do?" She laughs at her friend. "What did you just do?"

"God." Manning's wife gets up. "How desperate can

one woman be that she has to buy herself a date?" She looks over at Layla with disgust all over her face, and I have to admit she might be hot as fuck in a totally fake way, but her attitude just makes her ugly.

"I'll give you fifty thousand dollars not to come home," Manning says to her and pushes away from the table. "Fuck, I'd give you a million dollars to never talk to me again." He walks off, leaving her with her mouth hanging open, and the four of us just looking at her. She straightens her shoulders and turns and walks away in the other direction.

"Well, that was weird," Layla says, grabbing her empty champagne glass and bringing it to her lips for the last drop. "I wonder if I won the All-Star tickets?" she says, looking around.

"Well, there she is." I hear Nico now and turn to look at him as he walks to the table. He holds out his hand for Layla, who smiles and takes it, and I want to hit his hand away, but instead, I put my hands in my pockets. "We need a picture of the happy couple. Twenty-five thousand dollars."

"About that," Layla says, now standing up. "How bad would it be if I took the bid back?" she asks, looking around.

"Take it back?" I say, shaking my head and laughing. "Now, why would you do that?" I start to panic, thinking that she'll take it back and I won't get my only shot with her.

"Because the thought of going on a date with you," she starts to say, and I look down at her hand still in

Nico's. I look over at him, raising my eyebrows, and he drops her hand. Now that her hand is free, she throws it up in the air. "The thought of going on a date with you," she repeats herself. "It's preposterous."

"You just bid twenty-five thousand dollars to go out with me." I point at myself. "Now forgive me if I'm wrong, but I think that just tells you how much you want me." I smirk. "At least twenty-five thousand times."

"Oh, I want you all right," she says. "I want you to go fly a kite naked over a cactus farm." She winks. Nico and Ralph both wince and put their hands over their junk.

"This is perfect." A woman comes over with a camera hanging from around her neck. "Could we get a couple of pictures of the big-ticket item with the woman who shut it down?" She smiles and then motions with her hand to follow her.

"If you don't go with her," Nico says, "she'll just come back."

"Fine," Layla says, then turns to Candace. "How's my face?"

"Gorgeous." I answer for her, then reach out my hand and pull her with me as I walk after the lady. I hold her hand, and to my surprise, she doesn't yank it away. The woman stands in front of a huge white banner that has the foundation's name on it.

"Now, if I can get both of you in the middle." She motions to us. "There is a little X on the floor. Stand there."

"Do we have to take the picture together?" Layla asks as I look down and make sure that I'm standing on the X.

"What's the matter, gorgeous, scared that the picture

is going to show that you really, really want me after all?" I smirk, which makes her glare. She puts one hand on her hip, and the way she cocks her hip, her bare leg comes out, and I finally get a look at those black strappy heels she's wearing.

"I'm afraid the picture is going to be exhibit A at my trial when I kill you." She tosses her hair over her shoulder and looks away. "You can get one with one of the backup bids." She points at the women who bid but lost as they gather to watch us. I pull her to me and wrap my hand around her waist, and I swear she fits perfectly.

"That is perfect," the woman says as she snaps two and three pictures. She takes the camera away and looks down at the pictures, and it gives Layla the opportunity to step away from my touch. I look up at her and see that her light brown eyes are bright and her cheeks are pink. "We need a couple more."

"You know," Layla says. "This is so much fun, but wouldn't it look better if all the bidders get in on the picture?" I watch her trying to talk to the photographer. "Girls, why don't you get into this picture?" She motions to the women who are standing around, looking at us. They put their drinks down, and I watch them make their way over.

"This is brilliant," the photographer says. I'm about to say something when the photographer calls my name. "Look over here, Miller." I look her way ignoring the women gathering around me as she moves the women around, and when I turn around, I see that Layla is walking away.

"Layla!" I call her name, and she turns around, wearing the world's biggest smile, and she honestly is gorgeous. Hands down more gorgeous than any other woman I have ever met.

"Sorry," she says. "My ride is here." It's her turn now to wink at me. "Have fun with that." She points at the women around me. "Take care, slugger." She turns around, making her way through the crowd.

"Slugger," I repeat the word and then look at the photographer. "You have one shot, so make it count."

She nods her head, and after she snaps the picture, I clap my hands together and look at the women. "Ladies," I say in my charming voice. "It has been amazing, but I have to go. There is a big game tomorrow, and I have to be in tip-top shape." Some of them moan, and I swear a couple of them pout. I nod to the photographer and walk away, spotting Nico first. He is standing there talking to Manning, and the two of them are laughing at something.

"Mr. GQ." Manning chuckles and slaps my shoulder. "Twenty-five fucking grand."

I shake my head and look at Nico. "Listen, if she can't afford it," I start to say, looking around to make sure it's just the three of us, and people aren't eavesdropping. "I'll pay for it."

Nico shakes his head, laughing. "She already paid it," he tells me, and now my mouth hangs down. "She also said she would double it if you let it go."

I laugh now, putting my hands in my pockets. "I'm going to triple it if she actually goes out with me." I look at Manning. "Time for me to get going."

"Thank you," Nico says, "and I look forward to collecting that seventy-five grand from you."

I shake my head, laughing, and head out, not making eye contact with anyone. I get into the car and text Ralph.

Me: Did you take Layla home?

I start the car and make my way home, a text coming through as soon as I put the car in park.

Ralph: She said to tell you it's none of your business.

I laugh.

Me: Tell her she owes me a date and to get ready. I'm going to collect it.

He answers right away.

Ralph: She said words I don't want to repeat, but none of them were nice.

Me: Good. Tell her I like it when she's feisty, and I'll call her in the morning.

I throw my head back when the phone pings as I'm getting out of the car.

Ralph: BLOCKED, BLOCKED, AND BLOCKED.

Layla, Layla, Layla. I shake my head, walking into the house. You played your cards well the past four years, but tonight, you let one slip. She wants me. It's time for her to admit it to me, and oh, am I going to have fun making her say it.

FIVE

LAYLA

HEAT HITS MY face, and then a light, maybe a flashlight, is shone on me. My eyes try to flicker open, but then the brightness makes me shut my eyes again and groan. "What in the world is that hammering?" I roll over in my bed to lie on my back. The banging starts again, and this time, I pry one eye open, or at least I try to, but then have to shut my eye again. I put one of my arms over my eyes to block out the light and try to swallow, and that is the first indication that last night was either a good night or a bad night. My mouth feels like there is a cotton ball stuck on my tongue, and I roll over on my side. The cool sheets hit my naked body, and now I turn over and stick out my hand while my eyes are closed to make sure I'm by myself. The pounding starts again. "Oh, God," I say out loud, trying to sit up, and the minute I do, the room spins, and I fall back down on my back. "I'm dying," I say to no one since I'm all by myself.

The sound of my front door opening and closing makes me open one eye as I hear heels clicking all the way from the front door. The sound comes closer and closer to my room. "Oh, dear God!" I hear Candace shriek. "Why are you naked?" Her voice goes high, and I wince.

"I can't do anything with you unless you close the shades," I tell her, and I hear her walking over and closing them. Only when I don't feel the heat on me do I open my eyes and see that she is dressed in tight jeans, a jacket, and heels. "Thank you," I tell her, and she just smiles and shakes her head, walking into the master bathroom. "What are you doing?" I ask her and groan when my head pounds again.

"I'm getting you something," she says and comes back with a glass of water and two Tylenol. "There you go." She hands them to me, and I take them and swallow down the whole glass of water.

"You're the best," I say, and she crosses her arms over her chest.

"Why are you naked?" she asks me again, and I look down at myself.

"I'm not naked," I tell her, and her eyebrows pinch together. "I'm wearing shoes." I pick up one foot. "Okay, fine, I'm wearing a shoe." I close an eye now and look around. The dress that I was wearing last night is lying across the floor with my panties right next to it.

"Why don't you put on a robe, and I'll go start the coffee," she says, turning around.

"I swear if I were into women, I would give Ralph a run for his money," I tell her, and she throws her head back and laughs.

"Except he has something you don't," she says over her shoulder.

"It's called a strap-on. I can have one just as big as him, if not bigger!" I yell after her and then wince when my head pounds. I get out of bed, unstrapping the only shoe I have on and walk over to my walk-in closet to grab my white plush robe. I slip it on as I'm going to the bathroom, and I take one look at my face and wince. "What the hell happened last night?" Grabbing a towel, I clean the makeup off my face and tie my hair atop my head.

I walk out of my bedroom and straight into my family room. When I bought this house, I asked my realtor for one thing. I wanted a cozy home. I wanted to be able to have everything on one floor. I wanted a huge family room for gathering, and that is what I got. I immediately went in search of a couch because everyone knows that if your couch isn't comfy, it's useless. I found the perfect sectional couch with deep seats and more cushions than it'll ever need.

I then got the table that now sits in front of it, and I spot the reason I woke up the way I did. "Who thought that was a good idea?" I walk over and pick up the empty tequila bottle and then see an Uber eats bag right next to my phone. "I can not be trusted," I say and look over at Candace in my kitchen that is right off the family room. A white island separates the two rooms. The smell of coffee now fills the room. "Why did I think it was a good idea to order?" I peek into the bag. "Three double bacon cheeseburgers," I say to her, grabbing the paper receipt that is hanging on the bag. "At one a.m.?"

"I need coffee," she says before she turns around and looks at me. I sit on one of the brown cushioned stools at the counter as she sets a cup of coffee down in front of me and then grabs her own. She takes a sip and then smiles at me, and I can see that she is dying to tell me something, but I just don't know what it is.

"Are you pregnant?" I ask her, taking a sip of coffee and waiting for it to finally seep into my veins and wake me up a little.

"I am not pregnant," she says. "And I will not get pregnant unless I'm married."

"You can still wear white down the aisle even if you have a kid." I point at her. "It's the twenty-first century."

"Good to know," she says and then leans back on the counter and puts her coffee cup down. "Now, let's talk about last night."

"Ugh." I roll my eyes. "Can we not? I don't even re-member coming home." I look around. "Like, how did I even get here?"

"I drove you home." She fills me in. "You did the whole mic drop when we walked you into the door," she reminds me, and the memories come flooding back. Well, some of them.

"You walked me into the house and didn't think to help me change?" I shake my head. "Some friend you are."

"You started singing 'I am woman, hear me roar.'" She points at me, and another memory is put into place, and I laugh.

"That is always a good song. That and 'No Scrubs.'" I take another sip of coffee. "God, how much did I drink at that event?"

She grabs her cup of coffee, and I can swear she is like a cat that ate the canary because she just looks at me. "I would say enough."

"Why don't they serve food at those events?" I ask her, and the doorbell rings. I look at her, and she just shrugs. "Well, you can't expect me to get the door. I'm naked." I use my hands to point at my robe.

She pushes off from the counter and walks to the door. I peek around the corner, seeing the man standing there with a huge bouquet. "How many?" I hear Candace ask, and then she gasps. "Fifty."

"Yes, ma'am," he says, handing her the bouquet, and she turns around and spots me standing here.

"You got flowers." She holds up the huge bouquet of red roses that she has in her hands.

I clap my hands together. "Ohh, I love flowers. There must be at least two hundred in that," I say. "I must have been pretty fucking outstanding to get that bouquet," I say and then hear another knock on the door and see the man coming in with another one. "I must have drained that snake over and over." I wink at her as he puts down the two and then walks back out. It takes him thirty minutes to unload the fifty bouquets that are now all over my house. Every single color of roses that are out there are now in my house. From white to red to black to blue to even rainbow. There is not one space left that doesn't have flowers. "It smells like a flower shop in here." I look at her, shocked.

"Who do you think they're from?" she asks, and I shrug.

"I have no idea. I mean, to be honest, I haven't been with anyone in the past couple of months." I go from one to the other, looking for a card, and so does Candace.

"Found it," she says and looks at me. "Can I read it?"

"I mean, I guess so. It's not like you don't know how awesome and amazing I am," I say, looking around the house with my hands outstretched. "We also have to take a picture of this to show my future husband." Candace's mouth drops open. "He obviously has to beat this if he's going to marry me. God, Candace. I am shallow enough to admit I will throw this in his face, and we haven't even met yet." I shrug. "He has no idea that this will be brought up for the rest of his life."

She shakes her head and opens the white envelope and takes out the card. "Here are twenty-five thousand reasons to go out with me. Can't wait to cash in my voucher." She falls forward, laughing hysterically.

"Cash in a voucher?" I ask, looking around. "Who the hell sent them?" I place my hands on my hips.

"Oh, this is too good," she says, laughing. "I wish I could have this on video so you can see your face when I tell you."

"Tell me what?" I ask with my hands in the air.

"Last night at the event …" she starts to say and stops talking, looking to see if I remember anything.

"Yes, an event that was uneventful." I open my eyes

wide. "An event where I think the champagne was expired."

"There was nothing wrong with the champagne," Candace says. "Except maybe you had too much of it."

"Tomato, tomatoe," I say to her.

"I can't believe that you don't remember." She laughs, holding her stomach.

"Would you stop being so vague and just fucking tell me?" I shout now.

"Well, there was an auction," she says, and I gasp when she looks at me.

"Did I win the tickets to the All-Star game?" I cross my fingers. "Please tell me I won."

"Oh, you won, all right," she mumbles. "There was the auction and ..." she starts to say slowly. I just look at her, and I try to remember anything, but it's just coming up blank. "Well, it started at fifty cents," she tells me, "then it went all the way up to twenty-five thousand dollars."

"Holy shit, who the hell would bid twenty-five thousand dollars?" I ask, crossing my hands over my chest. And like a wave crashing into the sand, it all comes back to me. Sitting at the table, listening to those women bid on him. One trying to outbid the other like it was a pissing contest. The blonde who bid five thousand dollars, sitting there so smug. Like she owned the world just because she could bid that much. Then the sound of my voice echoes in my ears, followed by Nico's sold.

I gasp out and shout. "Nooooo," I say, shaking my head.

"Oh, but yes," Candace says. "Twenty-five thousand dollars."

"Oh my God," I say, putting my hands on my knees. "Oh my God, how could you make me do that?"

"How could I make you do that?" she asks me. "How can you do that? You hate him."

"I know," I tell her.

"Every single time he's asked you out, you denied him."

"You're not telling me anything that I don't know, Candace. I have to call Nico," I say, looking around for my phone. "I have to call him and tell him that I'm sorry, but that was a mistake." I rush around the house looking for my phone. My heart speeds up in my chest, my palms sweaty, and then I have the sudden urge to vomit when I pick up my phone and see the top notification.

Thank you so much for your donation of twenty-five thousand dollars. Your bid has now been accepted.

SIX

Miller

The door shuts behind me as I make my way into the practice facility. My phone's in my hand as I look for pictures of last night, hoping that I find one of just the two of us. "Hey, there he is." I look up, seeing one of the rookies who was for auction yesterday come out of the kitchen. "Mr. Twenty-five K."

I laugh at the nickname. "That would be me."

"It was insane." He starts to tell me, and I half-listen because I finally find a picture of us. She stands beside me, and all I can see is her leg coming out. I save the picture and send it to her with the caption.

Me: This is what twenty-five K looks like.

"So where do you think you're going to take her?" he asks, and I stop walking when we get to the door of the team's changing room. "For twenty-five K, you better get a private jet and fly her to Italy for pizza." He walks into the changing room, leaving me in the middle of the hallway, thinking.

"I can smell wood burning." I hear Ralph as he walks toward me, and I look up at him. "Jesus, did someone kick your dog?"

"I don't have a dog," I say, shaking my head.

"Then why the sad face?" he asks, stopping beside me but not before I look over his shoulder and see Manning coming in.

He's dressed in a tracksuit. "I thought this was an optional skate?"

"It is," Manning says. "But what does it say when your captain doesn't show up?" He looks at us. "What is going on here?"

"I was thinking about where to take Layla on our date." I look at the two of them.

Ralph laughs. "The question you should be asking yourself is if she is actually going to let you take her out?"

"She has no choice. She bought me." I point at myself.

"Don't say that again," Manning says, shaking his head. "You sound like a piece of meat."

"Seriously, guys, I have to wow the shit out of her." My stomach starts to sink, and I open Safari on my phone. "Siri," I say, pressing the button. "Tell me the top ten romantic things to do on a date." The two of them laugh out loud. "Don't knock this; you might get ideas."

"My idea of a romantic date is sitting down with Candace, just her and me and being next to her," Ralph says, and Manning looks at him.

"My idea of a romantic date is not having my so-called wife at home," Manning says. "Just me and my boy watching Netflix."

"Why do you even put up with her?" Ralph asks him. It's a question that everyone who knows him probably asks themselves.

"The last time I sent her divorce papers, she destroyed them, then she used my kid against me." He shakes his head. "It's not for much longer. Just until he can understand."

"Kids understand more than you know," Ralph says to him.

"Okay, can we focus on me, please?" I say now, throwing my hands in the air. "I finally get a shot with Layla, and I have to make it count."

"What does it say on the list?" Ralph asks, and I look down at the phone in my hand.

"Hit up a bar," I read, and they laugh.

"So she can drown her sorrow," Manning says. "What about number two?"

"Go grocery store shopping," I say, confused. "I'm not doing that. Take a boxing class together."

"You really want to put Layla in boxing gloves?" Ralph looks at me. "I haven't known her as long as you guys, but that sounds like a terrible idea." He grabs the phone from me, reading off the list. "Dude, this list is not anything I would do. One of them is play hide-and-seek."

"Oh," I say, smiling. "Naked. We can do it naked."

"You'll be lucky if she shows up. You are pushing it

if you think she is going to do it naked," Manning says. "I bet you ten thousand dollars that will never happen."

"I double that," Ralph says, still going through the list. "Go ax throwing." He laughs. "Are these romantic things or ways for your date to kill you?"

I grab my phone from him. "This looks fun. Go to the zoo." I look up at them.

"So she can feed you to the lions," Manning says, and I give up, putting my phone away now.

"Was she okay when you dropped her off last night?" I ask, and he nods his head. "Did she say anything?"

"Yeah," he says. "She said that it's ridiculous that they would offer people drinks and allow them to bid on stuff." I laugh now, seeing her face in my head. "She also said that the debutants need to get off your dick."

My eyes light up. "She was thinking about my dick." I slap him on the shoulder. "I knew she wanted me."

"I wouldn't say that," Ralph says. "She also said that you're gross, and you should be bathing in Purell."

"Now that," Manning says. "That's love."

"I know." I agree with him. "I'm going to send her flowers." I grab my phone. "One thousand roses." I look at them as their mouths hang open. "Is that overkill?"

"No." Ralph shakes his head. "Anything less is not even worth it."

"That's what I'm thinking," I say, walking away from them as I order them. I walk back into the room and see both of them lacing up their skates. "Order has been placed, boys."

"To be a fly on the wall," Manning says. Getting up

with his skates, he towers over six feet six. He turns, grabbing his gloves and helmet, and makes his way out to the ice.

Ralph and I follow him a couple of minutes later, and we are all on the ice. It's not a full roster today since it was optional, but we push the ones who are here hard, and when I walk off the ice, I'm drenched in sweat.

The rookies are still on the ice as I sit down with Ralph beside me, his phone pinging. He grabs it, taking off his gloves and helmet. His head goes back and he laughs. "She didn't remember."

"What?" I ask him, grabbing a bottle of Gatorade and gulping it down.

"Layla didn't remember bidding on you." He chuckles. "She is going nuts."

"But did she get the flowers?" I ask him.

"Oh, she got the flowers all right." He looks at me. "She's going to make potpourri with them after she shoves them up your ass."

"That woman loves me." My chest expands as I take my shirt off. "It's like elementary school when she says she hates you, but she really secretly loves you."

I grab my phone and see that I have fifty messages, and I laugh when I scroll and see that they are all from Layla.

Layla: How the hell did you get my number?

I laugh because, for the past four years, she's been giving me the wrong number every single time.

Layla: Are you out of your fucking mind?

Layla: I'm not going out with you.

Layla: If you look at the picture, it looks like I'm going to vomit.

Layla: I'm not going out with you.

Layla: I'm not going out with you.

She repeats the text over forty times. I put my phone down and go take a shower. When I come out, it looks like Manning and Ralph have left, and I'm alone. After I get dressed and walk out, I head out to my truck and call her once I climb inside.

Just the thought of talking to her makes my heart speed up. She answers after five rings. "What do you want?"

"Good afternoon, gorgeous," I say, ignoring her snippiness. "How are you doing?"

"How am I doing?" she asks, and I can tell she's flustered. "I'm not doing good."

"Are you sick?" I ask as suddenly something in me makes my head spin.

"No, I'm not sick," she huffs out. "Well, actually, maybe I am sick." She groans. "Maybe I have a brain tumor, and I don't even know. I mean, why else would I have done what I did?"

I laugh now. "Or maybe, you actually like me and want to date me, and your subconscious is finally breaking free."

"No," she says right away. "I'm going with a brain tumor. I have to go and call my doctor."

"Gorgeous," I say softly, and when all I get is silence, I look at the phone to see if she hung up on me or not. "Are you still there?"

"Miller, seriously, all jokes aside, this is a horrible, horrible idea," she says, and I have to wonder if she's home, and if she is home, is she sitting down with flowers all around her? Is she in bed, is she naked and thinking about me?

"This is not a horrible idea!" I yell. "This is the best idea that you have ever had."

"No, it's not!" she yells back at me. "Going to Cabo and sitting on the beach was a good idea. Me bidding twenty-five K to go on a date with you has to be the stupidest thing I've ever done. And I woke up one day with a tattoo."

I smile now. "A tattoo?" My voice comes out smooth. "I've never seen it."

"And you will never see it," she huffs out. "Ever."

"Oh, I think this is a challenge." I clap my hands together.

"There is no challenge!" she shouts. "There is nothing going on here."

"Oh, there is something going on here." I put the car in park. "Something big, and I can't wait for you to finally see it, gorgeous." She groans. "Be ready tonight. I'll be there at eight."

"No!" she shouts.

"See you later, gorgeous," I say and hang up the phone, smiling to myself. I get out of the truck and make my way over to the gym, where my trainer is waiting.

I walk in, and the cold air hits me right away. "You are five minutes late," he says, and I look down and see he's right. "Get on the treadmill." I nod at him, and for the next two hours, he pushes me until my legs feel like Jell-O.

"It's a good fucking thing I don't have to get back on the ice until Tuesday." My chest heaves up and down as I swallow a whole bottle of water. Sweat from my face drips down, and the phone beeps.

I walk over to the weight bench that has my keys, wallet, and phone, and I smile when I see Layla texted me.

Layla: One date. See you at eight.

I smile to myself like a giddy teenager. *I knew she wanted me*, I think to myself. "Come to Daddy."

SEVEN

Layla

Did he just hang up on me? I look down at the phone and see that the screen saver picture is up. How dare he hang up on me. I get up, storming over to my bedroom and falling on the bed, then turn to the side and see that it's just a little after one in the afternoon. I've just spent the past three hours trying to forget about what I did last night.

But the minute I try to forget, I take a deep breath, and all I can do is smell flowers. It brings me right back to the memories of last night. Sitting at the table watching all the women and then something happening, and I couldn't explain it. Bidding on him for twenty-five fucking thousand dollars, I close my eyes. Not only that, but I made the payment on the way to the car. They should have a code word before making a purchase that big. Like, were you or are you of sound mind. Because if I'd had that option, I would have failed.

I walked into the house and had a one-on-one with Don Julio, who did nothing but make me forget. He made sure that when I woke up this morning, the memories came slowly.

My phone pings, and I look down, seeing that it's a text from Miller, and I sit up in my bed. How did he get my number? For the past four years, I've given him a different number each time. Each time, he would blow up that number and then ask me why I never answered. I would laugh at him and inform him that he took it down wrong.

I call Candace, who answers right away, whispering, "Did you give Miller my phone number?" I hear a door close softly.

She answers right away. "No, why?" Her voice goes from a whisper to a normal voice. I hear her walking wherever she is.

"Well, he just texted me a picture of us from last night," I fill her in. "It came through. Like I actually got his text."

"Okay and …?" she asks, and I close my eyes, pinching the bridge of my nose. This is a dream; this has to be a dream or, better yet, a fucking nightmare. But then my eyes open, and I see it's not a dream.

"I never gave him my number," I tell her. "I gave him a number. All the fake numbers."

She gasps and then laughs. "Oh my God, you have to marry him," she sings with glee while I groan. "You said it yourself. If the guy finds your number, you'll marry him."

"I don't have time for this. I have to be at my grand-mother's place in thirty-five minutes." I don't even both-er answering or touching what she just said.

"Grandma Nancy," she says, her voice full of love. "Bring her some flowers," she says, then hangs up right after.

I slowly peel myself off my bed as I make my way to my walk-in closet. I grab my comfiest pair of black jeans, grabbing a white shirt with short sleeves that rests just above the top of the jeans. Gathering my hair, I tie it on top of my head in a high bun. I grab my purse, keys, and flip-flops. Bending down, I pick up a vase of roses in my arms and walk out of the house, trying not to fall. I walk as slowly as I can to my car, making sure I don't smash into anything. The flowers cover half my eyes. I buckle the bouquet in the front seat before making my way over to my grandmother's senior living home.

I stop on the way to pick up our favorite burgers and fries. When I pull up to her home, I'm thankful she's sitting outside in the front swing with four of her friends. She gets up as soon as she sees me park my car, waving and calling my name.

"Layla, honey." She walks over, and I look her up and down. She is still a beauty with her wild and curly salt and pepper hair that falls in the middle of her back. Her bright gray eyes shine as she looks at me. She's wearing a long orange dress with a bright yellow cover-up. The bangles on her arms clink when she spots the flowers and claps her hands together, each finger has a ring on it. It balances her aura, she always says. "Oh, you shouldn't have, dear." Her voice is soft and sweet.

"Can you grab the food?" I motion to the takeout bag that is on the floor of the car. She grabs the bag and my purse, then comes over to kiss my cheek. "Hi."

"You look like the cat just dragged you in and licked your hair," she says, and I laugh. She is full of all these strange sayings. She always had a saying about something. It's one of the things I think I love most about her.

"Well, after the night I had …" I walk with her up her concrete walkway as she says hello to the people she sees. "I'll take it."

"Oh!" she squeals with excitement. "I want to hear all about it," she tells me as she holds open the front door, and I step in and notice that all of her windows are open, and it looks foggy. I set the flowers on her glass table that is right off the small kitchen.

"What is that smell?" I ask her, looking around, and she smiles at me.

"I was making cannabutter this morning," she says. "And well, one thing led to another. I forgot about it, and it's burnt."

"Grandma," I say, putting my hands on my hips. "What the hell were you doing that you forgot you had it in the oven?"

"It's not what I was doing, dear," she says, winking at me. "It's who I was doing."

"Oh my God," I say, sitting down on one of the chairs before I fall on the floor. "That's so gross."

"I have needs," she says, walking to the table. "And sometimes those needs get met by a real willie instead of the plastic one in my drawer." Sitting down, she crosses her legs. Her feet are bare as they always are when she's home.

"This is all too much," I tell her, and she shrugs.

"Now, did you bring me a beyond meat burger?" she asks, grabbing the bag, and I nod my head. "Good." handing her a fry and her beyond meat burger. My whole life, she has been the one who guided me and stood by my side. My parents had me when they were both sixteen. They were best friends, and one night, they dropped me off to her, then went off to party. I was six months old, and that night, I became an orphan. My parents were killed in a hit-and-run accident, leaving my grandmother to raise me. She didn't bat an eye that she was fifty and now raising a child. She never made me feel that I stopped her from living. Instead, she said I was her second chance. Sure, she was unconventional, but so was life. "So tell me," she says, grabbing a french fry. "How was your night?"

"Not as eventful as yours," I say, taking a bite of the burger. "I mean, I spent twenty-five thousand dollars on a man." I take another bite, and my grandmother looks at me.

"You spent twenty-five thousand dollars on a man, and you're here?" She shakes her head. "Child, for that price, he better fan me after and feed me grapes." She takes a bite of her burger. "He also wouldn't be allowed to leave for a year."

"It was a children's auction." I put my burger down and grab a fry, avoiding her eyes. "And those other women were bidding and …"

"And you got jealous and said not today, Karen." She points at me. "That's my girl. You go get your man."

"He's not my man, Grandma." I push away from the table, going to get a bottle of water and spotting the brownies that are in the fridge. "I don't like him at all. He gets on my nerves. He's cocky." I put up my finger. "He's arrogant. He's rude. He's not my type." Okay, fine, he is my type.

"Is he hot?" she asks me with a smirk.

I shrug and grab my phone, opening to a picture of the both of us that he sent us and handing it to her. "I don't think so." She grabs it from me and puts on her glasses that are hanging around her neck.

"Are you blind?" she asks me, looking at me and then zooming in on the picture or rather the crotch of his picture.

"Grandma," I say, grabbing it from her. "I'm not blind. There is something about him that turns me off and makes me cringe."

"You like him," she says. "And you hate that you like him."

"One, I don't like him." I put my phone down and grab the burger, so I don't have to look into her eyes. Okay, fine, I might like him, or maybe I'm intrigued by him. Maybe I just need to have sex with him and be done with it. After that, the chase will be over, and he could move on and stop trying to get me to date him. "Two, I don't like him."

"You said that already." She smiles, folding her hands

together. "What else don't you like about him?"

"Fine." I throw up my hands. "This I can do. I can tell you all the ways I don't like Miller."

"I'm listening, dear," she says.

"One, he's pushy," I finally say. "He's always trying to get me to go out with him." She rolls her eyes. "Two, he's annoying. Three, he's crass. He sent a picture of his penis to his whole friend list."

She slaps the table, turning around to get her phone. "What friend list?" she asks. "Should I like him on Instagram, or is it the tik tok?"

"Grandma," I snap at her and then lean back in my chair. "If you like him so much, get dressed and you can go out with him."

She pushes away from the table and gets up. "Fine by me," she says and walks into her bedroom. "You won't have to ask me twice."

I smile. "This is perfect," I say, putting my hands together in front of my mouth. "Technically, I'm still going on a date with him. It's just going to be through my grandmother," I say to myself and look up when she sticks her head out of the bedroom.

"Panties or commando?" she asks me. "Should I go for easy access, or should I play hard to get?" She doesn't even wait for me to answer. "I'll see if you can see my panty lines and then decide," she says, going to the bathroom. I hear the shower turn on, and she walks back in naked. "I am going to rock his world."

It's my turn now to sit here with my mouth hanging open. *Oh, God, maybe this isn't a good idea*, I think to myself, but when my grandmother comes out of her room thirty minutes later all dressed up, I don't have the heart to tell her no. Her bright pink dress goes all the way to the floor, flowing around her legs. She walks over to grab the long yellow shawl she had before. She has a blue necklace and matching bracelets and rings.

"Honey, can you close the patio door for me," she says, and I get up and close it while she grabs her purse. She is stuffing something into it, and she turns to me. "Let's go so I can meet my man."

"Yes, I can't wait," I say to her, and we walk out of the house arm in arm. She stops on the way to the car to inform everyone we see that she has a hot date tonight. She gets in the car and opens the window to let the fresh air in.

"Are you sure you're up to this?" I look over at her, and she just pats her purse.

"The question you should be asking …" She moves her hair away from her face. "Is he up for all this?" She uses her fingers to point at herself.

EIGHT

MILLER

I GET OUT of the limousine as soon as the driver opens the door, and I smile at him. Okay, fine, maybe the limo was a touch extra, but what if she jumped my bones? I need to focus on one thing and one thing only. Her.

Walking up the steps toward her front door, I swear I feel like a kid on prom night. My palms are sweaty, and my heart is hammering in my chest. I look down and take a huge breath, and I press the doorbell. I put my head up and look at the stars, and then I hear the locks, and I wait for the door to open.

She stands there in black jeans and a white shirt. "Am I early?" I look at my watch and see I'm right on time. Okay, maybe she didn't know how to dress on a first date. I look at my blue suit.

"No, you are right on time," she says, smiling and then looks over her shoulder. "I'll get your date," she says.

"Wait, what is going on?" I ask her, confused.

"Grandma." She sings her voice cheerfully, and I can tell she is really enjoying this. "Your knight in shining armor is here."

"Layla." I say her name, and I am definitely not ready for what comes next. A beautiful older woman comes to the door. She walks to the door like she's on a catwalk, her curly hair is everywhere, and just with one look, I can see how Layla will look when she's older.

"Grandma Nancy," Layla says with a huge smile on her face. "This is your date, Miller." Layla waits for me to freak out or something, and I just look at her. She wants the chase, I think to myself she is going to get the chase of her life, but she better be ready for when I catch her.

I step into the house and take Nancy's hand and bend to kiss it. "The pleasure is all mine." I wink at her, and she smiles.

"Well, if the pleasure was all mine, I have another place you can put those lips," she says and stuns me by taking my face in her hands and kissing me right on the mouth. I pull away from her when her tongue tries to get into my mouth.

"Um," I say, shocked, and Layla folds her hands over her chest.

"Well, don't let me keep you two love birds." Layla ushers her out the door. "I won't wait up." I glare at her right before she closes the door. I don't even have time to think about it or to knock on the door and tell her that the joke is over before Nancy's arm slides through mine.

"So, tell me, hotcakes." She starts walking, and my

feet follow her. "Where are you taking me?" I walk back down the steps I just rushed up feeling nervous. She spots the limo right away and yells with glee. Putting her hands to her mouth, she smiles. "I've never been in a limo before." She jumps up and down and almost skips to the car, but she stops. "I've also never had sex in a limo before."

I swallow down and put my hands in my pockets. "We can at least cross one of those things off your list." I walk slowly to the car.

The driver holds open the door for her. "Pop the champagne." She throws her hands up in the air. "If the car is a rocking, don't come a knocking." The driver rolls his lips to stop from laughing as he looks over at me, and I nod my head. He walks to the trunk where he opens it and brings out the bottle of champagne I made him bring. I actually ordered two bottles of champagne. He also brings out just the one glass that I packed.

The front door opens as soon as the bottle of champagne is popped, and I look over my shoulder to see Layla coming out. "Grandma," she says, running to her, and I think she is about to tell me that I just got punked. She is going to come out and say gotcha and all of this was a joke, but she doesn't. "You forgot your purse." She hands her the purse. Turning, she walks to me. "I paid a lot of money for you," she says, stopping in front of me. "You better make it worth it."

I step into her, my hands ready to grab her hair and pull her head back and kiss the ever-loving shit out of her. I don't even care that she might knee me in the balls.

Actually, I'll be disappointed if she doesn't. "You can have your laugh now," I tell her and see her eyes get a deeper shade. "But know this, gorgeous." I step in, and our chests are practically touching. "At the end of the day, I'll collect that date." I lean my head in; she closes her mouth to swallow, and her breath hitches when she thinks I'm going to kiss her, but instead, I go to whisper in her ear. "You can bet on it." I walk around her now, going to the limo where Nancy is on her second glass of champagne, slapping my hands together. "Let's get the show on the road."

"Yes, let's," Nancy says, grabbing the bottle of champagne from the driver and getting in the car. I step and look at the driver and then look over my shoulder, seeing Layla just watching.

"Whatever you do," I say, my voice low. "You do not have the divider closed. I don't know if you have a lock system in the front, but it doesn't close."

"I'll handle it," he says, nodding, and I get into the limo, and not one second later, Nancy is practically in my lap. I have to fend her off, and I feel like I'm kung fu panda.

"You need another drink," I say, pointing at her empty glass and grabbing the bottle from the silver bucket. "So tell me about yourself, Nancy." I pour her some champagne.

"I'm an open book," she says, finishing the champagne, then holding out her glass for me to pour more. She slides herself close to me and puts a hand over my shoulder. Her finger taps my shoulder as I fill her glass.

She crosses her legs and put one of her legs over mine. "Tell me something, hotcakes." She takes a sip of the champagne. "Are you a grower or a shower or maybe a bit of both?" I am about to answer her when she keeps on talking, finishing the glass of champagne and then leaning over and placing it in one of the cupholders. "I think I need to find out," she says, and I don't have time to register what she says before her one hand flies to my cock, and the other one joins it. I try to protect my junk by trying to move her hands, but her face comes into my neck, and she licks me. She fucking licks me.

"Nancy," I huff out as I try to push her off me.

"I love when you moan out my name," she says, crawling onto my lap and straddling me. I put my hands on her hips to pick her up and move her off me.

"Nancy," I say, and she tries to stick her tongue into my mouth, but I turn my head to the side. I put her in the spot next to me, and I try to get away from her, but she locks her legs around my waist. She grabs my shirt and tries to bring me closer to her. "Nancy." I finally am able to push away from her, and this time, I sit as far away from her as I can. She looks as if she is going to come toward me, and I put my hand up. "Stay."

"But what fun is it if I'm over here, and you are all the way over there. For twenty-five K, I better be able to see skin." She winks at me. "I have a great idea."

I sit back with my guard up as my head spins as I try to come up with ways to end this date or at least get out with a little bit of my dignity. "Great," I say with a huge sigh. "What is this?"

"We should go painting." She grabs her phone. "I know a great artist who has lots of space."

"That sounds like fun." I agree. It's much better than the romantic gondola ride I had scheduled and then the picnic in the park under the stars. "I can do painting."

"Great." She claps her hands. "He's waiting for us. He is going to have to charge double since it's last minute."

"That's fine," I say, agreeing as she types and then gives me the address. The driver looks at me through his rearview mirror and nods as he makes his way there.

"I shall finish this champagne," she says, grabbing the bottle and filling her glass and then downing it. "It really goes down smooth, doesn't it?"

"It should; it's the best," I tell her. "But I don't think it's good if you finish the whole thing. I mean …" I try not to bring up her age. "Are you on any medications?" I try to find the right words.

"Nope," she says. "I'm as healthy as can be." I smile at her, and she winks. "They call me the Energizer Bunny."

"Is that so?" I nod again, and thankfully, the car comes to a stop.

She looks out the window at the white building. "Oh, good, we're here." She grabs her purse and is about to get out of the car when the door opens, and she stops to look at me. "Listen, before we get out, I should tell you that Luigi and I." She starts and then looks out the front. "We're friends."

"That's good to know," I tell her.

"With certain benefits," she says, and my mouth

hangs open. "Sexual benefits." She gets out of the limo, leaving me here in shock. But nothing could prepare me for the man who comes out of the door to greet her. He looks like he is in his early thirties. His long hair flows in the breeze. "Luigi," she says, and he holds out his hand for her.

"Nancy." He says her name in his thick accent. "This is a wonderful surprise." He kisses her on both cheeks, and I get out of the limo. He looks over at me, and you can see he is checking me out up and down.

"Luigi," she says. "This is hotcakes." She smiles at him.

"Miller," I say, holding out my hand, and he shakes it. "Thank you for squeezing us in."

"For Nancy," he says, bringing her hand to his mouth. "Anything. Shall we?" He turns and walks back into the house, and I look at the limo guy.

"If you hear screaming, you come and get me," I tell him, and he shakes his head and laughs. I walk into the house, and I'm surprised by the huge open concept room. A white sheet is in the middle of the room. Canvases are all around the room. Paintbrushes are in buckets everywhere. "Do you do classes?"

"Yes," Luigi says, going over to the paint in the corner, coming back with the two huge bottles. "It's where I met Nancy."

"Is there a bathroom I can use?" I ask him, and he points at the bathroom in the corner.

"You better hurry back," Nancy says, twirling. I walk into the bathroom, locking the door. I put my hands on the sink and let out a huge breath.

I'm in the bathroom for no more than a minute and then go back out. There is soft music playing now, and I look around and then stop in my tracks when Nancy stands in front of me naked. "What is going on?" I ask her. She winks at me, and I swear I don't think I've ever been so scared in my life.

"It's time to get you naked," she says, coming to me, and if I thought that this night had started off insane, nothing could have prepared me for Luigi coming back in the room naked also.

"Shall we start?" He claps his hands together. "Let's make art."

NINE

LAYLA

I SIT ON the couch to watch television, but I can't focus on it at all. I don't even know what's going on. I keep looking down at my phone to make sure I don't miss a text or a picture or anything and even keep checking his Instagram for a picture, but it's been radio silent for over two hours. I even texted Grandma, but she has yet to answer me.

Maybe pushing Grandma to go out with him was a bad idea. Maybe I should have just bitten the bullet and gone on the date with him. Fuck, it would have been one date, so one night for two hours tops. My mind goes around and around with scenarios as I tap my finger on my phone, and none of them are good. I finally give up, and I'm about to call her when the phone rings, and I see it's Miller.

"Hello," I say, putting the phone on speaker.

"Are you home?" he asks, and his voice is low, almost

in a whisper.

"Yes, why?" Throwing the cover off me, I walk to the front door, flip on the outside lights, then unlock the door and walk out. Miller stands leaning against the limo, and he puts his phone down as I make my way down to him. "What happened?" He looks exhausted.

"Oh, gorgeous," he says, and I hate that he gave me that nickname. Okay, I'm lying. I love when he calls me that. "I don't even know where to start with that question."

"Where is my grandmother?" I ask, looking around. "Is she here? Did you drop her off at home?"

"Oh, she's here," he says, walking over to the limo door and opening it. All I see is her hair, and when I lean in a bit, I notice she's sprawled out on the back seat.

"What did you do to her?" I ask, poking my head inside and calling her name. When she doesn't budge or stir, I get out of the limo and look at him with an arched brow, waiting for an answer.

"What did I do to her?" he asks, and his voice goes louder. "What did I do to her?" He shakes his head and runs his hands through his hair. "The question is, what did she do to me?" He points at himself.

"I don't understand." I look at my grandmother. "Grandma," I say, and she doesn't stir. "What did you give her?"

"What did I give her?" He laughs. "Me? The question you should ask right now is, how was your night, Miller."

I cross my hands over my chest and roll my eyes.

"Fine. How was your night, Miller?"

"Funny you should ask, gorgeous," he says. "It started off really well. Had this whole thing set up. We were going to go for a gondola ride and then have a picnic in the park under the stars, but hey, shit happens. Right?" He puts his hands on his hips. "Fast forward to getting in the car. Where your grandmother physically assaulted me." I roll my eyes now. "I thought I was going to be Bruce Lee at one point. She had her hands everywhere." His eyes go big. "Everywhere. It was like I was fighting with an octopus; her hands were everywhere all at the same time. She tried to get my dick out of my pants five minutes into the date." He points at his dick.

My eyes automatically go down to his area. "Did she succeed?" I ask, trying not to laugh.

"No, she did not succeed. I had to pry her off me, and when I tried to tell her to stop, she stuck her tongue into my mouth," he says, throwing his hands up in the air. "All the while, drinking champagne. I had to pick her up and put her in her seat. I almost jumped into the front seat with the driver."

"Oh, don't pretend you didn't like it." I cock my hip. "Let's be real. She's the best thing you've been with in a long time."

"I will agree with you on that," he tells me. "She asked me to take her painting. Said it would be nice." I look at him, waiting. "Why not? I thought."

"Oh." I put my hand to my mouth. "Like a painting class? That doesn't sound bad."

"That's what I thought, too. I see them on Facebook,

where everyone's painting the same thing. It should be nice. I can maybe ask her about you, try to connive her to tell you to date me," he says, going to the trunk of the limo and opening it. I wait as he takes a sheet out. "Painting. How bad could it be?" He opens the canvas, and all I see are different colors all smashed together. "I came out of the bathroom and came face-to-face with your grandmother." I look at him as he talks. "Naked." I try not to laugh. "Oh, and it gets so much better. Luigi, the painting instructor, was also naked."

"Maybe they wanted you to paint them. Like *David*." I try to make an excuse for it, but I swear it takes everything in me not to laugh out loud.

"Come to think of it, I wish that was the reason." He lets out a bitter chuckle. "No, you see, what they wanted to do was for all three of us to get naked." My eyes go big. "Paint each other and then have sex with each other while on said canvas," he says. "Luigi called it taste the rainbow."

I can't help it now as I bend over and laugh. "Like Skittles."

"Who knows?" He throws up his hands, and they fall by his sides. "I have no idea. I was trying not to look at the two naked people in front of me to ask him where he came up with the saying." He puts his hands in front of his mouth. "I saw things I shouldn't have today. Then Nancy came running up to me and said she baked me a brownie."

I run to him now. "Oh my God, tell me you didn't eat it." My eyes go wide.

"Are you crazy?" he asks. "I spit it out, but don't worry, she picked it up and ate it anyway."

"Is that why she's passed out?"

"Well, it could be that, or the two hours of sex that she and Luigi had." He puts his hands on his hips.

"You watched them?" I ask hesitantly, not sure what to think.

"Are you out of your mind?" He shakes his head. "I ran out of there and sat in the car eating the picnic I made for us," he says as he moves me to the side. "We couldn't get the music to go loud enough to drown out the moans." I have no words; all I can do is try not to laugh. "I swear I thought she was going to break a hip."

"She's fine," I tell him as he leans into the car to try to grab her.

"Is she covered in paint?" I ask, and he huffs out and grabs her enough to get out of the car with her.

"No, they both came out to show me the rainbow and then showered," he says, and all I can do is bite my lip. "Where do you want me to put her?"

"I guess you can put her in the spare bedroom," I tell him, and then walk by the canvas and stop. "Is that …?"

"Yup, that's their rainbow," he says. Looking at it, I swear I can see a ball sack outline and then an ass. "If you want it framed, I need to tell him by the end of the week."

"No." I shake my head. "I think I'm good."

"You sure?" he asks. Grandma groans in his arms, and her eyes flicker open.

"Oh, hotcakes," she says, cuddling into him and rubbing his chest as her eyes fall closed again. "Let me rest for a couple of hours, and then I'll be good to go." He glares at me while I laugh.

"Show me the spare bedroom," he says between clenched teeth. I turn to walk back into the house, and he follows me. Stepping into the bedroom, I toss the throw pillows to the side and move the duvet out of the way.

When he places her on the bed, she opens her eyes. "Okay, fine, sweet cheeks, but you are going to have to do all the work." She throws her hands out to the sides and spreads her legs. Miller backs away, shaking his head. I cover her with the duvet and then turn off the light before we walk out of the room.

"Well, this has been a night to remember," he says when we get to the door.

"It should have been for her since it cost me twenty-five thousand dollars," I tell him as we stand in the doorway.

"About that …" he says and looks at me. "When I was sitting in the limo tonight …" He starts talking, leaning closer to me. "While I ate the food and I tried not to think about what was happening inside." He continues stepping closer, and I suddenly move back, not sure I want him in my space. Not sure I want to be in his space. "I wondered why would she bid so high for me?"

"It was for charity," I say, feeling my back hit the wall.

"Is that the real reason?" He's standing so close now that our feet touch each other. "For charity?"

"Yes," I almost stutter and have to swallow because my mouth is suddenly dry. "Why else would I do it?"

"I think you did it because you were jealous." His hand reaches up to play with the hair that has fallen out of my ponytail, twirling it around his finger.

"I was not jealous." I want to push him away because I can't think when he's this close. "For me to be jealous, I would have to care."

He laughs now. "Oh, you care, gorgeous," he says. His voice goes low, and whereas before I thought he was going to kiss me, I don't think that this time. So I'm even more surprised when his mouth falls on mine. The kiss is so soft that if my eyes weren't open, I wouldn't realize it happens. "You owe me," he tells me softly, and I can still feel his lips on mine. "And just so you know, I'm going to collect." He moves away from me, going to the front door. "I'll text you tomorrow." He opens the door, and it slams behind him, and for the first time in a long time, I have no comeback.

TEN

MILLER

I WALK PAST the canvas and get into the limo. "Take me home, Jimmy," I say, closing my eyes to block the throbbing in my head. I thought I had seen it all. I thought that I was open to just about everything, but Nancy is way out of my league. Fuck, she's out of everyone's league. She's in a league of her own.

My phone beeps in my pocket, but when I see it's an email from Candace, I just turn my cell off. I can't even think right now, let alone answer her email.

When I get home, I don't even bother bringing in the blanket or the extra cases of wine that I brought just in case. After all the shit Jimmy saw and heard tonight, it's safe to say he'll never do me a favor again in this life-time.

Dragging my ass to my bedroom, I don't even bother to turn on any lights before I slip into bed naked and close my eyes. I toss and turn most of the night, the nightmare from the day before making me jump awake.

At six a.m., I finally give up and get out of bed, walking into the kitchen as soon as the coffee maker starts. Walking over to the big coffee table in the great room, I pick up the remote to turn the television on and switch it to *SportsCenter*. The ninety-five-inch screen lights up the whole room, so I don't have to turn on any lights. After pouring my coffee, I grab my laptop and head over to the couch, taking my first sip of coffee right before I sit down and watch the highlights from the night before. The season just started, so everyone is fresh out of the gate, including us.

My email is full of the same, and I answer the one from Candace first, asking about my calendar for the next two months. In the off-season, I usually do a lot of meet-and-greets. Last year, I did my first ever kids hockey camp in my hometown of Montreal. It was such a success that I'm spending most of the next summer there doing a whole month.

Tomorrow morning, we leave for a five-day road trip. We hit St. Louis, who won the cup last year, Detroit, and then Washington. Not only will it be hard mentally but it will also be physically grueling. Once I finish my coffee, I get up and walk over to the front door, putting on socks and my sneakers, then walk up the stairs to my home gym. The room has three walls of windows overlooking my backyard, so I grab the remote and open the pull-down shades. I also turn on the television before I climb on the bike.

I ride until my legs are jelly, then step off and grab a

towel. After wiping my face, I finish off a bottle of water. Looking up, I see it's almost eleven o'clock, and I smile, knowing I'm about to talk to Layla.

Walking over to the bike, I grab my phone and sit down on the workbench to call her number. I don't know if she's going to answer. She usually sends me to voice mail. Fuck, it took me two months to finally figure out her number, but I did.

As the phone rings, I put it on speakerphone and look out the window at the shining sun. After the fourth ring, I'm about to hang up when she answers the phone. "Hey there, hotcakes." She laughs, and I groan.

"It's all fun and games until people get naked," I tell her, and she laughs even louder. "How is Grandma today?"

"She's fabulous," she tells me. "Slept twelve straight hours, then woke up and decided to do a little yoga in my living room."

"Jesus, I guess Luigi really wore her out." I shake my head.

"You didn't let me get to the best part of the story. She did her yoga on her canvas that you left on my front lawn."

It's my turn to laugh now. "It's not funny." She tries not to laugh. "Do you know how much bacteria is on the mat?"

"I mean, the bodily fluid alone will have your house lighting up under a black light." I point out, taking another gulp of water.

"Yeah, whatever," she says. I hear her taking a sip of

something, and I wonder where she is right now. Is she in her kitchen at the table? Is she dressed or still in a robe? "At least I didn't want to cry when I saw a man naked."

"What are you talking about?" I huff out. "I see naked men almost every day." She laughs. "Not like that, pervert."

"According to Grandma, the minute you saw Luigi's sausage, you looked like you were going to cry." I love hearing her laughter. It's so carefree, and she's never really laughed around me before. I'm used to seeing her glare and having her be snippy.

"It was shock." I gape. "Shock at seeing not one person naked but two people in front of me naked. Two people I just met," I say, my voice going louder.

"Oh, please," she says, and I can almost see her rolling her eyes. "Like you've never had a threesome before."

"Okay, one." I start. "I've never been in or had a threesome."

"Yeah, right." She sings the words. "You don't have to lie to me."

"Gorgeous, there is one thing I never do, and that is lie." I look out the window. "There is nothing worth lying about. With that said, I've never had a threesome." My voice goes low. "Besides, when I'm with a woman, I want to spend all my time worshiping her. You'll see," I slip it in and then continue. "So when are you going to make it up to me?"

"How about tomorrow or the next five days?" she says.

"I get home Tuesday night, and then we have games

on Thursday and Saturday. But I have Sunday free before we leave on Monday for an eight-day road trip. God, this month is going to suck so bad." I close my eyes. Usually, I'm okay with travel. I've gotten used to it as the years passed by, but lately, it just sucks.

"Oh, stop acting like you don't like it. Besides, don't you have someone in each city to hook up with?" she asks, and I get up, walking downstairs.

"I used to." I am not going to lie to her. "When I was younger."

"Oh, because you are tipping the scale at thirty now." She laughs as I set the phone on the counter and open the fridge.

"Should I have chicken or steak?" I ask, looking down at two prepared meals. I usually get them five nights a week, so I know they are healthy and ready to eat. Otherwise, I would order pizza all the time.

"It depends," she says, and I hear rustling. "How is the steak cooked?"

"Medium with steamed veggies and a sweet potato," I tell her and then open the chicken one. "Grilled chicken, basmati rice, and steamed broccoli."

"Um, I would go for the chicken," she says, and I make a mental note of that. "I only like steak when it's grilled in front of me."

"Same," I tell her, putting the steak back into the fridge. "Now, what were we talking about?" I ask after I put the chicken in the microwave.

"I was trying to get off the phone with you when you started blabbing your mouth," she says, and I know she's lying. "But since you want to talk, we were discussing all the women you have sex with in the different cities."

I laugh. "That is not how I worded it at all."

"It is pretty much exactly what it is." She laughs. "You can sugarcoat it all you want. They are called puck bunnies, and they are everywhere."

"I know what they are called. I was telling you that I don't do that anymore." I stand at the island, waiting for the microwave to finish my food.

"But you did?" she counters.

"Everyone does," I tell her, taking the plate out of the microwave and going over to the stool to eat. "When you have all these girls throwing themselves at you as a rookie, you do it."

"So you are trying to tell me that you only did that when you were a rookie," she says. "I'm calling bullshit right now."

"Oh, I've had them. I'm saying that everyone does it. But after a while, it's just not that hot," I say, chewing chicken. "It's empty, and well, it sucks."

"Hold on a second," she says, and I can see her clearly in my mind as she sits up. "Are you telling me that you don't like meaningless sex?"

"You are the worst person to have a conversation with." I laugh while I eat. "You take one thing and spin it around. I like sex," I tell her. "Just like you like sex." I wait for her to answer or say something, but she doesn't. "I am just over the one night, never see you again sex."

"I live for those," she says. "I don't think I ever had sex with feelings before."

"Oh, come on, Layla. Are you saying you've never been in a relationship?" The thought is making my stomach sick.

"I have been, but I don't know, I think it's just better without strings," she says, her voice going low. "Anyway, I would love to dive more into this conversation, Dr. Phil, but I have to drive Grandma back home. She has Aquagym, and she can't miss it."

"I'll call you when I get back, but don't make any plans for next Sunday," I tell her, and she hangs up without answering me.

I text her now.

Me: I'm not messing around. You owe me a date next Sunday, and either you can come willingly or I can carry you.

I wait a minute to see if she is going to answer, and when I know she isn't, I follow up the text.

Me: Actually, come to think of it, I would love to carry you. Bottom line—I win, you lose.

I put the phone down and see the three dots come up and then disappear and then come up again, and finally, I see the text come through.

Layla: Go away. I'm about to block you.

Shaking my head, I finish my food. Once I clean up after myself, I get into the shower and slowly pack my bag for the flight the next day. I'm about to head to bed when I pick up my phone and snap a picture of myself lying on the couch shirtless.

Me: This could have been all yours yesterday.

I press send, wondering if she really is going to block

me. Either way, I know where she lives now, so it doesn't matter.

My phone pings two minutes later, and I see it's from Layla. I smile so big it hurts my face until I see the picture.

It's of Nancy naked again on her bed with the caption. *Layla: This could have been all yours yesterday.*

ELEVEN

Layla

"**W**HERE THE HELL is my cell phone?" I ask myself as I get off the couch and flip the cushions everywhere. "I swear I just had it." I put the cushions back and then walk back over to my purse at the front door. I turn on the hall light and look around to make sure that I didn't miss it, but after emptying half my purse, it's not in there either.

Going to the kitchen, I pick up the cordless phone and dial the number. My cell rings and then goes to voice mail right away. "Great," I say, hanging up the phone. Walking into my bedroom, I don't see it on the white duvet, and the bed is made since Grandma Nancy stayed over. She makes her bed every single day, so since she did it, I didn't have to. "Shit." I slap my head and walk over to the kitchen, picking the phone back up and calling Grandma Nancy.

"Hello." She answers right away.

"Grandma, did I forget my phone there?" I ask, closing my eyes and hoping like fuck she says yes.

"Yes," she says. "It died right after I sent a picture."

"Wait, what?" I ask, confused.

"Well, hotcakes sent a picture showing me what was under the suit," she says, and I run to get my iPad beside my bed. "And he taunted me. So I had to show him what he missed out on. Again," she says the last word, and I pull up the chat chain on my iPad.

"Grandma, it was just a picture of him on his couch," I tell her, and then I do what everyone would do. I zoom in on his chest and move it down to see if you can see any bulges in the shorts, and you can't. "Why are you sending him a nude shot of yourself?"

"He was baiting me," she says, huffing out. "Why couldn't he just get naked with me last night?"

"Grandma, we had this talk this morning," I tell her, reminding her as I shake my head. She rolled out of bed and came walking out of her room as if the night before hadn't happened. I sat on the stool, waiting for her to remember, and oh, did she remember. She got her cup of coffee and then sat next to me refreshed, she said. A little stiff but no worse for the wear. "Not everyone is okay with nudity."

"We are born naked, and we die naked." She repeats what she told me this morning. "I work hard for my body."

"No, you don't," I tell her. "You have amazing genes. It's what you've been telling me my whole life."

"Okay, fine." She finally gives in. "I was born with

an amazing body, and I shouldn't keep it to myself. It's a gift, and I have to share it with the world." I close my eyes. "Besides, I was just giving him a peek at what you are going to look like in the future."

"Grandma, who says I'm going to be with him in the future?" I gasp. "I'm never getting married."

"You're still young, so you might change your mind," she says, and I hear covers rustling. "And if you don't, well, at least he knows what he's going to get if he wants to tap that at seventy."

I laugh. "Thank you for showing him all that." I close my eyes. "I'll pick my phone up tomorrow. Do not send anymore nudes."

"I promise I won't," she says. "Unless he asks me for them." I want to say something, but she laughs. "You have to give the people what they want."

"Okay, fair," I say, taking a deep breath. "If he messages you for more, then by all means, give him what he wants."

"Good night, dear," she says and disconnects.

I take my iPad and send Miller a message.

Me: Sorry, I forgot my phone at my grandmother's.

I wonder now if he will even message me back. I mean, let's be real, I've put him through a traumatic event over the past two days. When we were talking on the phone, I almost forgot why I hated him. He made me smile, and talking to him was refreshing. He wasn't cocky. He was just a guy talking to me. Actually, he really threw me off when he spoke about meaningless sex and how he was over it. I mean, I know he's no virgin, but it's good to know he isn't banging a different chick every night.

I don't know why I'm sitting on my bed, waiting for him to text me back. I don't know why I even care that my grandmother sent him a nude. He started it by sending a picture of himself on the couch, smiling. Just last year, he tried to send me a dick pic, and it went to all his contacts. I look down, and the iPad bings.

Miller: Two dates. You owe me two dates. One for every time I saw your grandmother naked. Actually, I might ask her to send me one daily.

I answer him right away.

Me: EWWW, you are a pervert.

Miller: Only for you, gorgeous.

I take a deep breath, and my hands move without me even knowing what is going on.

Me: Fine, you earned it. I will go out with you. One date. That is it.

I put the iPad down and ignore the ping that comes after while I get up to take a shower. *What did I just do?* I ask myself once the water is raining down over me. Like what in the ever fuck did you just do, and why? This is a horrible idea, completely horrible. It's going to make things muddy. After I finish in the shower, I towel off and slide into bed. I look at my hands and then the iPad and then my hands again. "Don't do it," I tell myself, but my head is not really listening to me these days, so I press the middle button and see the text from him on the top line.

Miller: Gorgeous, that's all I need to show you how

much you actually like me.

Don't answer him. Don't answer him. Don't. Answer. Him.

Me: Or it'll push me over the edge, and I never talk to you.

I look at it and think about it and then erase it, shaking my hands out. "What the hell, Layla?"

Me: Hate like it's still an emotion.

After pressing send, I bring the iPad up and hit my head with it. "Stop while you're ahead." Placing the iPad on the table and grabbing the remote, I turn on the television. I flip through the channels but then finally give up and grab the iPad. I don't touch my texts even though I want to. No, I open Instagram instead and click the stories on the top and watch swiping right most of the time until I get to Candace, who's with Ari in matching shirts.

I cave then and type his name in, and his Instagram pops up first with the blue checkmark beside it. Obviously, it's public, and the first picture is of him eating, and the caption makes me smile.

When she says eat chicken over steak, you eat the chicken.

I shake my head and go down the rabbit hole, looking at all his posts. I smile through most of them, and then I see one of him with a weird face, and the caption is:

When you want to send your woman a picture and all your contacts get it.

Looking at the date, I see it matches the date of his Snapchat debacle, and I wonder who his woman was. The pit of my stomach burns. I turn off the iPad and put it on my side table, then turn off the television. "You need to get your head out of your ass," I tell myself as I close my eyes, but all I do that night is dream of Miller and his cocky fucking smirk.

When I wake up the next morning, I'm crabby and bitchy, and then I remember why I hate him. I hate him because he's irritating and cocky. Grabbing my coffee, I walk back to my bed to get my iPad to check my email. Opening it up, I see there is a text from the man in question.

Miller: Morning, gorgeous. Do you know what is happening in seven days?

Me: Zombie apocalypse?

Miller: Nope, better.

Me: Don't you have anything other to do?

Miller: I see you are a ray of sunshine when you wake up in the morning. I'll remember that for Monday.

Me: You are just full of yourself this morning.

Miller: Not just this morning, all the time. Have a great day, gorgeous.

Me: Stop calling me that.

I turn off my iPad and walk back to my bedroom, getting dressed and making my way over to Grandma's house. He doesn't send me a text for the rest of the day, but every morning, I wake up to an annoying good morning text with a countdown to our date.

I don't answer him for the whole week. I go about my day, and the only time I talk about him is when I'm on the air. The team road trip hasn't been too bad. They have won two and lost one, which is good, considering who they were facing.

The home games are even better, and I only admit it on the air, but Miller is having a great start to the season. His average is a plus six, and he's scored at least one goal in the past five games.

I try not to think about Miller when I open my eyes on Sunday, but I have no choice since he's already sent a text this morning.

Miller: It's today, gorgeous. I can't wait to see you. I'll pick you up at three.

Me: Are we senior citizens? Who eats at three p.m.?

He doesn't bother answering me, and at noon, I give up and call him. He sounds out of breath when he answers, and I wonder what he was doing. Obviously, I don't care, so I'm not even going to bother asking him. "Are you seriously picking me up at three?"

"Yeah," he says, and then I hear beeping. "Be ready or not. I can sit on your bed and watch you get ready."

"In your dreams." It's the only comeback I can think of because now my hands are getting clammy, and I'm suddenly nervous as fuck for this date or whatever it is. I'm going to call it a get-together.

"Oh, gorgeous, you do not want to know what you do to me in my dreams." He laughs.

"You dreaming of your death?" I roll my eyes. I'm so tempted to ask him exactly what I do in his dreams, but I'm not going to go there.

"Be ready at three," he says, laughing, and hangs up on me. I didn't even ask him what I should wear or where we are going.

I text him now.

Me: What should I wear?

I press send, and I know even before he answers that I should have rephrased it.

Miller: Naked with a smile.

A shiver courses down my spine when he says that, and I'm annoyed he makes me feel all giddy. Tossing the phone down, I think about it as I walk over to the closet. What should I wear that doesn't scream date? He's been chasing me nonstop since day one, but after I saw him with the girl, he just rubs me the wrong way. I'll never admit it to anyone, but every time he's around, my whole body wakes up. I make excuses because I'm not ready to admit he intrigues me. I am drawn to him, and I fight it every second of the way.

Grabbing a pair of white jeans, I slip them on and then choose a peach satin spaghetti strap blouse to go with it. Looking at myself in the mirror, I decide this is casual yet dressy with a pair of high heel gold wedges. Even though I take the time to curl my hair, I'll never admit that I spend way too much time on myself.

As soon as the doorbell rings, I grab my phone and take a deep breath. "Here goes nothing."

I walk to the door and open it to find him standing there in blue jeans and a navy blue T-shirt that molds to his body. His hands are tucked in his jean pockets, and his aviator glasses keep me from seeing his eyes. The minute he sees me, his face splits into a huge smile, making me smile. "What, no flowers?" I joke. He comes in, shocking me by putting his hand around my waist, and I wait for him to kiss my lips, but instead, he kisses my cheek.

"God, I missed you, gorgeous," he says and then looks at me. "You ready to go?"

"I mean, am I dressed okay?" I ask. Suddenly, I'm nervous about this date and worried I'm not dressed appropriately.

"You look gorgeous, no matter what you wear," he says, grabbing my hand and leading me out to his car. He opens the car door for me, and I get in and watch him walk around the front of the car. When he gets in and starts the car, he looks over at me, and his smile is still all over his face.

"I can't believe this is actually happening," he says as he backs out of my driveway.

"So are you going to tell me where you're taking me?" I look at him. "It's not like I can jump out of a moving car."

"I mean, if you say it like that," he says, laughing, "I'm actually taking you back to my house, and I'm going to cook for you." My stomach sinks because one, he's so fucking cute, and then two, he is actually going out of his way to cook for me.

"I can still jump out?" I look over at him and see his smirk, and for the first time in a long time, I laugh wholeheartedly.

TWELVE

Miller

As I gaze at her, I swear I wouldn't be able to frown, even if I wanted to. It's so good to finally see her. For the past week while I've been traveling, I sent her a text each day, even if she didn't respond. I knew she got them because they showed as read. "I'm going to get on the highway now." Her hands rest in her lap, and I wonder if she would hold my hand or try to break my fingers if I held out my hand.

"I can still jump out," she says, trying to hide her smile. When she opened the door, and I saw her, she took my breath away. She is always stunning, but knowing that she spent time to get dressed to go out with me did something. "If I tuck and roll, I might be okay." I reach out, not even caring, and grab her hand. "You can't drive a car and yank me back," she says, but she doesn't move her hand either. "How was your week?"

"Good," I say. "I don't want to jinx it, but …" I loosen my hold on her hand, expecting her to let go, but she doesn't.

"You guys are meshing well together," she adds in. "I mean, there are still a couple of things even you can work on." I laugh and look over at her. "What, you didn't think I would not tell you what you did wrong?"

"I know how much fun you have with it." I laugh. "So tell me."

"Well, number one, you need to hustle back a little faster," she says, and I know exactly what moment she is talking about. Manning lost the puck in the neutral zone, and by the time I looked back, it was a three on one. "Also, you get a little heated on the ice."

I laugh now. "Is that so?" I shake my head, and she shrugs.

"But all in all, it was a solid performance by you and the team. Manning, though …" She winks at me. "That man is a beast."

"He's married." My voice comes out harshly, and she raises her eyebrows at me. "I mean, maybe not happily, but still."

"Relax there, hotcakes. I was talking about him on the ice. Nothing more." She drops my hand and holds her hands up in surrender. "Besides, he's not really my type."

"Really?" I say. Looking over at her, I want to ask her what her type is. But I have to wait because I pull up to my gate and need to enter the code.

"Oh, look at you. So fancy," she says, laughing. "Is this to keep the harem away?"

"Something like that." Driving in, I park the car, then turn to her. "Welcome to my home."

"I would say thank you for having me." She leans over to open the door. "But you sort of forced me here."

I shrug, giving zero fucks about how she got here. I'm just fucking happy she's here. "Bottom line is you're here. So let's go with you being here."

"It's almost like a smoke mirror," she says as she gets out of the car. I shake my head and open my door, meeting her in front of the car. "This is nice," she says, and I nod my head. "Very you."

"What does that mean?" I ask her, looking back at my house. It's a two-story house, and from the front of the house, you can't tell how big it is because the upper balcony is covered, and you can only see one room on the side because the two-car garage is on the other side.

"It's sleek," she says, looking up, and she isn't wrong. The square stairs lead up to two gray pillars that hold up the upper balcony and cover the door. "Modern."

I grab her hand and link our fingers together, laughing. "Let me give you a tour." This is the second time she's let me do this. I keep expecting her to pull her hand away from mine, but she doesn't rip it away.

Walking up the five steps to the big brown door, I open it, and we are in the foyer. I don't think I've ever been this nervous about someone else seeing my house before. I also have never had anyone that I'm interested in over. This is my home, and I am not going to treat it like a revolving door. It is also my private space, and

I'm going to share it with a one-night stand. "This is the foyer," I say, and she looks at the pictures all along the wall. Each picture is a milestone in my life from my first time on the ice to the last season, when I scored my three hundredth point.

"It's very *GQ*," she says, pushing my shoulder with hers.

"Those stairs lead to the second floor." I point at the staircase on the side and then walk into the great room. And it really is a great room. It's the whole reason I bought this house to begin with. The whole back wall is windows, and to the left, I have two large white couches facing each other with a gray marble table in the middle. Four single chairs are at each end, almost like a box.

"This space is huge," she says, walking in to stand between the couches and the dining room table. "I love how it goes from family room to dining room to massive ass kitchen," she says, pointing toward the kitchen in the back. "Is that where you're going to cook for me?"

"It is," I say, walking into the kitchen and standing beside the big marble island.

"I love the high ceilings." She points at the ceiling. "This house is so you."

"Good," I say, walking to the big stainless steel fridge. "What would you like to drink?" I open the fridge. "Wine, beer, mimosa?"

"Mimosa." She answers right away as she walks over to put her purse on the dining room table. I grab the orange juice and the bottle of champagne.

"We should get a picture of this." I look over at her.

"It's like we are christening the house with you." I wink at her. "I mean, if it was up to me, I'd be licking the champagne off your naked body." Her mouth hangs open. "But for now, let's just go one step at a time."

"Nice save," she says and jumps when I pop the cork. "Also, why do you assume I would get naked for you?"

I shrug my shoulder as I walk to get a champagne glass and pour it, then grab the fresh orange juice I picked up this morning. "Wishful thinking," I say and hand the glass to her.

"Are you not drinking?" she asks, holding the glass at her mouth. I nod.

"I don't really drink," I tell her, "especially not during the season. But having you here is a special occasion." I open the fridge and grab a bottle of beer. "So I will bend the rules for you." I twist open the bottle. "To the beginning of a great—"

"Day." She finishes for me, and I just smirk. She clinks her glass to my bottle and takes a sip, then turns and looks out the window. "I will say that your backyard has to be the nicest backyard I've ever seen," she says, walking to the window.

"Let me show you," I say, putting down my bottle of beer. Walking over to the window, I slide it open. "All these windows open." I walk out, and she follows me to the covered lanai. "There are three seating areas." I point out as I walk down two steps toward the pool. "There is the hot tub," I tell her. "I've spent many nights soaking after a game in there."

"I thought you were going to say something else."

She shakes her head. "I hate hot tubs."

I look at her, shocked. "How can you hate hot tubs?"

"Because of all the sex people have in them." She scrunches up her nose. "It's just a pool of bacteria festering." She shakes her head. "But I love the infinity pool."

"Well, no one has had sex in that hot tub." I point at the tub. "And there are steps on each side leading down to the grass where I have my outside workouts," I say, pointing at the large green yard. I don't tell her that it's enough space to put a treehouse and for kids to run around free.

I point over to the second covered lanai in front of the great room. "And if you walk this way." I walk all across to the third covered lanai. There is an L-shaped couch set with a glass table in the middle, facing a wall with a television and a built-in fireplace. I stop and point at the windows. "This is my bedroom."

"Smooth," she says. "Trying to lure me into your bedroom." She finishes her drink. "I'm going to need a lot more than one mimosa." She chuckles, and I step closer to her. Grabbing her empty glass, I put it on the table next to me.

Walking back to her, I see her eyes follow me, and if someone asked me, I would say she looks nervous. "When I get you in my bedroom," I say, my voice going low, "it's not going to be because you're drunk. It'll be because you are begging me."

She shakes her head. "That's a lot of confidence for a man who has been chasing me for the past four years."

"Well, I was confident enough to get you here," I say

and then lean in. "Even if you did have to buy my time."

She pushes me now. "Fuck off. It was for charity."

"Is that your story?" I say, tucking my hands in my back pockets. Otherwise, I would reach out and touch her, and the last thing I want to do is push her away. I already feel like she has her guard up.

"That's my story, and I'm sticking to it," she says, folding her arms across her chest.

I throw my head back and laugh. "Does that mean you don't want the grand tour of the house?" I point toward the bedroom where you can see the chair in the corner as well as the white cover on the big king-size bed.

"I think we can save that tour for another time," she says. I clap my hands and smile so big my face feels like it's going to hurt. "What are you clapping about?"

"You," I say, getting close enough to her that I can feel her breath on me. "Just admit that this"—I point at her and then at me—"will happen." Her mouth falls open, and I lean in farther. "Good to know we are on the same page," I tell her right before I kiss the corner of her mouth. "Now, let me refill your drink."

THIRTEEN

Layla

I CAN'T SEEM to take my eyes off him while he walks away. The date or whatever we are calling this is going great. I look around the yard and then back at the window that I now know belongs to his bedroom, and I wonder what it looks like. I mean, not that I care, but I do wonder if it matches the rest of the house.

I will admit I thought I would see a bachelor pad with a man cave, but instead, I found a sleek modern home. "Here you go." I hear him say and look back at the sound of his voice. "Were you trying to peek in my room?" he says, and I roll my eyes.

"You caught me," I say. Our fingers graze as I grab the glass of mimosa that he's holding up for me, making me shiver. I blame it on the wind right away, but the tree leaves haven't moved. "I was wondering how fast I can get in and out." I take a sip of the mimosa, hoping like fuck my mouth just stops talking at this point.

"Oh, gorgeous," he says, winking at me. "If you're in my bed, nothing is going to be fast."

"Oh, good God," I say, trying to show him that I'm not affected by his words. He throws his head back and laughs. "Good one." I point at him. He walks toward the door, but I don't follow him. He looks over his shoulder.

"Come on and check it out." He opens the two doors. "I promise I won't bite." He takes one step in and then smirks at me. "I mean, unless you want me to."

"You are the most annoying man," I say, walking to him. "I'm going to check out the bedroom just to prove to you that I don't care."

I walk in ahead of him, and if I wasn't trying to prove a point, I would gush about how beautiful his room is. The ceilings are high with exposed gray beams. The king-size bed sits in the middle with a white duvet on it, a gray throw blanket is across the foot of the bed, and about fifteen throw pillows. "Do you really make your bed every day?"

He shrugs. "Not every day, but I like things clean," he says. I check out the gray velvet couch in front of the bed facing the fireplace with two round gray velvet chairs in front. The lights hanging from the ceiling look like light bulbs on a chain—it's modern and masculine all at the same time. "The master bathroom is in there." He points at the arched doorway in the corner. My feet move on their own, and again, I'm awestruck when I walk into the bathroom. The floor has transitioned from the gray rustic wood planks in his bedroom to a darkish gray marble. The massive shower has mirrors all the way around with what looks like jets everywhere, and it faces a big deep tub that has a marble step to get into it. Candles line the back of the tub, and I can just imagine how it would be.

"It's so …" I try to find the words. "It's so …"

"I love it, too," he says. "Come and let me show you upstairs."

"You really don't have to give me a whole tour," I tell him, but I follow him out of the bathroom past his walk-in closet, and we end up in the great room. "I will give you this; the layout is perfect."

"It's not the only thing that's perfect," he says, and I groan.

"I know," I tell him. "I know you're perfect, too."

He stops and turns around to face me. We're suddenly standing way too close, and our chests are practically touching. He lifts his hand and rubs my cheek with his thumb. I think I hold my breath because I'm not sure what's going on. Maybe the champagne is just fucking with my head. "I was going to say that you're perfect, but thank you for thinking I'm perfect, gorgeous." He winks at me, walking away to the stairs. I put the glass of mimosa down as I follow him.

When I get to the top of the stairs, there is another living room that leads to an outside patio, but I don't stop there. My eyes roam to the hallway and what looks like a game room. "Oh my gosh," I say, looking at the framed jerseys all along the walls around the room. "Are all these yours?"

He nods his head. "This one was when I was drafted." He points at the one all the way at the far end. "That one was the first jersey I wore in the NHL," he says, pointing at the next one. I walk toward the wall and start going from one to the other. "What are these?" I ask him of the wall of pucks all in separate glass boxes.

"That was from my first goal ever." He points at the box on the top with a smile. "I was five, and my mother kept it." I look at him as he stands next to me.

"You, Miller," I say to him, standing in front of him. "You are definitely unexpected."

"Gorgeous," he says, stepping closer to me. "We have just begun." I'm waiting for him to lean in closer to me, waiting for him to kiss me. This is it, but am I going to let him kiss me? Do I really want to do that and confuse him and lead him on? This can't go anywhere; my mind is fighting with itself. "Now let's go start dinner," he says, walking past me and toward the stairs, leaving me here suddenly wishing that he fucking kissed me.

I follow him down the stairs, and he points at the stool in front of the island. "Sit," he tells me, and I raise an eyebrow at him. "Please."

"That's better," I say and sit on the stool. He walks over and gets my glass and puts it in front of me. "What is on the menu?"

"Steak," he says. Walking over to the fridge, he takes the steak out and puts it on the counter while grabbing other things.

"Do you want me to help?" I ask him.

"Are you kidding me?" He laughs, turning to grab the bowls. "You paid twenty-five thousand dollars for me, so the least I can do is cook for you."

I laugh now. "I mean, for twenty-five K, I think you're right." I watch as he marinates the meat.

"What's your favorite music?" he asks, grabbing a remote, and I shrug. "Michael Buble it is."

I laugh when his voice comes out of the speakers. "Are you trying to seduce me?" I ask as he grabs something else and chuckles.

"Gorgeous," he says, "if I was trying to seduce you, I would put on Barry White." He looks up at me and winks.

I laugh so hard my stomach hurts, but I don't say anything as he prepares the steak and then starts on the salad. "Do you always cook?"

"When I have the time, yeah," he says. "It helps me de-stress. I can just focus on the food and not stress about anything else."

"Is it hard to go from a hockey player to a normal human?" I ask, wanting to know everything about him.

"Well, I think I'm a human, to begin with, and being a hockey player is just my job." He walks over and opens a bottle of red wine and grabs a clean wine glass. He pours me some wine and smiles at me. "My job is just under the microscope."

"And when you fuck up, the whole world sees," he says. "I mean, if other people fuck up at work, reporters aren't there shoving a microphone in your face to ask you why you fucked up so bad."

I never actually thought about that. "I guess I do it also then." Taking a sip of my wine, I say, "I get on the air the day after and …"

"You discuss what we did wrong, but"—he looks up at me—"you also discuss what we are doing to fix things or not."

I tilt my head to the side. "Not always." I swallow the wine down. "I mean, when you fuck up."

"Oh, I know." He chuckles. "Also." He leans in and whispers, "Sometimes, I listen just to hear you say my name." I don't know what to say to that, so instead, I just take another gulp of wine. "Do you want to sit by the pool while I barbecue?"

"No," I say, getting up. "I'm going to set the table and make myself useful."

"Well, gorgeous, if you want to make yourself useful …" he says, and I know I set myself up for something. "You can stand next to me in a bikini and feed me grapes while I cook for you."

I can't help the laughter that escapes me. "But if you feel more comfortable with setting the table, that is good, too." He grabs the plate of meat and the bowl of veggies and walks out toward the grill.

"Where do you want to eat?" I ask right before he starts the grill.

"Wherever you want, gorgeous." He places the veggies on the counter next to the grill.

"You know I have a name, right?" I ask. "It's two syllables. Lay-la."

He laughs. "So is gor-geous." Shrugging, he says, "So same."

Shaking my head, I walk back into the house and go to the kitchen, opening drawers to find a tablecloth and then the plates and utensils. I carry the stuff outside, putting it down on the white round table right next to the grill. "Is it okay if we eat outside?"

"More than okay," he says, opening the grill lid and walking away from the smoke that comes out. "If you want, we can play music outside."

"It's totally up to you," I say, setting the table for the two of us. "Should I bring out the salad that you left on the counter?"

"Yes," he says, and when I walk in and then walk back out, he has the food on the table.

"I didn't know how you liked your steak, so I made it medium, and if you need it cooked more, then I can put it back on the grill," he says as I place the salad in the middle of the table.

"That should be perfect," I say, looking down at the food he grilled. The steaks look perfect. He has baked potatoes, some asparagus, and then some veggies in a tin platter that he cooked on the grill, and I'm shocked he did all this. I don't think anyone has actually cooked me a meal before.

"Where do you sit?" I ask. He comes over to the table with two bottles of water that he got out of the fridge that is under the counter. He pulls out one of the chairs and waits for me to sit down. "Thank you," I say, trying to ignore the heavy beating of my heart and the dryness in my mouth.

"You forgot your wine?" he says, putting the bottles of water on the table. I can't say anything to him, so I just nod my head. He walks back into the kitchen, and

I see him coming out with the bottle of wine and my glass, but he is also carrying a glass bowl under his arm. He puts the bottle down, then grabs the bowl and sets it down. The glass bowl has folded paper inside it, and I watch him put down the glass and then pour me some more wine. He walks over to his chair and sits down. "Serve yourself," he says. I grab my fork and place a steak on my plate and then serve him one, too. He grabs the veggies and places some on his plate and then hands it over to me.

"Okay, the suspense is killing me," I say when I grab my fork and knife and cut into the steak.

"What's with the bowl?" I look at him and take a bite of the steak, the meat melting on my tongue.

"That," he says, grabbing his own fork and knife and cutting into his steak and popping a piece into his mouth, "is the question bowl."

"A question bowl?" I ask, taking another bite of the steak.

"It's to get to know each other," he says, and I look at him, shocked that he set this up. "Figured this is one way to get to know you." He winks at me. I have never had a guy try this hard. I have never had a guy want to try this hard. And before he even says the next line, I already know that I'm in uncharted territory. "And it'll be a step to you giving me a chance."

FOURTEEN

MILLER

I WATCH HER face as I say the words. "And it'll be a step to you giving me a chance." She is mid chew when I say it, and she just looks at me. I know I should go easy, but I finally have my chance to lay it out on the line. "Besides, all the other things I've tried to get your attention with have fallen flat." I ignore my sweaty palms, trying to stay cool, calm, and collected, and I hope to fuck she can't hear the pounding of my heart.

"By getting my attention," she says now, cutting her steak roughly. I can tell by her tone that nothing good is going to come from this. "Was it flirting with me and leaving with a different woman each time?" She looks up at me. "I mean, that first time I met you. I left you, and by the time I finished peeing, you were dry humping someone by the bathroom door."

My mouth hangs open now. "I'm not just about the women," I tell her and cut my own steak. "Do you want me to grab a paper, or do you want to go first?"

"Did you actually write the questions?" she asks before she takes another bite.

"I did," I tell her. "This morning when I was having coffee."

Her eyes go back to looking at her plate and coming up. She puts down her fork and knife and puts her hand in the bowl to grab a piece of paper. "So I ask you this question, and then do I have to answer it?"

"If you want to," I tell her. "What's the first question?"

"What do you like to do on your day off?" she asks.

"Is it off-season or during the season?" I counter her, and she sits back in the chair. "Off-season just chill at home and watch a couple of movies. During the season, same," I say, chewing a piece of steak. "What about you?"

"On my day off, I usually go for a run, depending on how hot it is, and then I hit up a market, and then"—she looks down—"I like to bake."

"Really?" I say, shocked. "Baking like Grandma Nancy's brownies or baking like banana bread?"

She laughs now. "My favorite is key lime pie with a graham cracker crust."

"Will you marry me?" I ask, laughing, and she shakes her head, putting down the piece of paper on the table. "My turn." I pick a paper out of the bowl and open it. "Name a moment that changed your life."

"My parents dying," she says right away. "Even though I was too young to understand it or even realize it, it changed my life."

"I'm sorry," I say, putting the paper down and placing my hand on hers. "I didn't know."

"I sometimes wonder how different my life would be if they were still alive," she says. "Now don't get me wrong, Grandma Nancy was the best, and I wouldn't change her for the world. But I sometimes wonder if I would even still be in Dallas if they were alive." I watch her eyes blink away tears.

"You're a strong, strong woman," I say, and she doesn't say anything.

"So what is yours?" I can see her trying to take the focus off herself.

"That's easy."

"I swear." She grabs the glass of wine. "If you say this date, I'm going to drown you in the pool."

I slap my hand on the table and laugh. "For the re-cord, that wasn't what I was going to say." I smile when she glares at me. "Seventeen years old. Second overtime period, game-winning goal in the playoffs." I think back to that moment. "There was a scout in the stands, and I didn't even know."

"That must have been the best night," she says, and I love that she gets it. "I can't imagine."

"It was a good one," I say. "Your turn." I point at the bowl. She sits up and mixes the papers around.

"Watch it, I put the dirty ones on the bottom," I say when she picks the last one on the bottom. She looks at me and then looks at the paper. "I'm just kidding." She opens it. "Or am I?"

She reads the question and just looks at me. "It's not a dirty one."

I snap my fingers. "Shucks. I really wanted to know what color of panties you were wearing."

She shakes her head, ignoring what I just said. "What is one thing that you can't stand in a relationship?"

"That's an easy one," I say, grabbing my water bottle and taking a long sip. "Untruthfulness. Lying. Secrets. All of it. I can't do it." I look at her. "No matter what you say about me or what you think about me, I will never lie or keep anything from you. Ever. Even when I would meet girls, they knew going in that even one lie was a game changer for me. I won't do it to you, so you don't do it to me."

"That's a big, big declaration," she says, looking down as she sets the paper on the table.

"It is what it is. If there is no trust, there is no relationship," I say. She just nods, not adding anything else. I reach into the bowl. "Favorite season."

"That's easy, winter," she says, and I raise an eyebrow.

"Me, too," I reply. "Is it because of hockey?"

"That, and we live in Dallas. There are only so many one hundred degree days I can take."

She leans over and grabs a paper. "What was your longest relationship?" She folds the paper and looks at me expectantly.

"Seven months," I answer her. "Five years ago."

"What?" she gasps. "That is your longest relationship?"

I nod my head. "It was."

"Seven months?" she repeats. "Seven?" She holds up her fingers.

I nod my head, chewing. "She wasn't the one. So I wasn't going to waste her time or mine," I say, and look at her. "I was also twenty-five, but still."

"How do you know that after only seven months?" she asks.

"It was just a feeling I got. I wasn't head over heels for her." I try to find the words to explain. "My parents have been married for forty-six years," I say. "They were both eighteen when they got married. From the first day my dad laid eyes on my mother, he knew. She says the same thing. It's actually really cute when she tells the story. Her eyes light up like it was yesterday. It was a chance meeting, and back then, there were no cell phones and social media to stalk each other." I smile, and she just laughs. "It was a knock on the door, and can I take you out for ice cream kind of times."

"Oh my God," she says, leaning forward with her arms crossed on the table. "That is so fucking cute. Tell me everything."

I chuckle, taking a sip of my water. "There really isn't much to tell. They dated for six months before he saved enough money to buy her a ring. It was a tiny thing, and even though he has money now and wants to replace it, she refuses to have it replaced."

"Do you have a picture of them?" she asks, and her eyes light up. I take out my phone and open my photos and find the one I took of them at Christmas in front of the Christmas tree. Mom's hugging his waist while his arm is around her shoulders.

"Here they are at Christmas. We had it here since it was easier with my schedule." I hand her the phone, and she just smiles and looks up at me.

"You look like your dad." I nod my head. "Can I swipe, or will there be surprise pictures?"

I shake my head and chuckle at her ridiculousness but then nod my head for her to continue. She keeps swiping, looking at all the pictures.

"The two of them have been inseparable since they got married," I say as she looks at the pictures. "The minute she is sad or upset, he can feel it. If he's having a bad day, she knows it even before he comes home. They laugh together, and they celebrate together. There were times that she would be cooking, and he would walk up to her just so he could kiss her. I want that."

"Forgive me for saying this," she says, putting my phone down, "but you aren't exactly seeking the kind of woman who wants the white picket fence."

I chuckle and lean back in my chair. "You got me there." She takes a drink of her wine. "But that was then, and this is now. I'm thirty years old. It's time for me to grow up, as my father and mother say. Besides, I want that. I want to have the white fence and to love someone so much that I feel lost without them."

She laughs. "It's cute that you are still scared of your parents."

I roll my eyes. "I'm not scared of my parents. I just don't want to let them down." I watch her when I say the next sentence. "It's why I will only get married once. When I say the vows, it's going to be forever, and it's going to be to someone who is as head over heels for me as I am for her." She swallows and avoids making eye contact with me.

"Things change," she says, looking at me. "People can change over time. Sometimes divorce is better than staying in a marriage that is empty." She shrugs and smiles. "I'm going to start cleaning up," she says, pushing away from the table.

"But we still have more questions," I say. I'm tempted to ask her about her last relationship, but something tells me it's not what she wants to discuss. I lean in now and take the top paper. "What is the most romantic thing that someone has done for you?"

As I watch her, I wonder if she'll sit down and answer or just ignore it. I'm holding my breath, hoping she just goes with it. "I don't want to answer that," she says, sitting down and pouring herself another glass of wine. I can see that she's nervous.

"Why not?" I ask, tapping the paper on the table. "Okay, fine, I'll ask you another question."

I put the paper down and take out another question. "A movie you can watch over and over again."

"*Notting Hill*." She answers this one without thinking twice. "I'm just a girl in front of a boy asking him to love her." Her eyes shine. "What about you?"

"*Mighty Ducks*. The Flying V gets me every time," I say, and she just throws her head back and laughs. *I can watch her every night*, I think to myself. I can sit down with her every night and ask her questions. The feeling scares me just a bit, and I grab my water just to keep my hands busy.

She finally stops laughing and looks at me. "Ask me the question again," she says, her voice going low. I don't move. I just look at her. "The last one."

I sit up again and grab the paper, opening it. "What is the most romantic thing that someone has done for you?"

She looks up at me and then looks down at her hands. Her hair falls in front of her face, and she tucks in a piece behind her ear. Her eyes are so light as a shy smile curls her lips. "I don't want you to make too much of this," she says and finishes her wine for the liquid courage. "This," she says softly. "This, right here, is the most romantic thing someone has ever done for me."

FIFTEEN

Layla

MY HEART HAMMERS in my chest almost as if it's trying to get out, and my mouth is as dry as the desert. "This, right here, is the most romantic thing someone has ever done for me," I admit, and just from his smile, I know it was the right thing to say. This whole dinner has knocked me on my ass.

"Is it really?" he asks. His brown eyes turn a soft amber color, and I wonder if his cheeks hurt from smiling.

"It really is," I admit. "It's also the most thoughtful."

"Does this mean you might say yes to a second date?" He winks, and I throw my head back and laugh. I don't think I've ever laughed this much on a date before. It's so carefree.

"Relax there, Romeo," I say and finally get up and start clearing the plates. "Why don't we see how the rest of the date goes first?" Standing, he places his hands on mine to take the plates from my hands and puts them back on the table.

"You are not cleaning the table," he says. "I'll clean it up later."

"I think there is a universal rule that the cook doesn't clean."

"There is also a universal rule that says when a gorgeous woman agrees to have dinner with you, you don't make her waste her time cleaning up." He smirks, and I roll my eyes.

I shake my head. "Okay, fine." I sit down. "Let's finish these questions."

He slaps his hands together. "Please pick the what color is your panties one."

I slap the table, laughing. "White," I tell him, and he laughs. For the rest of the night, we go through the questions, and none of them are about my panties. They are actually all thoughtful, and we get to know each other better.

"I have to get going," I say, getting up. "I have a show to prepare for."

"I'll go and get my keys," he says and walks into the house.

"I can take an Uber," I tell him.

He looks back over his shoulder at me. "For twenty-five K, you best believe I will deliver you to your front door," he says. I watch his ass as he walks away. "I know you're watching me," he says, not turning around.

"How do you know that?" I shout.

"Because if you walked away from me," he says, stopping and looking at me, "you can bet your sweet ass that I'd be looking at you. Now let's go." He motions with his head. I start walking toward him, and he puts his hands on his hips. "See, I'm totally checking you out."

"Smooth," I say, and we walk through his house together toward the front door. The car is parked right out front. He opens the car door for me, and when we get to my house, I look over at him as my hand comes out to grab the door handle. "Thank you."

He puts his back to the car door, keeping one hand on the steering wheel. "The pleasure was all mine." He looks at my house and then back at me. "I know that you're expecting me to kiss you right now."

"Oh my God," I say, opening the door and putting one foot out. His hand wraps around my wrist, stopping me from getting out of the car.

"I want to kiss you," he says softly. "But I don't want you to kiss me because you think you have to. I want you to kiss me because you just can't help yourself." He lets go of my hand. "One of these days, gorgeous, you are going to beg me to kiss you."

"Always so sure of yourself." I get out of the car but then lean back in. "And just for the record, I would have let you kiss me." His mouth opens wide in shock, and I close the door.

Walking up to my front door, I feel his eyes on me as I put my code into the front door. As soon as I get into the house, I slam the door without looking back to see if he was watching. I lock the door, and only when I hear his car drive away do I drop my head against the door and let myself relax.

"What the fuck are you doing?" I ask, expecting someone to answer me. Pushing away from the door, I walk farther into the house without bothering to turn on any lights. Hearing my phone ding in my purse puts a smile across my face.

Miller: I had the most amazing time with you. Thank you for making today MY most romantic date ever.

I sit on the bed looking at the text but don't respond. I'm not sure what to say when another text comes through.

Miller: Also I totally checked you out when you were walking away.

With a laugh, I put the phone down and slip off my shoes. Heading into the bathroom, I turn on the dim lights as I walk to the shower. The whole day plays over in my head as I lean back under the stream and let the warm water flow over me. His words play over and over in my mind. *Marriage is a one-time thing for him.* I can honestly say that he shocked the shit out of me with that one because I had him pegged as a bachelor for life—a wham, bam, thank you, ma'am kind of guy—and nothing like the man who had dinner with me.

He was compassionate, he was kind, he was genuine, and he was attentive. He wasn't the cocky, arrogant guy I had built up in my head over these years, and for that, I felt horrible. I turn the water off and step out of the shower. Grabbing the white plush towel, I wrap it around me. I slip into bed naked and close my eyes, and all I can see is his smile. My night is filled with dreams of the kiss he never gave me.

The next morning when my alarm goes off, I stretch to grab my phone, then scroll up to see what I missed while I was asleep. A couple of emails, an Instagram alert, and then finally a text from Miller about an hour ago.

Miller: Have a great day, gorgeous.

I think about answering him, but instead, I open my emails, and I get sucked into Instagram. I scroll my feed and then my notifications when I see that Candace commented on Miller's latest post. My curiosity gets the better of me, and I click the picture.

It's the picture of the dishes on the table, and the caption is:

When you'd rather look into her eyes and hear her laughter than clean up.

I click on the comments and see several hundred women begging to have dinner with him. Candace leaves one, calling him a smooth operator. By the time I reach the end of the thread, I'm rolling my eyes, irritated that it bothers me. I make my coffee and go back to my bedroom to dress for work.

After grabbing a pair of blue jeans and a white spaghetti strap shirt that I tuck into the front, I slip my beige cashmere long sweater over it. My open-toed boots complete the look. I toss my phone into my bag without looking at it again and then grab my coffee and make my way over to the studio.

I see Brian when I walk into the studio, and he holds up his hand to wave to me. I put my coffee and my water down on the desk and grab the earphones. "Testing," I say, and he nods.

The show begins, and I start off. "Hello, everyone, and welcome to the show. I'm your host Layla Paterson with my trusted producer, Brian."

"Happy Monday, everyone," Brian says. "How was your weekend?"

"Uneventful." I look at him, and he just smiles at me like he knows something.

"Well, I heard that you won a certain auction over the weekend," he says, and I nod my head.

"I did, and I'm so excited to say that one lucky listener is going to be attending the winter classic game right here in Dallas." He shakes his head. "With a meet and greet with five of the Dallas players."

"Wow," Brian says. "Nice giveaway."

"It is. Why don't we take a caller and see what they thought of the game on Saturday," I say, and I click on the first flashing button. "Welcome to the show."

"Hey, Layla," the male caller says. "Hey, Brian. I have a beef to pick with the team."

"I'm here for all this," I say, leaning back and waiting.

"I just think they had an amazing time on the road. They won games by playing some smart hockey, but then they come home and play like amateurs."

"Well," I say, "I think they played a good game. It wasn't their best game, but I've seen them play worse."

"Oh, that is for sure. Miller looked like he had two left skates on," he says, "and Manning and Ralph played like they had oil on their gloves."

"I'm going to disagree with you on those," I say, trying not to get irritated about him talking about Miller.

"They had a couple of bad shifts, that is for sure, but by the second period, I think everyone was doing what needed to be done. They went into the third period trailing by two goals to come out and win in overtime. They hustled their asses. Thanks for calling. Who do we have next?" I ask the next caller, and we go on and on until I sign off at the end of the show.

"That was a good show," Brian says, coming into the room when I take off my headphones and place them down. "Word on the street is your bank account is twenty-five K lighter."

"It's for charity," I say, getting up. "It's a tax write-off." I get up and grab my stuff, listening to him laugh. "See you tomorrow." I walk out of the door and into my office, grabbing my bag and phone.

"You're running out already?" the receptionist asks. "Beat the Monday traffic."

"You got it," I say, getting into the elevator. I check my phone and see that I have four texts from Miller.

Miller: *Your voice is that of an angel.*

Miller: *That guy was a dick.*

Miller: *Do you want to go out for ice cream tonight?*

Miller: *Unless you want to have dinner also.*

I don't answer him back because the elevator door opens, and I walk to my car. I make my way home, singing at the top of my lungs to the radio.

Slipping off my jeans and putting on my shorts and a tank top, I grab my hair and pin it at the top of my head. I click on the television while I go to the fridge to start preparing my dinner. I'm just turning off the stove when

I hear the doorbell ring, so I put the pan down and grab a cloth to wipe my hands. The doorbell rings again as I head to the front door.

"I'm coming!" I shout and then open the door, coming face-to-face with the man I've been avoiding all day.

"Figured it would be hard to ignore me if I was right in front of you," he says, coming into the house and kissing my cheek. "It smells great in here."

SIXTEEN

MILLER

STANDING AT HER front door, I'm not sure I'm doing the right thing as I wipe my clammy hands on my jeans and ring the bell. "Here goes nothing," I tell myself, and I'm that much of a creep that I lean in and put my ear to the door. The sound of the television is playing. "Is that *SportsCenter*?" I try to listen for a second more. "God, this woman is all that," I say and ring the bell again.

"I'm coming!" I hear her shout, and the smile fills my face. All day, I've been texting her, and it's been radio silence. The sound of the door unlocking makes my heart speed up even more.

Now I have to wonder if this was actually a good idea. Fuck, maybe I should have thought things through before I just showed up here unannounced. Yet the minute I see her in her shorts and tank top, I know I made the right decision. "Figured it would be hard to ignore me if I was right in front of you." I walk into the house, her shocked mouth hanging open. I want nothing more than to kiss her, but instead, I kiss her right on the cheek. "It smells great in here."

I step into the foyer and wait for her to close the door. "What are you doing here?"

"I sent you more than five texts," I say. "According to Google, I should give you until tomorrow to get back to me." I shrug, thinking about the list that told me not to come over here, not to mention the texts, and, more importantly, give her space. "I'm not one to follow the rules."

"You don't say," she says, shaking her head. "What if I was with someone?"

I look past her into the house. "Are you really with someone?" I ask, suddenly pissed that she would do that.

"No," she says, rolling her eyes. "But still."

"That isn't funny," I say. She walks away from me, and I can see the cheeks of her ass in those shorts. My cock suddenly wakes up, and I don't move. She stops and looks over at me. "Just checking out the view," I say, and she throws her head back and groans.

"Walk in front of me," she says, and I smirk at her.

"Want to check out the goods?" I say, walking past her. "I can walk backward if you want to check out the main event."

"What are you doing here?" she asks me, walking with me into the main room, and I follow her into the kitchen.

"I wanted to take you for ice cream," I say, and she

looks at me. "And I wanted to see you."

"Did you eat?" she asks, and I shake my head. "I was too busy trying to text you and then reading bad information online about this."

She laughs then, and I finally feel my stomach settle and don't feel like an idiot for just showing up. "What did you make?"

"Crispy chicken, honey parsley carrots, and basmati rice," she says, and I just look at her. "What? I like to cook."

She places two plates on the counter and scoops the food onto them. Walking over, she sets them on the counter. "Do you want some water?"

"Yes, please." I pull out the chair and sit down, waiting for her to come back. I see her plate is half the size of my portion. "Thank you," I say when she sits next to me. "I wasn't expecting this."

She shakes her head. "I wasn't going to be rude and eat in front of you without offering you some." I grab the knife and pick up a carrot. "And I figured you wouldn't leave anyway."

"It's like we've been together forever." I wink at her. "These are the best carrots I've ever had."

"You don't have to pretend," she says while eating a carrot from her plate. "So what else did Google say?"

"Well, I'm not supposed to discuss the text, which is stupid," I tell her as I chew another piece. "One piece of advice was to wait five days," I huff out. "Five days is equivalent to a year." She laughs. "It also said not to ask you out again. But that shit was too late since we're going for ice cream."

"So you basically just made your own rule book." She chews a piece of chicken.

I put my fork down. "I've never been in this position before."

"The one where the girls don't text you back?" she asks, not making eye contact as she scoots the food around her plate.

"I mean, yes and no," I tell her. "I've never had to jump through hoops."

She pushes away from the counter and takes her plate with her, tossing half of it in the garbage. "No one is asking you to jump through hoops." She crosses her arms over her chest. "I didn't ask you to come over here."

I look at her now, trying to read her. "Oh, trust me, I know." I finish eating my plate. "I like this."

"Me glaring at you while you eat the dinner I made for myself?" she says, and I clap my hands, laughing.

"This," I say, pointing at her and then at me. "And for the record, I want to jump through hoops for you." I see her shield come down just a bit. "Now, can I please take you for ice cream?"

"I'm lactose intolerant," she fires back with attitude.

"Really?" I say. I fold my arms over my chest, knowing full well she's lying. "So if I get up right now and look in your fridge, I won't find ice cream?"

"Um," she starts, and then I can see her thinking of an excuse. "It's for when Ari comes over."

I laugh. "At Ari's birthday party, you ate a piece of cake." I point out, not mentioning how I watched her from across the room.

"Okay and?" She looks at me, not sure where I am going with all this information.

"Gorgeous"—I laugh—"it was ice cream cake." I see her mouth hang open in surprise. "Now, can you please go get some pants on so I can take you to get some ice cream?"

"Okay, fine." She pushes away from the counter. "But for the record, I found out I was lactose intolerant after that party."

"They have sorbet," I tell her as she walks away from me, and I watch her ass.

"Stop watching me, pervert!" she shouts, and I laugh. Getting up, I walk over to the sink, then rinse off our plates and load the dishwasher.

"Okay, fine, I'm ready," she huffs, and I look over and see her wearing tight jeans with the same tank top, but she's wrapped a sweater over her shoulders.

"You look gorgeous," I tell her, and she shakes her head, making me laugh. "It's going to be fucking amazing."

I walk toward the door and hear her. "What is going to be amazing?"

Stopping at the door, I turn, and when she almost bumps into me, my hands grasp her hips to steady her. The only lights are coming from the kitchen. I bend my head and lean close to her. "When you finally let me kiss you," I say in a whisper. "Now, let's get going. I don't want to keep you out too late and have you come up with another excuse for why I can't see you tomorrow." I turn and unlock the door, my hands and body itching to hold her hand in mine, but I have to go slow and not jump in feet first.

"I'm busy tomorrow," she says before I open the car door for her.

"Obviously," I say, and she laughs.

"I have no idea what to do with you," she says right before she gets into the car.

"Good," I tell her. "Because I have no idea what the fuck I'm doing with me either." I close the door and head over to the driver's seat.

After starting the car, I make my way over to the ice cream parlor I frequent. I'm surprised to see so many people there. I get out, and I'm not even five steps from the car before someone notices me. "Fuck," I say to myself when she gets out of the car.

"You ready?" I ask, and she nods. We walk toward the door when someone calls my name, and I look over. The blonde is there with three friends. I smile and pick up my hand to wave.

I walk another couple of steps, and the same blonde comes over to us. "Can I have a picture?" she asks, and I smile.

"Sure you can," I say and look over at Layla, who just watches from the side.

"I'm going to put this on my Instagram right away," the blonde says, holding up the phone and snapping a selfie of us. "Do you mind if my friends join in?"

"The more, the merrier," I say, and the three girls come over. "We are going to have to squeeze in to get the picture." I look at the camera. "How lucky can one guy be?" I laugh with them, and she tells me she'll tag me on Instagram.

"Thank you guys so much," I say to them and then turn around to see that Layla has taken off. I look around and see that she is standing in line in the store.

"There you are," I say, walking to stand next to her. "I was looking for you. You just took off."

"Figured you had enough attention on you," she says, and I don't have a chance to say anything when she smiles at the girl behind the counter who looks at her and then at me and then comes back when it finally clicks who I am. Hockey is a big deal in Dallas, so it's no surprise that people notice me. "Hi, can I get one scoop of strawberry in a cup, please," she says, and the lady nods at her.

"Is that all?" she asks when she hands her the cup. Layla takes the cup and moves away toward the cashier.

"I'll have the same," I tell the girl, and she makes me the same cup. I walk to Layla and see that she's already paid for the two ice creams.

"I was going to pay for it," I tell her as she grabs a couple of napkins.

"It's fine," she says the two words, and that's it.

"Do you want to eat in here or outside?" I ask, looking around and see two more girls notice who I am.

"Can we have a picture?" one of them asks. I smile and nod, posing for the picture. It takes Layla two seconds to walk back to the car, and that is where I find her waiting for me.

"Sorry about that," I say. "It's not usually like that."

She laughs, and I realize she's pissed off. "It's always like that. You just never notice."

"What's that supposed to mean?" I ask her. "It's my job."

"It's your job to play hockey," she says. "I don't think your job description includes flirting."

I want to take a step back. "I wasn't flirting," I tell her and think about the whole conversation. "I was being nice."

"I've been around other people who are in the same position as you, and there is a way to be nice without flirting." She shrugs. "I mean, I don't really care. That's a you problem."

"Oh my God," I say, laughing. "You're jealous."

SEVENTEEN

LAYLA

I WATCH HIM, my blood to the point of boiling. He went through all this to get me to come out with him and then blatantly flirts with other girls in front of me. And then he thinks I'm jealous. He has lost his goddamn mind. "You're jealous." He laughs, and I stand here in front of him with my mouth hanging open.

"You have got to be kidding me?" I'm shocked, and the ice cream is now making my stomach curl. I walk over to the garbage can and toss the ice cream away. "I'm ready to go."

"Why can't you just admit it?" he says, looking at me. I look around to see if anyone is looking in our direction. A couple of people are watching us, making me look down at the ground and then back up. "There is nothing wrong with you being jealous."

I don't know if I trust myself not to kick him in the balls, so instead, I just grab my phone out of my pocket.

"I'll catch an Uber," I tell him, trying to get my heart rate to go down and focus on the phone in front of me.

"I'll drive you," he says, walking past me and going to throw his ice cream in the garbage. I walk to the car and open my door and close it before he even turns around to walk back. He gets into the car, not saying a word until we are far away from the ice cream place.

"I was just joking with you," he says, his voice low, and I look over.

"It's fine," I tell him, and I just look out the window.

"I didn't mean anything by it," he says, and I look at him. "I was just …" he starts to say and then stops.

"You were just what?" I'm so curious to see if he gets it.

"I was just happy that you might have been jealous," he says, and I take a deep breath. "That's all."

"For the record, I was not jealous. I was annoyed, but that's a me problem, and it's not a you problem, so don't worry about it," I tell him as he pulls into my driveway. "Thank you for the ice cream." I get out of the car as fast as I can. "Good luck in Denver," I say before I slam the car door.

I practically run into my house and lock the door. Only then do I let the hurt set in and kick myself for even making me feel this way. I ignore the ping of my phone, and I ignore the hurt in my chest by burying it just like I always have.

The next day, it lingers on my mind more than I care, pissing me off that I'm letting it even bother me. I know he's texted me, but I leave the messages unread, which just makes my phone heavier and heavier.

I'm just getting home a couple of days later when the phone rings. I check the name before I even answer it. "Well, well, well," I say with a smile. "If it isn't my best friend."

Candace laughs right away, and I can hear that I'm on speaker in her car. "Well, well, well, if it isn't my best friend, the big spender," she says, and I groan.

"Am I never going to live that down?" I unlock the door and walk into my house, tossing my keys on the table in the foyer. I kick off my ballerina flats, dumping my purse and the sweater at the same time at the door.

"Not anytime soon," she says.

"Is that the only reason you called me?" I shake my head. "Don't you have something better to do?"

"It's actually the reason I'm calling," she says. "Ari and I were wondering if you wanted to come over and have dinner with us." She mentions her little girl. "Make it a girls' night."

I sit on the couch with the phone to my ear and then press speaker. "That sounds like the best idea ever. Is she going to be wearing her Halloween costume?" I smile, thinking of the pictures I saw on Instagram this morning of Ariella dressed up as Minnie Mouse.

"I think I can arrange that since she had a tantrum this morning when I told her that she couldn't wear it out to our mommy and me class." I laugh until my stomach hurts. "It's not funny. I swear I think she said bitch."

"She did not," I say. "What time were you thinking?"

"I'm pulling up to my house now," she says, and I

hear the car stop. "So now would be good."

"Perfect. I'll leave now." I get up. "What should I bring?"

"Nothing," she says, her voice tight. "And I mean nothing."

"Listen, that tone might work with Ralph and Ari, but you are not the boss of me," I say, and it makes her laugh. "I'll be there shortly."

I walk to my bedroom, changing out of my jeans for yoga pants and a sweater. Slipping on my slides, I grab my purse on the way out. I make a pit stop on the way, and when I pull up to her house, I'm shocked to see a for sale sign. I grab the two bags and the white box of cupcakes, and then snatch the balloon and walk to the front door.

"Knock, knock, knock," I say when I walk into the house, and I hear Ariella squeal. "Where is my favorite girl in the whole world?" I sing-song, stopping in the middle of the family room as she runs to me, still a little unsteady. Candace follows, ready to catch her if she falls down. I squat down in time to catch her when she falls forward. "There she is." I kiss her neck, and she laughs. "I brought you a balloon," I say, and her blue eyes light up.

"Loon," she says and looks back at Candace. "Mama, ook loon."

"I see that, princess." She smiles and then spots the other bags. "I see also that Auntie Layla didn't listen to Mommy."

I laugh at the way she just sang the sentence. "I'll

save the cupcake for after dinner."

I take the doll I just bought her out of the bag, and she claps her hands and gives it to Candace. "Mama, open."

"Another doll?" Candace says.

"I'm obviously buying her love. Can you just give me this one thing?" I squeeze her to me. "But enough of that. You're moving?" I ask her as she sits down next to me and opens the doll for Ari.

"Ralph said that if he can't pay me for this house, then we have to move," she says, handing the doll to Ari. "And when I didn't accept the money, he put a for sale sign on the lawn." I throw my head back and laugh. Ralph and Candace met a little more than six months ago. He was a single dad and needed help with his social media. Enter Candace and by the time both of them knew what was happening, they were in love with each other. "Little does he know that I already picked out the perfect house."

"Sneaky," I tell her, and she shrugs.

"What's new with you?" I look at her. "How did the date with Miller go?"

"Grandma Nancy loved him." I fill her in on the date that he had with Nancy, and her laughter has tears streaming down her face. "Then the next day, I felt sorry for him and went out on a date with him."

She stops laughing and looks at me, shock filling her face. "Wait, what?" She looks confused. "You went out on a date?" I nod my head. "With Miller?" Again, I nod my head, not sure I can put it into words. "The guy you loathe?" I roll my eyes at that. "The guy you paid twenty-five thousand for?"

I throw up my hands. "It was for charity," I tell her, and she just raises her eyebrows at me. "But yes, I went out on a date with him. I mean, technically. We didn't really go out."

She gasps. "Oh my God, you had sex with him?"

"Oh my God." I put my head back. "I did not have sex with him. He picked me up and took me over to his house and made me dinner."

She shakes her head. "I'm sorry, I'm just …" Her hands come up. "I'm …" She puts her hands on her face. "You need to just go slow."

"It's not a big deal," I say, getting up now and bringing the white box to the counter. "I owed him a date, so I went out with him. He made me dinner."

"Hold on." She grabs her phone. "This is the dinner he made for you?" She shows me the picture that I already saw, and I nod. She gets up now and walks over to the fridge. "I need wine."

"Yeah, well," I tell her. "I also let him take me out for ice cream," I tell her, hoping she'll let it go, but she doesn't. "It's like a miracle."

"Well, it ended in a disaster, so it's safe to say that will never happen again," I tell her, getting a sinking feeling in my stomach. She picks up her phone and orders pizza and then turns to me while keeping one eye on Ari. "It really isn't that big of a deal. He came over a couple of days ago to thank me for going out with him. Then asked me to go have ice cream with him."

"And …" She waits for me to finish.

"And nothing." I tap my fingers on the counter. "We were there a whole five minutes, if not less." She doesn't say anything as she waits for me to finish. "Fine," I snap. "He flirted with girls right in front of me. I got salty, and I asked him to drive me home."

"You mean, you got jealous," she says the same thing that Miller said, but I glare at her.

"I wasn't jealous. I was annoyed that he blatantly flirted with other women in front of me. Who does that? It's disrespectful. I was right there. He came over to my house to take me out. I didn't call him to beg him to take me out; he showed up out of the blue. *After* I ignored his texts all day." The pitch of my voice rises, and I'm suddenly angry. "Google even told him not to call me but Mr. I Go By My Own Rules decided to show up at my door." She doesn't say anything, which frustrates me even further. "What?" I snap at her. "What are you thinking?"

"You aren't going to like what I have to say," she says, and I fold my hands over my chest. "Could it be that you got upset because you like him?" I open my mouth to scream, but she puts her hand up. "He should not have flirted with other women in front of you. That was disrespectful but think about it. If you didn't care about him, would you really care?"

I stare at her, opening my mouth and closing it and then opening it again. "If you went out with Ralph and he flirted with other women, would you care?"

"I'd cut his balls off." I point at her.

"Okay, fine. If you went out with Brian, and he flirted

with other women, would you care?"

I glare at her. "No, I would give him a high-five."

"Which means …" She looks at me, and all I can do is glare at her.

"I don't like him," I tell her, and she rolls her lips. "Fuck," I say, slapping my palm to my forehead. "I might like him."

EIGHTEEN

MILLER

SHE HASN'T ANSWERED one of my texts in three days. Three long fucking days. My head is spinning, and I literally have no idea what to do. I text her before I left for Denver, and she never answered me.

I arrive at the arena at the scheduled time for our Saturday game. My body's still sore from the grueling physical game we played last night. We flew back home right after the game, and I had no time to do anything but sleep. Walking into the locker room carrying a cup of coffee, I'm one of the last to arrive. "Gentlemen," I say. The rookies nod at me, some in their workout clothes already. I sit in my spot next to Manning, who is undressing. "My ass is tired," I say, putting my coffee next to me and just taking a second to breathe.

"If you think your ass is tired now," Manning says, "wait until next week when we play four games in six days." Thinking about next week makes me groan. We leave tomorrow night and are away the whole week.

"I hate those long stretches," Ralph says, taking a drink of his protein shake. "I can do two days, but a whole seven?" He shakes his head. "Get ready for cranky Ralph."

I laugh at him as I shrug off my jacket. "When don't we have cranky Ralph?" Manning laughs with me. "Him, I get," I say, pointing my thumb at Manning. "With his wife and all."

"Can we not talk about her," he says. Sitting down, he puts a baseball hat on his head. I look around and see that the rookies have gone and are no doubt in the gym working on their cardio. "I showed up at home last night, and she greeted me naked."

I laugh. "I don't know why that would make you cranky."

"She had hickeys on her tits," he says, and my mouth hangs open. "Yeah. I don't even care, to be honest. I haven't felt anything for her in years, and I just want fucking out."

"I don't know how you do it," Ralph says. "At some point, you are just going to have to leave her and brace yourself for the worst."

"I don't want to put my son through that." He shakes his head. "Worst case, I have another four years, and then I can let him decide." He gets up. "Time to get my head into the game." He walks out of the room.

"Time to get my legs working," Ralph says. "Show off for my girls." He winks at me.

"Is Candace coming tonight?" I ask, and he nods, his whole face lighting up with a smile. I smile back at him, and my chest suddenly hurts. *I want that*, I think to my-self. I take out my phone when Ralph walks out and send her a text.

Me: This is officially the third day with no response. According to Google, I should wait at least five days before I message you again, or I'm going to look des-perate. I guess it's too late for that. Although, accord-ing to another Google article, after twenty-four hours, I should give up. LOL. I hope you are doing well. I was wondering if you would like to go and get coffee tomorrow? I would ask you to have lunch with me, but something tells me that you would say no to that. But coffee is safe, or is it?

I press send and then look at how long the message is. It's been three days with no response, and I'm get-ting a bit scared I said or did something to offend her. I mean, I probably did say something, but in my defense, I was probably nervous. I replay the night over and over in my head to see if I can pinpoint exactly what it was that would make her not answer. Getting to know her is even better than I thought it would be. I knew she was hot, but she's funny as hell, and she just has a way about her that makes you want to sit down and talk to her about literally anything from the day's events in the media to paint drying on a wall.

As I'm holding the phone in my hand, my leg starts to move up and down with the nervous energy flowing through me again. My fingers start to move before I even know what is happening.

Me: Wow, I didn't know it would be that long. But

seriously, gorgeous, let me bring you coffee, or you can bring me coffee. Whatever you want.

I put the phone down and start getting ready for the game. Slipping into my workout clothes, I ride the bike for an hour to warm up my legs. After a light dinner, I walk back to the locker room and finish getting ready. We skate on the ice, and the fans are cheering already. Ralph stands by the glass looking at Ari and Candace, and right behind him is the woman who has been driving me mad. She's looking more beautiful than ever.

I skate next to him and wave at Ari and then point at Layla. "You!" I shout at her, and she just looks at me. "Answer your goddamn texts, woman." Ralph shakes his head while Candace and Layla just laugh.

Her eyes go light, and she flips me the bird. "She likes me," I say, nodding my head. I blow her a kiss, and she ducks to get out of the way. I wait for her to stand and look at me. "Answer your text." Then it finally dawns on me. "Oh my God, did you block me?" I ask her through the glass and hear Manning now laughing behind me.

"Layla, do us all a favor," he says to her. "Answer his text before he cries."

"Fuck you," I tell him, then turn back to Layla. "I'm picking you up tomorrow at ten."

"I can't hear you?" she jokes, and finally Candace answers.

"She'll be ready." I put my hands in the air as if I just scored an overtime goal.

"See you later, gorgeous," I say, skating away before she says something to me.

The game is brutal, but we end up winning, surprising even us. When I skate off the ice, I give my stick to the equipment guy and then walk into the locker room. The away bags are already set up for us to pack our stuff. It's only after I get out of the shower do I walk over and grab my phone. I usually have a shit ton of notifications after the game with people tagging me in pictures. I scroll down until I see a text alert.

Layla: There is a little café I know of. I'll be there until ten thirty.

She follows it with the address of the coffee shop. I smile so big, and I don't bother answering her back in case she decides to leave. I walk out of the arena, saying bye to the guys, and go straight home. Usually, I head to the bar with some of the boys, but I've stopped doing that lately. I get home and walk to the kitchen, then heat some food and go straight to bed after eating.

The next day, I get to the coffee shop at nine forty-five. Pulling open the door, I step in, sliding my glasses off and hanging them on my shirt. I look around the café at the three walls painted black and a wall with exposed brick. Black tables are all around the room with a brown couch in the corner. The coffee bar is along the brick wall, and I smile at the guy behind the counter. I order two lattes, and he tells me to grab a seat, and he'll bring them to me. I look over and see that they have fresh muffins and croissants. I order two of each and then walk to the open door in the back of the room. It leads to a back patio filled with the same black tables and a huge white awning over it. I grab a table in the corner and text her that I'm already here.

I watch the door the whole time, and I start to panic when it's past ten o'clock. I'm about to call her when I see her walking into the back. Her eyes roam the room until she spots me. I get a chance to look at her. She is wearing dark blue jeans with a beige sweater tucked into the front and a leather jacket that hangs open. She looks so fucking sexy. She walks over as soon as she sees me, and I get up. "Morning, gorgeous," I say, shocking her when I lean down and kiss her cheek.

"Sorry I'm late," she says. I grab the empty chair and hold it for her to sit down in. "Thank you."

"I ordered you a latte," I tell her. "But I think it's cold."

"That's okay," she says. I sit next to her, and I'm so happy that she came. She picks up a cup and takes a sip. "It's still warm."

"I can get you another one," I say, and she just shakes her head. "It's fine."

"How have you been?" I ask awkwardly, and she laughs.

"This is awkward, right?" she says, and I want to take her hand in mine. "It's weird."

"It's because you didn't answer my text." She laughs.

"Which one?" she answers, and it's my turn to laugh now.

"I wouldn't have had to send you all those texts if you'd just answered me back," I tell her.

"You are persistent. I will give you that," she says. "But honestly, you didn't need to be." She takes another sip of her coffee and tucks her hair behind her ear.

"Look, if I did or said anything that offended you …" I start, and I'm suddenly nervous that she is going to get up and leave. "I'm sorry."

She doesn't say anything. She just looks at me, and I wish I knew how to read her. "Thank you," she says softly, "for not meaning to offend me."

"I seriously missed talking to you," I tell her. "Even though we never really talked before, I missed joking with you and asking you questions."

"That's a really nice thing to say." She looks down.

"I have to be somewhere in twenty minutes," I tell her when I see it's almost ten twenty. "Will you come with me?"

"So you double-booked yourself?" She laughs. "I'm shocked."

"Will you come with me?" I ask her, not willing to tell her that this is something I do once a month.

"I don't know," she answers, not sure.

Standing, I grab her hand in mine. "I promise you are going to love it."

She rolls her eyes, and I laugh, relieving the tightness in my chest. "Fine, let's go."

We walk out, and I put my glasses on and open the car door for her. "I can take my car," she says, stopping.

"So you can take off on me?" I joke. "Not a chance."

With a laugh, she gets in the car. I close the door after her and get into the car and make my way over to the standing engagement I have. We park in the parking lot, and when we get out, she looks over at me. "Are we here to get your monthly STI check?" She looks at the hospital building. I clap my hands together and laugh.

"That was a good one," I say, "and if you are keeping track, I had mine two months ago, and I'm clean."

"A lot can change in two months." She looks over at me as we walk into the hospital lobby and head straight to the elevator. I laugh and press the button for the fourth floor. "Seriously, though," she says quietly, "what are we doing here?" The elevator doors open, and I put out my hand so she can walk, and she stops in the middle of the room. "What?" she asks, looking around, and I'm about to tell her when the doctor comes toward us.

"There you are," he says to me. "We are all set up."

"Rudy," I say. "This is Layla. Layla, this is Dr. Rudy. He runs the children's oncology wing." I see her mouth hang open, and I don't think she is ready for the rest. I don't think she expected the rest.

Rudy puts his hand out to shake Layla's hand, and she smiles at him. "It's good to meet you," Rudy says. "Let's get story time with Miller started, shall we?"

NINETEEN

LAYLA

MY HEAD IS swimming, and I look around, not sure I heard the words properly. "Miller," I say his name softly as we are ushered to the room. His hand rests at my back as he talks to Dr. Rudy.

"What are you doing here?" I ask him, and he smiles at me, stopping to look at me.

"On the first Sunday of the month, I read to the kids," he tells me like it's no big deal, and I swear to God this man gives me whiplash. "It's something I've been doing for the past four or five years."

I don't get a chance to ask him another question because we stop at a room, and I hear Dr. Rudy talk. "Okay, everybody." He claps his hands. "He's finally here." I stand with him at the doorway as the kids cheer and clap. He raises his hand to say hello to everyone. I stay at the door and watch him walk in. He high-fives some of the kids that he knows, calling them by their first name. I see a couple of the dads raise their hands to say hello to him.

He finally makes it to the chair set up at the back of the room, facing out to everyone. He is dressed in jeans and a Dallas shirt with a green bomber jacket on. He sits in the chair, taking off and hanging his glasses on his shirt. "Hello, boys and girls," he says with a smile as the kids greet him back. "I'm so happy to be back again." He smiles at them. "I see some old faces." He makes eye contact with the kids he must know. "And then I see some new kids who I hope to get to know." He points at a couple of them, and some of them wave enthusiastically.

They are all sitting on the floor in a circle, their parents are scattered around the room, and I'm blown away that not one cell phone is out and no one is asking him for a selfie. No one is filming; it's just a man reading to a group of sick kids.

I wipe away the tear leaking out of my eye. "He really is a class act," Rudy says, and I just nod. "For a couple of hours, these kids forget they are sick."

I listen to him read at least five stories. He never rushes through them and always asks the kids questions. When he is done reading, he sits with them for some questions and answers, and he stays to sign whatever they bring to him. He smiles with them all and hugs them and jokes with them. He also chats and shakes hands with the parents. My heart is literally going to explode in my chest because nothing could have prepared me for this.

I turn and walk away for a second, looking for a bathroom to make sure you can't tell that I'm crying. I follow the signs to the bathroom and look at my reflection in the mirror. My eyes look a little bloodshot, and my nose has just a touch of redness to it. I shake my head, walking out of the bathroom, and stop when I see Miller standing by a nurse. She has blond hair, and I hear her first.

"Don't tell me you were going to leave without saying hello," she says to him with a huge smile as she steps in closer to him.

He smiles at her, and my heart sinks. "Not a chance in hell, beautiful." He puts his hand around her shoulder, and they walk away from me. This, I shake my head, this is not for me. Just when I'm about to turn around and head out the nearest exit, I hear him call my name. "Layla." I look up and smile at him, game face on. "There you are. I was looking everywhere for you."

"I just went to the bathroom." I fold my arms over my chest so he doesn't try to hold my hand.

"You can go ahead and finish your conversation." I point at the blonde, who is just standing there. "I'll wait over here."

"I wasn't having a conversation," he says, and I want to roll my eyes so hard, but I don't. "Are you ready to go?" he asks, and I just nod and then look around.

"I was going to thank Dr. Rudy for letting me stay," I tell him as we walk to the elevator. The blonde is still looking at us.

"You can thank him next time you come," he says. We get into the elevator, and I stand as far away from him as I can.

"That was really amazing," I say, and he smiles. "Have you been doing it long?"

"I've been coming here for about four years. I came with the guys once, and then I forgot something and came back, and well …" He shrugs and smiles. "I love it. It's hands down the best feeling in the world to come in and be a little bit of light for them."

Goddammit, I yell at myself when he says that. I walk out of the elevator and to the car, and I get in when he opens the door for me. "Thank you," I tell him, and he just looks at me as though he is trying to figure out something.

He gets in the car and looks over at me. "Want to go and get something to eat?" he asks, and I shake my head.

"Not really," I say. "If you can just drop me off at my car, I have a couple of things to do today."

He just nods and starts the car. I look out the window the whole time. My emotions are so up and down I can't even begin to explain them. He pulls into the parking lot of the coffee shop.

"Thank you for sharing today with me," I tell him when I reach for the door handle. "It was hands down the best day I've had in a long time."

He smiles at me. "Anytime, gorgeous." He says my nickname, and I want to cringe. I also make the mistake of thinking about how many other people might have had that nickname.

"Take care, Miller," I say, getting out of the car and walking to mine. I ignore the beating of my heart in my chest and the stinging in my eyes. I ignore the anger while I make my way home. I ignore it all, burying it deep inside me. I unlock the door and slam it shut, and only then do I let my shoulders slump. I'm not in the house for longer than a minute when the doorbell rings.

I open the door, expecting it to be anyone else but him. "Miller?" I say his name in almost a whisper.

"What exactly is going on right now?" he asks me, walking into the house, and I close the door softly. "We were having the best day. And then. It's like a switch went off, and I just don't understand it."

"It's nothing," I tell him, and he just stands there with his hands on his hips.

"At least be honest with me." His eyes look at me like they dare me to say something.

"Be honest with you?" I laugh now, and he looks at me, shocked at the way it came out.

"Okay, you want me to be honest with you," I say. "Here it is. I don't know what goes on in your head some-times," I tell him, and I don't give him a chance to even answer it. "I finally came to the conclusion that I liked you." His eyes light up. "Oh, don't celebrate just yet. So I decided that I like you, and maybe we can be friends."

"I don't want to be friends with you," he says, and it's now my turn to stare at him. "After all this time, you have to know that friendship is not what I want from you."

"Well, it's about the only thing that you are going to get from me," I tell him.

"Why?" he asks.

"Why?" I counter him. "Why? Seriously. I can't take the two sides to Miller," I tell him, my voice rising a bit. "I'm with this funny Miller, who makes me laugh and cooks me dinner and is considerate and kind."

"That's me." He points at himself proudly.

"And then there is the idiot Miller, who takes me out and flirts with girls right in front of my face. Who has the audacity to just straight-up disrespect me to my face." His face falls. "Yeah, that's also you."

"But that isn't the real me," he tells me. "The guy in my house is the real me. The guy at coffee shop is the real me. The guy reading to those kids? That is the real me." He shakes his head. "That other guy, he's the hockey player."

"You got at least one thing right; he's the player." He rolls his eyes. "What would you say if we went out, and you saw me with a male fan of the show, and I hug him and call him honey?" His eyes glare at me. "If I let him put his arm around my shoulder and walk away while we have a conversation together, letting you watch."

"I'm not like that," he says, huffing out.

"That is exactly who you are. Now you have to decide what kind of man do you want to be?"

"I want to be me!" he shouts, making me glare at him.

"Then be you," I tell him.

"So, you can't be with that person," he says. "The second guy."

"I won't be with that person ever. I won't be in a relationship if I have to second-guess my worth." I wipe the tear away, feeling more hurt than I thought I would. "I will not second-guess my worth."

"No one is asking you to," he says.

"But you do—every single time you grab the blonde

or the brunette and squeeze them in for a picture. I can't do it," I say softly. "I wouldn't expect you to accept me that way, just as I don't expect you to make me accept you like that."

"I'm sorry I hurt your feelings," he says and then walks to the door. "And for the record, they don't mean anything to me. It's just a part of my job. Take care, Layla." He says my name and walks out of my house. I wait a few minutes before I move and lock the door, walking then to my purse and taking out my phone.

I look at his contact, and everything in me screams to block his number. But my fingers don't do it. I don't touch anything. I press the button, closing off the screen, and then a text comes through.

Miller: I'm sorry I can't be that guy.

I power off my phone. "I'm sorry, too," I say to the universe.

TWENTY

MILLER

AS I DRIVE away from her house, my heart is crushed like it's never been before. I play the day over and over in my head. Showing her that part of me was something I didn't take lightly. I'm not ashamed of it, but I love doing it just because there isn't a big deal made from it. When I walk onto that fourth floor, I'm just a regular guy being invited in to help these kids forget they are sick for just a little bit.

When I pull up to my house, I see she hasn't texted me back. To be honest, there really isn't anything she can say. Unlocking the door, I make my way to my bedroom without turning on any lights.

I pack my bag to pass the time and try not to think about what she said, but I hear the words over and over again. *I don't have two sides*, I tell myself, and when I go to bed that night, all I can do is hear "I like you but ..."

I'm cranky as fuck when I get to the airport and park my car. My shades are blocking the circles around my eyes from having the worst night of my life. I grumble to a couple of the guys who say hello to me and stand on the side while they bring the stairs out to load the plane that is parked there.

"Hey," Manning says when he walks in a couple of minutes later. I nod at him, and he just stands there with his phone in his hand. I don't even know what he's scrolling since the guy refuses to be on social media. "This week is going to be a long one."

I look over at him. "It'll be good to get away," I finally say, and I see he wants to ask me something, but he just looks ahead as Ralph gets here. With his bag hanging on his shoulder, he grumbles hello to us, and we grumble back.

We load up the plane. I sit by myself, and I look back to see Manning sitting by himself, and Ralph sitting across from me by himself. I take the baseball cap on my head and put it over my face and just zone out while we fly to Winnipeg.

When the plane touches down, I look out the window and am shocked by the amount of snow on the ground. "Shit," I say. "I didn't pack a jacket," I say, looking at Ralph, who just furrows his eyebrows.

"Dude, we're on a road trip to Canada in November. Were you expecting palm trees?" He laughs at me.

"I think someone is going to have to go shopping," Manning says from behind me.

I get up and grab my bag. My balls freeze the minute I step out of the plane, and apparently, I'm the only one who didn't pack for this trip properly. "Rookie mistake,"

Ralph says, shaking his head as we walk to the waiting bus. I rush in taking the first open seat, rubbing my hand together.

"So does that mean you won't come shopping with me?" I ask, and he puts his head back.

"No," he says and then looks at me.

"Don't make me go by myself," I say. "I don't want to be the only one."

"Ask Manning," he says. I turn in my seat, and I don't even have to ask him.

"No," he snaps out. "It's a mall."

"Exactly! You can, I don't know, start your Christmas shopping," I tell him, and he just glares at me.

"You're my captain. You don't leave anyone behind," I tell him, trying not to laugh.

"This is hockey, not the military," Manning says, and then huffs out. "Fine, Ralph and I will both come."

"Hey," Ralph says. "How did I get sucked into this?"

"Assistant captain," Manning says. "We leave no man down."

He shakes his head, and when we get to the hotel, we dump our bags and rush out to the mall. Ralph is typing away on his phone, and so is Manning. "You guys are worse than girls."

"The question is why aren't you texting Layla?" Manning asks right before we get into the waiting van that the hotel got for us.

"That's over," I say, my voice low, and they both look at me. "What?"

"That's over?" Ralph asks. "I'm so confused. When

did it start?"

"Fuck you," I say, flipping him the bird. "She's so …"
I shake my head. "She's so …"

"She's so all up in your head." Manning laughs.

"She told me yesterday she can't date me because I'm two different people," I say out of frustration, and I look at them.

"What does that mean?" Manning asks, and I shrug.

"She had to have told you more than that," Ralph says. "She's not just going to leave you hanging like that. No girl would."

"So she loves the Miller who cooks her dinner and does stuff, but she hates the Miller who flirts with girls in front of her."

"You flirt with girls in front of her?" Manning folds his hands together.

"No," I say, shaking my head. "They were fans. They came up to me, and you know you have to be nice to them."

"Were these fans women?" Ralph asks, and I nod.

"Don't even start," I say to them. "You pose for pictures with girls."

"I do," Manning says, and so does Ralph.

"But," Manning says, "I don't call them sweetie and beautiful."

I look at him. "I don't do that."

He and Ralph both laugh. Ralph talks before Manning. "You always do. And you put your—"

"Arm around them, bringing them close to you," Manning finishes.

"Don't you?"

"Fuck no," Ralph says. "One, I would never even do that for fear she might think something else, and two, that sends the wrong message."

"It does not," I tell them.

"When you pose with guys, do you call them handsome?" Manning asks, and I just glare at him. "Do you hug them and pull them closer?"

"Exactly," Ralph says.

"Whatever. It means nothing," I tell them. "That is a part of the job."

"What job?" Manning asks, and Ralph just looks at me. "I don't think she's telling you not to be nice to the fans. I think she's telling you to stop with the smiling and the joking and the touching."

"You can be nice without all that. It also blurs the lines. It makes them think you want them or they actually have a chance," Ralph says. "What would you do if you walked with her, and she did that with guys? Called them hot stuff and shit. Makes them hug her and pose for a picture." The thought makes me bite down on my jaw. "Exactly."

We get to the mall and step in, and I can tell already that a couple of people recognize us. "Great," I say and look over at Manning. "Why do you have to stick out like a sore thumb?"

"I'm six feet six," he says. "There's nothing I can do."

A couple of kids come up to us and ask us for our autograph and to take pictures, and then I look over and see three girls twirling their hair. "Incoming," Ralph says, and I look up.

"Oh my God," one of them says. "Are you guys hockey players?"

"We are," Manning says. "Have a great night."

"That's how it's done," Ralph says, and I walk ahead when one of the girls asks for a picture.

"Sure," I say, then turn to the guys. "Look at this." The guys walk over to the girls. "Are we taking selfies?" I say, and I almost call them beautiful, but I stop myself. My mouth almost drops open in shock that they might actually be right. One of the girls slides up to me, but I put my hands in my pockets and pose with a smile. "Have a great night."

"Oh, we will now," one of them says, and I turn to walk away without saying anything.

"How's it going?" Manning asks when we walk into the store.

"She was right," I say softly. "Like I didn't see it before."

"Look, you can be professional without the touching and the flirting," Manning says. He picks up a jacket for me, and I try it on as the sales lady walks over with a smile.

"Can I help you guys with anything?" she asks, and I look up at her.

"We are just looking," I say, turning around now as she steps away.

"Was that hard?" Manning asks.

"It must kill him," Ralph says. And I just look at them.

"I don't know what you're talking about," I say to

them.

"This is what would have happened," Manning says to me and then looks at Ralph. "You be the girl."

"Hi, can I help you guys with something?" he says to Manning and pretends to throw his hair behind his shoulder, and I laugh at him.

"Not yet, sugar," Manning says. "But as soon as I see something I like"—he winks at Ralph—"you'll be the first to know."

"I am not like that," I say as Ralph laughs.

"Manning," Ralph says, "you nailed that part and the wink."

I shake my head. "You are both assholes." I grab the jacket and go to the cashier, whipping out my card when she asks how I'm paying. "Thank you." I grab the jacket. "Actually …" I smile at her. "Do you think you can cut off the tags for me?" And I swear I have to stop my eye from winking.

"Sure thing," she says, cutting off the tags and the instructions. "If you have any questions, my number is on the bill."

"Thank you." I smile at her and walk out.

When we walk past a group of girls, one of them spots us, and you can tell her eyes light up. "Oh my God, you guys are my favorite players," she says, and even I want to roll my eyes. "Can I get a picture with the three of you?"

"Sure," we all say. I watch Ralph and Manning walk to her, and all they do is stand next to her. Actually, their bodies are away from her, and they just lean in their heads. I walk over when the girl tries to put her arm through Ralph's and Manning's. They stick their hands in their pockets so she knows they don't really want her touching. "Thank you, guys," she says and walks away.

"She touched you." I point at the guys and mimic her holding their arms.

"Yes," Ralph says, "but that picture will show I had my hands in my pockets, and she touched me and not I wanted her to."

I don't say anything, and for the next three days, I watch and learn basically. I break the habit of smiling so much while still remaining polite.

Right before we load the plane to go home, Ralph walks past me and says, "He's learning, grasshopper." I've just left three girls who all wanted a selfie with me. I posed with my head leaning into them and not my body.

"He looks like a cardboard cut out," Manning says. "But at least I didn't hear any sweeties or beautiful." I shove his shoulder, and he just laughs. "But seriously, do you see it now?"

I look right and left and then down. "I do. I just never really paid attention or thought twice about it."

"That's because you were single," Ralph says. "It's a different ball game when you are with someone, and you have to take their feelings into consideration."

"I am single," I tell them, and they both laugh.

"Don't be an idiot," Manning says. "Layla is the best."

I glare at him, and my hands clench into fists. "Aren't you not available?" He laughs and shakes his head.

"You have to say you're sorry," Ralph says.

"What if she slams the door in my face?" I ask them, and they both shrug.

"What if she doesn't?" Manning says and walks ahead of me to get onto the plane, leaving me in the middle of the steps with people walking around me.

"What if she doesn't?" I repeat to myself and make a plan to go and give it one last shot.

TWENTY-ONE

Layla

I OPEN THE shades leading out to the backyard. The bright sun shines in right away, making me close one eye. "Too bright to start the day," I grumble, walking to start my coffee while I turn on the television, and the sound of *SportsCenter* plays. I turn my attention to the television when they bring up the game yesterday against Edmonton.

"Someone has lit a fire under Adams's skates because he is having the week of his life," one of the broadcasters says of Miller, and I have to agree. He is on fire. He scored a goal in every game along with an assist. He was named player of the game for the past two games.

"I guess he's handling the breakup better than you," I say to myself and then shake my head. "Breakup? You need to date someone in order to break up with them."

I watch another play that happened last night, and I couldn't agree with them more. "He is on fucking fire."

The play shows his skating into the zone, leaving the puck so fast no one sees that it's not on his blade anymore when Ralph picks it up and shoots it five hole. "Cocky Adams, very, very cocky."

I hear a knock on the door and lower the volume of the television, waiting to see if perhaps I was mistaken, but the knock comes again. I look at the clock on the wall and see that it's just a little past nine thirty in the morning. "Who on earth," I say, walking to the door and unlocking it.

My heart speeds up when I see it's him. It's not like I haven't seen him in the past week. I've seen him when I was watching the game. I might have even taped the games and then rewound when I knew he was going to be on. But now he's standing there in front of me wearing jeans and a T-shirt with a leather jacket. His aviator glasses hide his eyes. I made myself bury the hurt that I felt all week. I forced myself to literally wash him out of my hair, but now here he is, and I'll be damned if I admit that I'm happy to see him. I don't even know why I feel like this since the last time I saw him, I was telling him how I didn't like half of him.

"Good morning," he says, his smirk coming out. "I brought you coffee," he says, holding up two cups of coffee. I didn't even see them in his hands because I was trying to get my heart to beat properly and my breathing to slow from panting.

"Um," I say, trying to sound smooth, but my mouth is so dry I can't even swallow.

"You look nice," he says with a smile, and all I can

do is stand here holding the door handle. "Can I come in?" He smirks now again. I move aside so he can walk in, not sure I can talk without stuttering. "It's good to see you, gorgeous," he says, stopping beside me and leaning down to kiss the corner of my mouth.

I close the door, turning to see him walking into the house. "What are you doing here?" I ask him when I finally get my words to come back to me. "I mean, why are you here?"

"I'm here to bring you coffee," he tells me. "And because I missed you."

"Miller." I say his name.

"Did you miss me?" he asks, and I just look at him. "Honestly."

I fold my arms over my chest. "I mean, I saw you at least four nights."

He laughs now. "I heard your voice every day." My stomach gets a little flutter. "Listen, about what you said," he says as he puts the coffees down on the counter. "You were right."

My mouth hangs open, and my heart that never really got to a normal heartbeat since I opened the door speeds up even more. My palms feel sweaty, so I rub them together. "What was I right about?"

"You were right about the way I acted in front of you," he says, and I cross my arms over my chest to keep them from shaking. "The way I act with fans in general, especially women." I look at him and tilt my head to the side. "I didn't get it until …"

"Until?" I ask, waiting for him to continue.

"Until I spoke with the guys about it," he says, and I now laugh.

"Which guys exactly did you talk to about this?" I ask, suddenly wondering who he would even discuss this with.

"Ralph and Manning." He smiles shyly. "It was bothering me." His voice goes lower when he says the next sentence. "And I was in a really shitty mood. I landed in Edmonton and didn't have a coat."

"It's winter," I tell him, and he rolls his eyes at me.

"Trust me, I'm aware. My balls froze and shriveled up," he says. "But anyway, I realized that how I acted with them was not okay, and it was inappropriate." I just listen to him, not wanting to smile too big. "I've been watching my every move."

"I don't want you to change," I tell him.

"I'm not changing for you," he tells me. "I'm changing for me. I don't want to be that guy," he says. I can see he's nervous, so I get up and go to him. Standing in front of him, I can smell his aftershave. "I want to be the one who flirts with only you." He smirks at me. "I want to be the one who sends naughty pictures only to you." I laugh, shaking my head.

"How about we refrain from sending any dirty pictures?" I joke, but his face doesn't turn up into the smile I want to see.

He still looks at me, his face showing me that he isn't joking about this. "I want to be with you." He comes closer, his voice going really low. "And only you." I look down and then look up again, and he tucks the hair behind my ear. "And I never want you to doubt that." He uses his thumbs to rub my cheeks. "You never have to doubt your worth with me, gorgeous." He uses the nickname I've come to love. "Because, to me, you are worth everything."

"Smooth," I say, trying to make light of what just happened. My feet move on their own as I step closer to him. "Very smooth, Adams." My hands go to his waist. "Very smooth."

"I'm going to kiss you," he says. "I know that I wanted you to beg for it. But …" His head moves closer to me.

"Please." My voice comes out almost cracking. "Kiss me."

His hands never leave from my face, and he moves them to cup my cheeks. "I don't know why," he says and chuckles, "but I'm so fucking nervous." My stomach does flips, knowing that he's just as nervous as I am. "Here goes nothing," he says, and he closes the distance between us. I close my eyes right before his lips fall on mine.

His tongue slowly comes out, and I think I sigh when it touches my lips. My mouth opens for his tongue, and the second his tongue touches mine, my back arches into him. My hands squeeze his jacket into my fists. His tongue goes around with mine. His hands move from my face to my hair now as he turns his head, going to the other side. The kiss is soft at first as our tongues get to know each other, and after a couple of minutes, I step closer to him and press my front to him. My hands move from his waist and his jacket to around his neck. His hand drops from my head to my neck, his thumbs holding my chin. He lets go of my lips, and I groan, wanting his lips back.

Slowly opening my eyes, I feel almost in a daze. His lips move from the corner of my lips to my cheek and then down to my jaw. "Miller." I whisper his name, not sure if I'm going to ask him something or not. His tongue traces my jaw, and my head falls back to give him better access as my eyes close.

"I always knew," he says, coming back and taking my mouth again. This time, my mouth opens for him, and my tongue is waiting. He twirls his tongue around mine twice, then kisses my lips softly. "That kissing you would be out of this world," he says, his voice low as he takes my lips again. "I just never thought that it would be like fireworks at Disney."

I laugh, putting my head back, and he takes this chance to lean forward and kiss my throat.

"Fireworks at Disney?" I make fun of him.

"What?" he says, looking at me. His eyes are a soft amber color. "Whenever something amazing happens, they ask you what are you going to do now?" His hands go to my waist. "And every single time, it's I'm going to Disney. Well, you are my Disney."

My hand moves to his face, and I touch him for the first time, rubbing my thumb along his bottom lip. "I'll take it," I guess. "I can't believe you're here."

"I can't believe you didn't slam the door in my face," he says, laughing. "Now, can we go out for breakfast?" He looks at me. "Or lunch?"

I look at him, and I take the biggest leap I have in a long time. "I'd love to go to brunch with you."

"You can't go out like this," he says, looking down at my shorts and tank top.

"Fine," I say, grabbing the coffee and then walking back to my room. "Do you want to come and watch?" I ask, and his eyes go wide. "I don't mean me getting naked." He frowns now. "I mean, come and choose my outfit."

He nods, and I wait for him to walk beside me. He puts his arm around my shoulder as we walk back to the bedroom. "Welcome to my bedroom," I say, and he whistles when he walks in. "You can sit on the couch." I point at the loveseat right in front of the king-size bed.

"What if I wanted to lie on the bed and smell your pillow?" He winks at me.

"You can lie on the bed, just don't put your shoes on the bed," I tell him and walk away as he watches me.

"I won't put my shoes on the bed," he says, and I look over my shoulder. "But one of these days, my shoes are going to be under this bed," he says, throwing my cover over to sit on it as I swallow around the lump in my throat. He plops down on the bed, grabbing a couple of pillows to prop behind his head. "Now, start the fashion show."

TWENTY-TWO

MILLER

SITTING ON HER bed, I swear she can hear the sound of my heart hammering in my chest. It echoes in my ears. The team opted to fly through the night to get home a day early, so I crawled into bed at five a.m., setting my alarm for eight, knowing I was going to try to get her to talk to me.

Showing up with the coffee was a chance I took. I didn't set my hopes high. In fact, I thought she would slam the door in my face. When she opened the door, I almost forgot everything that I planned to tell her. The sleep was still in her eyes, and her hair piled and flipped to the side. I poured my heart out to her and held my breath while I waited for her to either kick me out or take another chance with me.

Now I'm in her bedroom waiting for her to get changed. I look around the white bedroom at the gold light hanging in the middle of the room. The king-size bed has a white duvet, and a gray quilt is folded by the foot. My eyes move to her white and gray nightstand that holds a single gold lamp with a white shade, and a picture of two people holding a baby. "Where are we going?" she asks from her closet.

"Wherever you want to," I say to her as she walks out wearing black jeans and a white shirt. "What happened to my fashion show?" I put my hands behind my head. "First, you had to start with the lingerie."

She throws her head back and laughs. "Nice try there." She goes to her bathroom, and I get up to follow her. She stands by the sinks, grabbing her toothbrush, and looks into the mirror at me. "Are you going to watch?"

"Does that bother you?" I lean against the doorframe. "Voyeurism."

"Are you asking me if it bothers me that you are watching me brush my teeth?" She turns to lean against the counter. "Or are you asking me to have sex with someone in front of you?"

I glare at her. "I don't share what's mine." I put my hand in my pocket. "I failed that in kindergarten," I tell her, and she turns back around to brush her teeth. "After only one month, they called my parents in and said I had trouble sharing."

She stops brushing. "You're kidding."

I shake my head. "I'm not. This whole sharing is caring is bullshit. I have mine, get your own was what I said."

She rinses off her toothbrush, wiping her lips with a hand towel. "Well, good to know," she says, stopping in front of me. "I don't share my toys, either."

"Are your toys in the top drawer of that side table?" I wink at her, and she laughs.

"I have too many to fit in that little drawer," she says, getting closer to me and kissing my lips. I grab her hip, bringing her to me. My cock springs into action as her tongue slips into my mouth, and I want to drag her back into her bedroom and throw her on the bed. She lets go of my lips. "My treasure chest is under the bed." She walks back into her closet, and I think she is going to bring out the chest and show me, but instead, she comes out with a plaid scarf wrapped around her neck, carrying her leather jacket in her hand.

"A treasure chest?" I ask as she slips on the jacket and then the black ballerina shoes that she had beside her closet door. "Is it like a big chest?"

"It's about this big." She shows me with her hands, and my eyes go big. "Big enough for me." She winks at me and then looks down to see my cock pressing against the fly of my jeans. "Is that going to be a problem?" she asks, pointing at my hard-on.

"Do you want to go and take care of that before we leave?" She rolls her lips together. "I can talk you through it." She laughs now.

"Laugh all you want now," I tell her, "but one of these days, we're going to do a whole show and tell with that chest of yours." I walk to her and bend to suck on her neck. "And I'll be the one talking you through it." She swallows now, and I try to ignore the pressure from my jeans. "Now, let's go before I do something that we are not ready for," I say, smacking her ass as I walk by it. "Fuck, I've waited four years to do that."

Shaking her head, she walks beside me out of the house. I open the car door for her, and she stops in front of me. Getting on her tippy toes, she kisses under my jaw at the same time her hand cups my cock. "I've been waiting four years to see what you do kiss me willingly" She winks at me, and I close the door, blocking out her laughter. I look up at the sky and close my eyes, counting to ten, but nothing helps me. She knocks on the window. "Are you going to be much longer?" She rolls her lips, trying not to laugh.

I walk around the car and get in, slamming the door. "That mouth of yours," I say, starting the car, "is going to get you in a lot of trouble."

"Promise?" She leans over and kisses my lips, slipping her tongue into my mouth. She lets me go a second later and goes back to her seat. "It's just as good as it was inside."

"Fireworks at Disney," I say, putting my glasses on. I make my way over to one of the hottest spots in Dallas. When we pull up, the valet opens the passenger door for Layla, and I get out, walking around to grab her hand in mine. "Is this okay?" I ask, and she nods her head. We walk in, and the hostess smiles at me. I nod to her. "A table for two please." She grabs two menus, and we walk into the dining room but see that most of the tables are taken. "Are there any tables outside?" She nods her head and walks outside to the almost empty dining area. "Can we have that table in the corner?" I ask, and she walks over to it. I grab the seat for Layla to sit down and then walk around to sit in front of her. She hands Layla a menu and then hands me mine. I open the menu, my stomach now growling. "I'm starving."

"Me, too," Layla says as she looks around. "Incoming," she says, and two kids walk up to us.

"Sorry to bother you," the little boy says, "but can we get a picture with you?"

I look at Layla, who smiles at them. "Sure," I say and get up to crouch down. "Do you guys play hockey?" They both nod their heads.

"I can take the picture," Layla says, getting up and grabbing the phone from one of them. "Smile," she says and takes the picture. The kids walk away, saying how cool it was.

We order the food, and I talk to her about her week. We eat without being interrupted, and I hold her hand as we leave.

We stand here waiting for the car, and it happens. I knew it was going to happen when I walked through the dining room and saw a table of girls in the corner , and then the finger-pointing started. "Hi, can we get a picture?" the girl asks, and I just nod at her.

"Sure," I say, leaning my head into her and smiling.

"Thank you," she says, and I nod at her and then look at Layla.

"Manning taught me that," I say, pointing. "The whole lean in with your head thing."

"Did he?" she says, trying not to laugh. "I'm sure, after a while, it will look much better and less like you are afraid of women."

"It does not look like I'm afraid of women," I say, almost huffing out. "Okay, fine, I'm a bit stiff." I open the car door for her when the valet stops the car.

"Thank you," she says and then waits before she gets into the car. "For taking my feelings into consideration." The wind blows her hair across her face.

"Thank you," I say, bending down and kissing her lips. "For not throwing the coffee in my face." She laughs now. "Do you want to go back to my house and see if we can get some fireworks going?"

I kiss her lips. "I have a firework in my pants that wants to go off," I tell her. She pushes me away from her, then gets into the car. I get into the car and hold her hand as I make my way to her house. We walk into the house together, and the minute the door closes behind me, she is the one who is on me. As she pushes me against the wall, my hands fly to her ass, bringing her to me, and in the entryway, I attack her mouth. Her hands are all over me, my hands cupping her ass to pick her up as she wraps her legs around my waist, and I turn to put her back against the wall. Her pussy rubs my cock over our clothes, and both of us let each other go to moan. I look at her as her eyes flicker open. "I can't think when I'm around you," I tell her. I kiss her neck and then take off the scarf. "I have to woo you."

"Considere me wooed," she says, leaning in to suck my neck into her mouth. "Now, how about I see that firework you have in your pants?"

With a groan, I let her go. "I can't believe these words

are coming out of my mouth," I tell her, kissing her again. Always wanting to kiss her. "I want to savor this."

"I have a couple of places on me that need savoring." She winks at me, and I turn and walk into the house as she tightens her legs around me. I walk over to the couch, and she slips off me. I shrug off my jacket to toss it to the side, and she does the same.

"I want to do this the right way," I tell her, and she looks at me, confused. "I want you so much." I swallow. "More than I want to go to Disney and a bit less than I want to win the Stanley Cup."

She laughs now. "I'm glad I made that list." She pulls me down to sit next to me. "But you're right." She snuggles next to me. "I haven't dated someone in a long, long time." I try not to let it get to me. "I haven't wanted to date someone in a long, long time."

I grab the phone out of my jacket. "I'm going to google what couples do on the first date."

She laughs now, filling the room. "Please tell me what it says."

"Laugh all you want …" I look down at the phone. "Google has not led me wrong."

"Google told you not to contact me for five days." She points out, and I shrug. "So what does it say?"

"Be confident is the first one," I tell her, smiling. "Check that one off the list." I look down and read the rest to her. "Pay attention to her body language."

"My body language was dry humping you at the front door," she says, and I swear I haven't laughed so hard in my life. She grabs the phone from me.

"What are you doing?" I ask her.

"I'm going to google how many people have sex on the first date," she tells me and then gasps. "I'm the man in the relationship." I grab the phone from her, looking down at it and scrolling.

"Oh, look at the survey," I tell her. "We should do it." She takes the phone from my hand and tosses it aside and then straddles me. My cock is pushing to get out.

"How about we do us?" she says. "We go at our speed. Let's start with us making out on this couch." She leans forward, and her tongue slips into my mouth. My hands want to move from her hips and cup her tits. She lets go of my mouth. "And if we end up naked, then we end up naked. If we end up with my shirt on the floor, then that is okay, too."

"Why are you asking? This is so hard," I groan as her hips rotate on my lap.

"Oh, baby," she says. "I'm not the hard one." She laughs, and I snap, turning her on her back. It's me who rotates my hips now, making her shift her hips up. "Yes," she hisses out, then looks at me. "I would be okay with your shirt coming off," she says, and her hands are already under my shirt.

"Okay, but that's it," I tell her, and for the rest of the day, we make out on her couch with my shirt off. When I leave her right before dinner, both of us are wired. "Are you going to miss me?" I ask her when she walks me to the door.

"Honestly," she says. "I'm going to go into the tub and bring a friend with me."

My mouth opens in shock. "Are you going to think about me when you play with yourself?" I kiss her when she nods. "I approve of this."

I walk out of the house without looking back, my whole body one tense nerve. I call her as soon as I get into the car. "What?" she answers, and I laugh.

"I want to listen," I tell her, and she laughs. We discuss the game tomorrow night, and when I get home, she still hasn't stepped into the bathtub. Hanging up the phone, I walk into the house, and I'm going to the fridge when I get a ping. I see that she sent me a picture. I open it up, seeing her kneecap and what looks like bubbles around her.

I call her on FaceTime right away. "Are you in the bath?" I ask her when she answers, and I hear the water around her. She comes into view with her hair tied up.

"I am." She looks at the camera mischievously. "And I'm not alone."

"No," I say to her. "Changed my mind. You can't play with yourself."

"What?" she shrieks out. "That's not fair. You left me all pent-up and needing release."

"How is this," I tell her. "Tomorrow, after the game, you come home with me, and we can go to second base?"

She shakes her head. "How about I do this, and we still go to second base?"

"Just think how good it'll be," I tell her, and she rolls her eyes.

"Then you can't drain your snake either," she says, and I laugh. "What's good for the gander is good for the geese."

"I don't think that's the way that goes," I tell her, and my cock is screaming at me not to agree to her requests.

"So we both wait until tomorrow then?" she asks, and I nod my head. "I want five," she says, huffing out. "You have to make me come five times."

"I think I can do that," I say, and she hangs up the phone with me.

I slip into bed without touching my cock, and the next day, I arrive at the arena grouchy. All day, she's sent me messages about places that are itching, and all of them are below her waist.

I walk into the locker room and send her the last text, telling her where to meet me after the game. She got a lift in with Candace. I nod to the boys when I get in and grab my workout stuff, hoping an hour on the bike will help, but it doesn't.

I walk to the ice, carrying my gloves under my arms, and finally put them on before I take the ice. I hear some of the fans cheer and then stop by the glass, not even noticing her. She knocks on the glass, and I smile at her. Taking her in, I see her cheeks are a bit pink.

I wink at her and then look at the side to see Candace smiling at me as she holds Ari in her arms. She turns, and I see that the Dallas jersey she is wearing has my number on it. I laugh now as she turns around. "Thought you might like this."

"You know what that means," I tell her, almost

screaming, not even caring that people are around and that reporters might see or hear this. "That means you're my girlfriend."

TWENTY-THREE

Layla

"You know what that means!" he screams through the glass, with not a care in the world. "That means you're my girlfriend." I throw my head back and laugh while he presses his lips to the glass.

"Eww," Candace says from beside me. I look over and see her nose scrunching up, making me laugh even more. "That's gross." I look back at the glass. His lips are still on the glass while Manning pushes him away. "Ari, tell Auntie Layla that's gross," she says to her daughter, who scrunches up her nose like her mother.

"Dad!" I hear being yelled and look over at Manning's son, who wears his jersey. He slaps the glass, and I see some of the other guys try to throw a puck over the glass for him. I smile and

look back to see if his wife is around. I don't know why I'm shocked that she isn't here. He's a seven-year-old kid, so anything can happen to him.

Manning smiles at his son and puts his glove against the glass as his son puts his hand on his. "Score a goal for me tonight." He jumps up and down, and Manning just laughs.

"Where is the mother?" I lean and whisper to Candace, who looks around. I help her look around also, and I don't see her anywhere.

"Probably somewhere pretending to be the perfect captain's wife," she says and then looks at Manning, who just smiles at his son. "So"—she points her finger at me—"does this mean you are officially Miller Adams's girlfriend?" Her finger moves up and down, pointing at the jersey, and I roll my eyes, trying not to let her see the happiness in my eyes.

"Do people in their thirties still need labels on things?" I turn to her as we watch the practice. "We are two adults who want to spend time with each other." Slowly, the players skate off the ice, and I see Manning look over at his son, who is watching the other team. He looks up at Candace and me. She nods her head when he points at his son, and then I see him bend his head and shake it.

Candace walks down to his son, tells him something that makes him smile, and he grabs her hand as we walk back to the family lounge. I usually stay in the press box, but when Candace is here, I stay with her. We walk into the room, and we both look around for the mother, who is standing there with a glass of wine in her hand as she talks to a couple of the other wives. "There is your mom," Candace says. He walks up to her, and she smiles at him and bends to kiss his head. The massive rock on her hand glistens as she rubs his shoulder.

"Okay, I'm not a mother or anything like that," I say, my voice low. "But that was fake, right?"

"That was totally fake," she says and kisses Ari on the head, who puts her arms around her neck and hugs her.

"Can your daughter be cuter?" I ask, rubbing Ari's back.

"Nope," she says. "Let's go sit down and get our seats." I walk with her outside the box to sit in two seats. Ari sits on her lap and claps, saying da-da. "So you and Miller?"

"Okay, fine," I say. "Get it out now."

She laughs. "It was a ticking time bomb just festering until I knew it would explode one day," I gasp, and she shakes her head. "Oh, I always knew once you got to know him, you would cave."

"I did not cave," I tell her and lean back in the chair, turning to her and folding my arms over my chest. "Okay, fine," I huff out. "I might have caved a little bit." I hold out my thumb and forefinger. "He cooked dinner for me." I'm trying to come up with reasons as to why I caved, trying to convince her of the reasons. "From scratch as if he cooked it all." I don't add in that no one has ever done that for me. I don't tell her how it threw me off the path of hatred that I had for him. Okay, maybe not hatred, but I definitely didn't like him.

"Well, I don't know how it happened, but I'm happy for you," she says. "You look happy."

"What the hell does that mean?" I ask, and she just shrugs. I've always smiled when needed, and I'm always in a good mood.

"I don't know how to explain it. You are the same as before, but now there is just something about you that, I don't know, lights up. It's that glow," she gasps. "Did you have sex with him already?"

"Fuck, I wish," I tell her. "I basically handed myself to him on a silver platter, and he said no." She goes wide-eyed. "Well, he didn't because Google told him it wasn't a good idea." She laughs now, and I get angry, thinking about it. "That fucking bitch Google." I explain to her how he goes to Google for everything. "Anyway," I tell her, "he owes me five orgasms tonight, so he better save some of his energy because I'm ready to collect."

The guys skate onto the ice, and the game is intense. Boston is out for blood, literally. One of the rookies has to leave the ice after getting body checked at center ice. His head was down. It's Rookie Mistake 101: always skate with your head high. Manning was the first one to skate over and fight the attacker. His gloves were off even before he got to the scene, and by the time the referees got it under control, there were four other fights.

It isn't the first time I've seen fights on the ice, but then when I saw Miller skate up and toss his stick to the ice, my heart sped up, and my mouth suddenly got dry. He holds another guy, who then knocks his arm away, and I see the smirk come out. I can read his lips. Well, almost. The only words I can actually see are Pussy. Ass. Dick. Suck. Fuck You. Fight Me. Little bitch is the last thing that he says before the guy swings at him. I grip the armrests of the seat, seeing that he's ducked and swings up with a punch, the guy going down. The referee is there to stop Miller from doing anything else. He points at the box, and Miller shakes his head and skates to the box, pulling up his sleeves. The crowd behind him is banging on the glass as he sits there next to Manning.

The game ends with us sealing the deal with an empty-net goal in the third period with ten seconds to go. I help Candace walk down to her truck and then text Miller that I am waiting for him at his car. I take my phone out and scroll through the pictures of tonight's game. I hear footsteps coming closer and look up to see Miller coming out, holding his suit jacket in his hand.

His crisp white dress shirt fits him too perfectly. The top two buttons are undone, his custom-made blue pants hug his thick thighs, and I swear my mouth waters when he looks up. His hair is still wet, and you can see that he brushed his hands through it. His scruff on his face makes my hands tingle, just thinking of feeling it.

"Well, look who it is," I say, pushing off the car. "If it isn't Rocky Balboa." He shakes his head and walks to me. Wrapping his free hand around my waist, he kisses my lips. It feels like we've done this a thousand times before, which is weird since I know that we haven't.

"Hi," I say softly to him. With my hands on his chest, I lean into him a bit more, so I smell his aftershave all over me.

"Hi," he says back softly. "Gotta say, I like you waiting for me." He rubs his nose against mine as he kisses me again lightly. "You hungry?" he asks, stepping away from me.

"A little bit," I say, and he opens the car door for me. "I mean, I'm more horny than hungry." He laughs now.

"You and me both," he says, closing the door behind me and walking over to get into the car. He tosses his jacket in the back seat, and we take off for his house. "Did you enjoy the game?" he asks.

"I mean, it's different now that you know I'm a girlfriend," I say, and when he looks over at me smirking, I wink at him.

"When I saw you wearing my jersey, I got a hard-on, and let me tell you. A hard-on and a jockstrap do not go well together," he says, and I laugh. The car ride home is quiet as the two of us remain in our own world. I'm not going to admit this to him, but I'm nervous. It's silly and crazy, and I can't even begin to explain it to myself, let alone him.

When we pull up to his house, my hand comes out to grab the door handle to open it. "I hope you saved your energy, Adams." He looks over at me. "You owe me five orgasms, and I bumped it up to seven for fighting." I get out of the car and wait for him to meet me. He charges to me and pushes me against the car door. "Miller," I say almost breathlessly.

"All night," he says. "I was holding on by a string." His mouth devours mine, his hands come up to cup my tits, and I let go of his mouth to moan. "All I could see was you in my jersey." He lifts the hem of the jersey, and right here in the middle of his driveway in the dark, he slips his hand into my jeans. I try to open my legs, but the restriction of the jeans doesn't let me.

"Wet," he says when his hand rubs up and down my covered slit. "Right, though." His mouth finds mine again as he rubs up and down. I'm aching to get him to touch me skin to skin, aching to feel his fingers in me. "All I could see," he says again when he lets go of my mouth, "is fucking your mouth with my cock while you wore this jersey." I close my eyes, picturing the same thing he is picturing, and I come, just like that. My legs squeeze together, and I shake. A moan escapes me, and he rubs up and down, and when I finally open my eyes, I see the smirk on his face. "Six more to go." I take his hand out of my jeans and stick his finger in his mouth. "Shall we?" he says, and I finally realize that right here in the middle of his fucking driveway with only his fingers in my pants, not even in my vagina that I came for him.

"Um," I start to say to him as he pulls me to the front door. "I—"

He unlocks the door and steps in with me following him. I'm about to say something else, but I can't because I'm pushed up against the door. "Do you know what I did last night?" he asks as he devours my neck, and I can't even see in the darkness. I see a little bit of light coming from somewhere in the house, but I can't focus on anything else but him. He's all around me, yet I can't get enough of him.

"What?" I ask almost in a daze.

"I fell asleep with the thought of you sitting on my face," he tells me, and my head falls back against the door. "Time to find out if you taste like strawberries."

TWENTY-FOUR

MILLER

My heart hammers in my chest, my cock is harder than a rock, and all I can think about is getting her naked and pleasing her. I attack her neck, sucking in and tasting her. She moans softly, and all the plans that I had are out the window. Taking my time with her and savoring her are out the window. Making her come on my tongue is the new plan. My hands roam from her neck to her tits, and I wish I could feel them better, but with the fucking jersey on, I can't tease her nipples the way I want to. "I want to rip the jersey off you," I tell her right before my tongue slips into her mouth for a bit. My hand goes to her hips and then her ass.

"Take it off," she says breathlessly when I let go of her mouth. "Let's take it all off." Her hands go to the hem, and she tries to take off the jersey. I grab her hand in mine and then take the other in mine and raise them to the side of her head. "Miller," she groans, and her fingers fling to mine.

My mouth goes to her ear. "Don't move your hands," I tell her, slipping my fingers out of her. "The minute you move your hand is the minute I stop." I wish there was more light shining through, so I can see her eyes, I wish I could see her eyes when she comes. I drop down to my knees, coming face-to-face with her pussy. My finger comes out, and I move over the zipper of her jeans right where I know her clit is. "All night," I tell her, slipping the button out. "I was hard." The sound of the zipper opens, filling the room, both of us not breathing. "Thinking of this." I kiss her right above her lace panties. "Thinking of how you taste," I say, pushing down her jeans over her hips. Leaning in and licking her right over her lace thong.

"Miller." She hisses out my name, and I look up to see that her hands are still above her head.

I push her pants down and remove her right shoe, tossing it over my shoulder, and the minute her foot is free from the boot, I peel her pants leg off. I kiss up her bare leg, stopping to bite it and then suck at certain places. The sound of her heavy breathing fills the room. It would take nothing to move her over to the couch and have her sit and spread for me, but I have to taste her. I move the jersey up and see her white lace thong, my tongue comes out to lick up again. My finger moves the lace to the side, and I see her little landing strip, my tongue comes out and licks between her lips, and now, it's both of us who moan.

"Honey," I tell her, putting one leg over my shoulder

to make her open for me. "Fuck," I say, going in again, and this time, I lick all the way up to her clit. She moves her hips side to side, trying to get my tongue on her. I use my thumb to open her up for me, sucking on her clit while I slip my other finger into her. I close my eyes as I bite her clit and add another finger inside her. "Gorgeous," I say, licking her up and down and then slipping my tongue into her with my fingers. "I could spend all day here." My finger moves in and out of her as her back arches off the door, and her hands slip down a bit. "Tell me." My fingers are slick with her juices. "Did you think of me?"

"Yes," she says, her eyes now looking down at me.

"Did you touch yourself thinking of me?" I ask, biting her clit and then sucking in, and she comes on my fingers.

Her hands bury themselves in my hair, and I stop my fingers from fucking her while she comes. She groans out in frustration now. "Miller."

"Put your hands back up, and I'll make you come again," I tell her, and she moves her hands back up beside her head. My fingers now fuck her faster and harder than I did before. My mouth sucks in her clit and her slit all in one. I can tell she is close again because my fingers are getting tighter and tight.

"Miller," she says my name again.

"Shh," I tell her. "I'm eating," I say, devouring her pussy with my mouth. With my fingers and tongue, I make her come again, and right before she finishes, I rub her G-spot with my fingers and make her come again. I lick her clean, and when I slip my fingers out of her, she watches me lick them clean.

"That was …" she starts to say, her hands falling by her sides like cooked noodles. "That was …" I put her leg down. "That was …"

I laugh. "Was it that?" I joke with her, and she just looks at me. Her head comes forward as she attacks my mouth. Her tongue slips into my mouth as she grips my chest now. I feel her pull the shirt up. One hand slipping under the shirt while the other hand palms my cock.

"Is there a light?" she asks when she lets go of my mouth, and her fingers work the button of my shirt.

"Why?" I ask her.

"I want to see it all," she says, and I throw my head back and laugh. She lets go of me, walking to the wall. Kicking off her other shoe, she then takes her pants off. She turns on the soft light that is on the table. She stands there wearing just the jersey that covers her. "That's better."

"Is it?" I ask, and she nods, coming over to me, she gets on her tippy toes and kisses under my chin right before she bites it. "Now," she says, unbuttoning my white shirt. "Let's see what all the fuss is about." She winks at me.

"I don't even know what to say to that," I tell her, and she slips the shirt over my shoulders, and I let it fall to the floor where it lies right next to her jeans.

"I like," she says, using her finger to trail down the middle of my chest. "Now for the main event." She winks at me. I watch her small hands unbutton my pants, and they fall to the floor, leaving me in my black Hugo Boss boxers, and the tip of my cock trying to push out. "Oh, I really like this," she says, and before she says anything else, she is on her knees in front of me. My boxers are now under my ass, and my cock is in her mouth. My eyes close as I feel her mouth take my whole cock. I look down, seeing my name on the jersey as she sucks my cock with everything that she has. I move my hips, putting my hands in her hair as I fuck her mouth.

"I think," she says, taking her mouth off my cock and licking up my shaft. "I love your cock." She twirls her tongue around the tip. "Fuck, it's perfect," she says. Her hand fists it, moving it up and down. "Long, thick …" She takes it in her mouth.

"I'm glad you approve," I say, my hips moving front and back. It doesn't take me long to feel the need to come. After going all night and all day thinking about her and making her come, I knew that I wouldn't last long the first time. "I'm going to come."

"Good," she says, taking her mouth off my cock, and she surprises me by putting her mouth back on my cock.

Her hand moves up and down faster. "Gorgeous," I say right before I shoot in her mouth. She swallows it all, never letting it go until the last drop. "Fuck."

"Not yet," she says, getting up. "But yes, please."

I push the hair away from her face and kiss her lips. "Not tonight," I tell her, and she glares at me.

"We just went to third base," I tell her, and she throws her head back.

"Yeah, I want a home run." She practically stomps

her foot, making me laugh. I grab her and throw her over my shoulder, slapping her ass. "Miller."

"I have to still make you come five times," I remind her.

"One of those times can be you fucking my brains out," she tells me as I walk through my house to my bedroom. I toss her on the bed, and she just looks at me. Her hair all over the place, her legs spread as I get on the bed with her. "Don't bring that cock here unless you plan on using it."

"Oh, I'm going to use it," I tell her, and the smile fills her face. "I'm planning on using it right now."

She slaps her hands together in glee. "Condom?" she says, looking at me, and I finally take the jersey off her. She sits in the middle of my bed now, her perfect round tits sitting in a lace bra being pushed up.

"Hmm," I say, moving the cup down off a nipple and seeing it ready to be played with. "Hello." Leaning down, I twirl my tongue around it. Her legs open, and I see that her panties are still pushed to the side, leaving her open. I move over to the other nipple, and my finger slips into her at the same time I bite down and suck it.

"Condom," she says, almost panting. I smile now, slipping my finger out and rubbing her wetness on her nipple, then bending to clean it off. "Miller," she huffs out.

I put my knees by her hips and rip her bra off her. "You know what else kept me up?" I ask, her mouth hanging open at the torn bra that I toss to the side. "These," I say, grabbing her tits and rolling the nipples. "Your tits are perfect."

"Good, they cost me a fortune," she says, and it's my turn now to look shocked. I feel her tits again. "A perfect size B," she says. I push them together, and my cock is at full salute now.

"I want you to watch," I tell her as my hips push forward, "while I fuck your tits and fuck you with my fingers." She looks down as I slip my cock between her tits. "Hold your tits tight for me," I tell her, and her hands come up and squeeze her tits together as I move up and down. My hand reaches behind me to slip into her. "I'm going to destroy you," I tell her, my hips moving faster, and the little minx sticks out her tongue to lick the tip of my cock. "When I finally fuck you, I'm going to fuck you so hard you're going to feel me for a whole week."

"Yes," she says, moving her hips up to meet my fingers. "I'm going to come," she says, and her head falls back as she comes again. Her juices run down my fingers as I slip them out of her. "I can't move."

I move away from her now and smirk at her. "Gorgeous," I say, leaning down and slipping my tongue into her mouth. "We've only just started." She looks at me, her eyes heavy, and I lie on the bed on my back. "Now," I tell her. "Climb on me and ride my face."

TWENTY-FIVE

Layla

"I'M LAYLA PATERSON, and I wish you a great weekend," I say, leaning back in my chair. "And don't forget to tune into the game tonight and then again on Sunday."

"It is going to be a tough weekend," Brian says. "Vegas is coming to town, and they are on a winning streak."

"They are," I agree, "but so is Dallas."

"I think they need to win the next two games because then they go on the road for six days, and you know that it's going to be rough," he says. I try not to let it bother me that Miller is going to be gone.

"Well, we will be back Monday with all the news. Stay safe, everybody." I take my headphones off. "That was a good show," I say. He nods, and I get up, putting my hand up to tell him goodbye.

I make my way to my office, where I grab my laptop and my bag, checking my phone and seeing that I have a text from Candace.

Candace: Are you ever going to call me back?

I laugh, thinking of when she called me on Wednesday while I was in the middle of watching a movie with Miller. I couldn't even think about answering because he had my shirt up to my neck, my tits loose while he fucked me with his fingers. For the past five days, we've been together every single night. He usually picks me up, and we have dinner. Then we get hot and heavy right before he drops me off at home. I swear, this man is going to make me rip my hair out.

I dial her number as I walk out of the office. "Well, look at what the cat dragged in," she says, answering after one ring, and I laugh.

"I am a cat," I tell her, getting into the car. "A cat in motherfucking heat." I slam the door and pull out of the parking lot.

"It's been a week," she says, shocked.

"It's been eight days," I huff out. "Eight days. I can't even count the hours."

"I have no words," she says.

"Well, I have a couple of words," I say. "He's a grower, he's a shower, and so help me God, he better be a plower."

Candace laughs now. "I'm not kidding. He's given me more orgasms than I can count, and still he hasn't given me the proper fucking he claims he's going to give me," I huff out.

"Why don't you just take things in your own hands?" She pushes me. "Climb that man like a tree."

"You don't think I've tried." I roll my eyes. "He just picks me up and tosses me around like a rag doll and then eats my pussy until I forget everything."

"Ewww," she says, and I laugh. "You were on speakerphone."

"I think I'm going to be sick." I hear Ralph and laugh.

"Ralph, do me a favor and ask him why he isn't giving me the dick," I say loudly, and he groans out.

"The last thing I'm going to talk to Miller about is his dick and where he puts it," he says. "Now, I'm going to go and pretend I didn't have this conversation."

"I can tell you right now where he should put it," I say, laughing. "I'll see you guys later." I hang up and then call the man we are talking about.

"Hey there, gorgeous," he says, and I smile like a love-sick idiot. "I was just thinking about you."

"Really?" I say, tapping the steering wheel. "Well, were your ears ringing because I was just talking about you." He laughs. "I was telling Candace and Ralph about how you don't want to give me your dick."

"Layla." When he says my name, I know he's mad. Over the past five days, the only time he has called me Layla was when he was pissed about something. "You did not talk about my dick with Ralph."

"Yes," I say, and he groans.

"I thought we said we would be private," he says.

"I thought you said you were going to fuck me senseless!" I shout. He laughs now.

"Are you coming to the game tonight?" he asks, and I want to tell him no. "Why don't you pack a bag and stay the night?"

"Are you going to give me what I want?" I ask, and he laughs. "I'm not kidding."

"Text me to tell me if you are going to meet me at the game or be at my house after," he says. "Be safe, gorgeous."

I arrive at the game with Candace, wearing black jeans and a thick brown sweater with a thick collar. He notices my suede knee-high boots right away. He winks at me during his warm-up, and they end up winning the game with ten seconds to go when the puck bounces off his stick by accident. It's a great game, and he walks out, smiling at the end of the game carrying his jacket. "There he is," I say, pushing away from the car. "The number one star."

"Ohh," he says, putting his arm around my waist. "Are you my prize?"

"I'm whatever you want me to be." I kiss him, and he opens the door for me.

"Those boots …" He shakes his head. "Got my cock hard already."

I sit in the seat. "If this got you hot"—I wink at him—"wait until you see what I have on under this." He hisses. Shutting the door, we get to the house, and he looks at me. "You didn't pack a bag."

"No." I shake my head. "I plan on being naked all weekend long. What do I need clothes for?"

I get out of the car and walk into the house, and I'm surprised that he hasn't already attacked me. "What is going on?" I ask when we step into the living room.

He looks at me. "What do you mean?" My heart speeds up when I see a look I haven't seen before on his face.

"I mean, you didn't attack me when we walked in," I say. "You didn't even try to feel me up in the car." He looks at me. "Oh my God, you don't find me attractive," I finally say, my stomach falling. "Is that why you haven't had sex with me? Oh my God," I say, wanting to escape or have the floor open and swallow me.

"Are you insane?" he tells me. "I've been walking around with my cock hard for the past eight days."

"So then why?" I ask him. "Why haven't we had sex?"

"Because," he shouts, "I don't want it to just be sex! I want this to be more. I want to cook for you and for it to be romantic," he says, and I look at him. "I've never been down this road before." I don't have a chance to say anything. "I don't want us to just have sex, and then that's it.."

"Is that why you haven't had sex with me?" I ask, my heart pounding in my chest.

"Us having sex will be the final step, and," he says, putting his hands in his pockets, "I don't want this to be over."

"What do you want?" I ask, holding my hands together so he doesn't see them shaking.

"I want a relationship with you," he says. "I want to have sex with you but not be scared that you're going to walk out of that door tomorrow, and it'll be over." He sits down on his couch. "We've both had no-strings sex." His voice goes low. "I don't want that to be with us."

"You want a relationship with me?" I know he said more after that, but that's the only thing I actually heard. "I mean."

"I don't want you to date anyone else," he finally says. "I don't want to date anyone else."

"I'm not dating anyone else," I say. "I also don't want you dating anyone else."

"So you like me?" he asks, smirking at me.

"Of course, I like you," I say, trying to be smooth about this by ignoring the way my heart is pounding in my chest. "Do you think I would still be here after eight days if I didn't like you?"

"I don't know," he answers honestly. "I haven't really done this thing before." I swallow when he says that. "I've never been with someone who I want to see all the time. I haven't been with someone who drives me crazy and then makes me laugh all in the same breath." I laugh and go sit next to him. "I want you to know that this isn't just to get you into my bed," he says, and I smile now, looking down and feeling my wide smile hurting my cheeks. "Layla, I've chased you for four years, not even thinking about the day after. But now that I've been with you, I don't just want to be that one night."

I lean over and whisper, "I don't want it to be just one night, either." I don't tell him that I like him so much it scares me. I don't tell him that I've been trying not to overthink things or read too much into things. I don't tell him that if he didn't call me tomorrow, I would be heartbroken. I don't tell him that for the past eight days, I've woken up thinking about him. I think about him all day, and when I go to bed at night, I want to be with him.

I watch him get up, and then he holds out his hand for me, and I put my hand in his. "I have a surprise for you," he says softly, and I laugh.

"I've already seen your surprise," I say, and he laughs, now his eyes light are brown.

"Not that," he says. He pulls me to his bedroom, and I stay stopped at the doorway when I see what he meant by a surprise. The whole bedroom has candles lit. I look around, and I swear I've never seen so many candles in my life. "I was going to do the whole roses things, but I thought it might have been overkill."

I ignore the pain in my chest and put my hands to my face, blinking away the stinging of my eyes. "You know," I say, "when you asked me what was the most romantic thing someone has ever done for me?"

"Yeah," he says, standing in the middle of his bedroom at the foot of his bed.

"I want to change that answer," I say, walking to him. "This," I say, opening my arms and turning around in a circle. "This right here is the most romantic thing someone has ever done for me."

"Good," he says, coming to me and grabbing my face in his hand. "You, gorgeous," he says, "are worth it all." He leans forward to slowly take my lips. The kiss is not rushed like all the other ones. This kiss is slow, almost as if he's savoring it. I close my eyes and get lost in all of him.

TWENTY-SIX

MILLER

I WANTED TO cook for her. I wanted to make her see that this isn't just another night for me. I wanted it all, but then she looked at me, and I could see she had doubts that I even liked her. I can't even wrap my head around what we are doing. Neither of us has put a label on it. I mean, I called her my girlfriend in front of about fifty people, but for the past eight days, we haven't spoken about it.

Could I just have sex with her? Yes. Did I want to just have sex with her? No. I wanted her to know I wanted more. The kiss is soft, unlike all the others we've had over the past week. "I can never get enough," I say, peeling her sweater over her head. "You leave me always wanting more."

"You always leave me breathless," she says, unbuttoning my white shirt. "Every night, I wanted you to stay with me," she says, looking up at me, shocking me. "I wanted you to stay with me if only to hold me."

"If I stayed with you, gorgeous," I tell her when she slips the shirt over my shoulders, "I wouldn't have been able to just hold you."

She smirks at me. "I would have been okay with that." Her hands go to my pants, and I push her back before she slips off my pants.

"If my cock comes out," I tell her, "I won't be able to stop from burying myself in you."

"I am more than okay with that," she says, kicking off her boots and then slipping her pants off. Standing in front of me wearing just a bra and panties, she comes to me. "Make me yours." She puts her hands around my neck.

I attack her mouth this time, not sure I can stop myself. My hand goes around her waist as I pick her up, and she wraps her legs around my waist. I walk to the bed, our mouths never letting the other go. My knee hits the bed, and she only lets me go when I lay her in the middle of the bed. I lean over to grab a condom out of the side drawer. She sits up in the middle of the bed and kisses my stomach. "I've never done this," I tell her as she looks up at me. "Here."

"You've never had sex in your bed?" she asks, confused, and then looks down and then up. "I've never had sex in my bed, either." She unbuttons my pants and pulls them down over my hips.

"This is not what I thought it would be like," I tell her, ripping the condom with my teeth.

"How did you think it would have been?" she asks as

I unclip her bra and toss it to the side.

"I thought it would be smoother," I say as she pulls down my boxers and my cock springs out. I roll the condom down my length. "I thought it would be after I make you come a couple of times with my tongue and my fingers."

"You can still do that." She lies back and spreads her legs, and I see her pussy out and open for me. Her panties are crotchless. "Just after you make me come with your cock."

"You got it," I say, taking my cock in my hand and rubbing it up and down her slit. "Are you going to watch?" I ask as the tip of my cock slips into her. Her eyes never leave my cock as she takes me in one smooth move.

Her heat all around me as she pulls her legs back. "Fuck me," she says, still looking down at where we are joined. I pull my cock out and then slam into her again. I try to go slow, but she keeps asking me to go harder.

"More," she says, her hips coming up to meet my thrusts. Snapping, I grab her hips in my hands and pull her onto my cock each time I slam into her. The sound of skin slapping fills the room.

"I'm going to come," she says. I slip out of her and flip her over to her knees, then slam into her from behind. The sound of her moans, along with my panting, fills the room. I wait for her to come, and when she finally does, I pick her off her knees and slam into her one more time until my balls hit her clit and I come inside the condom.

Once I slip out of her, I walk to the bathroom, taking the condom off and then kicking off my pants. When I return to my bedroom, I see Layla lying exactly how I left her. "I need a minute," she says when she sees me. I lean down and snap her panties off her. I toss them over with her bra and then grab another condom out of the drawer.

Climbing back on the bed, I admire her fine ass as I put the condom beside her on the pillow. She looks over her shoulder at me, and again, I grip her hips and turn her around.

"You have to stop throwing me around like a rag doll," she says. My mouth devours her for a second, and then my face slips down to her pussy where I eat her until she has come two more times. She's about to come again when I stop and put the condom on.

I lie on my back now. "You said you want to be in charge." She smirks at me and puts her leg over my hips to straddle me.

"Oh, I'm going to like this," she says, sliding down my cock and leaning forward to grab the top of the headboard. She uses her legs to rise and fall on my cock. My hand rests on her hips and then plays with her nipples as she goes faster and faster.

"I'm getting close," she says in a whisper, and one of my hands goes down to play with her clit. "Harder," she says. "God, right there," she moans as she comes all over my cock.

She rides it out and then collapses on my chest, and I roll her over with my cock still buried in her. "My turn." I smirk at her. "Roll your hips back," I tell her, and she opens her hips wider as she puts them on my shoulders, I lean forward a bit, going deeper than before. Her eyes close, and we both groan. I lean forward a bit more, my hands going under her, and I squeeze her shoulders. "This is going to be hard," I tell her, pulling my cock out and then slamming back into her. "It's going to be fast."

"Give it to me," she says as my mouth finds her, and my hips go into overdrive. I slam my cock into her over and over again, holding her shoulders and making her meet my slams. She cries out. "Miller," she says as she lets go of my lips, and I suck on her neck. My thrusting never stops, and as my balls start to get tight, the thrusts get shorter and shorter. She comes again on my cock, and it drips all the way down to my balls. "This can't be," she says, and she comes right after, but this time, I follow her. Her legs fall from my shoulders to my arms and then onto the bed. Her arms that were around my neck fall limp, too. "I don't think …"

"We still have a lot of night left," I tell her, and she just moans as I slip out of her.

"I don't think I can close my legs," she says, just lying there.

"If you stay open for me all night …" I lean over and move my finger over her clit, and she tries to push my hand away. "Let's go take a shower." I grab her and carry her to the shower, placing her on the bench. I run back to the drawer, grabbing another condom, and when I go back, she is sitting on the bench with her head back. I turn the water on and grab the soap in my hands. "Let's get you clean."

"Why? Does that mean you are going to get me dirtier before you actually clean me?" She stands, letting the water fall all around her. She moves her neck to the side as the water flows down her tits. I bring the bar of soap to her tits and wash them, her nipples perky and ready. I grab the body wash that she brought over last week when she showered here, and I pour some in my hand, the suds starting right away. I wash her tits again, and she laughs. "I think they are clean," she says. I rub down to her stomach, the water making the soap suds more. I wash her hips when I bend to kiss her mouth.

The water falls onto my back as her tongue goes into my mouth. My hand goes to her ass, rubbing it and squeezing it. I turn her around and wash her back, my cock rubbing between her ass cheeks. I turn her back around and slip my hand between her legs. It goes all the way up to her ass, the slipperiness of the soap making me slip a finger inside.

"Hmm," she groans as my hand grabs her ass with one hand while the other hand goes in again and slips inside. "Miller," she says my name as my finger then slips into her pussy and comes back out to wash her all the way up to her clit.

"Fuck," she says. I look into her eyes and see her eyes looking down at my cock. Her hand comes out to fist my cock, and I turn to push her against the tiled wall. She lifts her foot to rest on the bench.

"Make me come," she says as my forehead rests on hers. "Let's make each other come," she says, her hands moving up and down my cock. My two fingers are now finger fucking her as the water cascades around my shoulders. I take my hand out and move it over her clit back and forth.

"More," she says. "Faster." Our hands now move in unison as she jerks me off, and I finger fuck her. I look into her eyes when I know I'm about to come, and she can feel it. "I'm going to come."

"Me, too," I pant out and come all over her hand while she comes on mine. My lips fall onto hers, and when she lets go of my cock, she puts her foot down, making my fingers slip out of her.

She grabs the condom in her hand, tearing the corner off. "You need to clean inside me." She winks, getting on her knees in front of me. "But first, let me clean you with my mouth."

TWENTY-SEVEN

Layla

My eyes flicker open when I hear a pot bang, but then they fall back closed. I turn from my right side to my left side, and my whole body screams at me. I feel like I went through a marathon but not just any marathon. The marathon the Navy SEALs do when they throw them in the water at night, and they have to swim to survive. I stretch my arms over my head, and my arms and legs scream at me.

I blink my eyes open again when the smell of coffee fills the room, and I see the bed empty beside me. I prop myself up on one arm, looking around the room to see if he's here and listening to hear if he's maybe in the bathroom. I see the candles that took us forty-five minutes to blow out. Every time I would bend over, he would slide his cock in me, teasing me. By the end, I pushed him on one of the velour couches and fucked him until we both were sweaty. Which then meant we had to take another shower.

Getting up now, I put one foot on the floor and look over at the empty condom wrappers on the nightstand. My vagina aches as I walk. "He was not kidding," I tell myself while I gather them all in my hand, counting seven of them as I walk to the bathroom. I literally feel him still inside me. "How?" I toss the wrappers in the garbage where I see another four. Twelve, I count. "No wonder my vagina feels raw," I say, washing my face and then using the bathroom.

I look around the room for something to wear, hoping to see a robe hanging in the bathroom. Opening the linen closet, I don't see anything there, so I walk into his walk-in closet. "Holy shit." Looking around, I see a room filled with only suits in every color you can have a suit made. I walk into the second closet and see a whole wall of jeans and then sweaters and another full of shoes. Looking at the other side, I see T-shirts hanging up. "Who hangs up T-shirts?" I ask myself as I grab one to slip on. It falls to the middle of my thigh, and my nipples are sensitive to the cotton of the shirt. I lift the shirt up to inspect them to see them red with little dots all over them from his scruff. I don't know why, but it makes me smile like a fool. I take a second to check out the rest of my body. The same little dots are all over my thighs, and some are on my hips.

I make my way to the kitchen, tying my hair on top of my head, and even that hurts. It could have been when he yanked my head back while plowing into me. Remembering that sends a shiver down my spine.

I see him before he sees me, and I take a second to watch him in front of the stove, cooking something that smells delicious and has my mouth watering. I mean, it could also be the sight of him in basketball shorts that are riding low on one side. His back is perfect, his thick ass is perfect, his thighs are perfect, and his cock … well, his cock should be molded and sold in sex stores.

"Good morning," I say softly. He looks over his shoulder at me, and his smirk turns into a full-blown smile.

"Good morning, gorgeous," he says and turns back around to the pot, turning off the stove. "You got up just in time."

"In time for what?" I ask, walking to him. He bends his head when I get beside him, kissing my neck.

"I made you an omelet," he says. "I figured you needed protein." He winks at me, and I look him up and down. His battle scars are barely visible. He has a bite mark beside his nipple, and he also has one beside his hip that I gave to him while I was riding his face and then fell forward right before I came. "Do you want to eat outside?" he asks, turning to plate one omelet and then opening the oven to take out a bigger plate that has to be his.

"We can eat on the couch outside your bedroom," I tell him, and he nods his head. "What can I carry?"

"There is a tray in that cabinet." He points at the cabinet in the corner. "You can make coffee and bring some juice and a couple of water bottles." I nod and walk over, bending to grab the tray, and I hear his groan behind me. "If you keep shoving your ass in my face, we are not going to be eating anything."

I laugh now. "I'm not shoving anything in your face." I put the tray on the counter and grab two cups, milk, cream, water, juice, and the pot of coffee. He places the two plates on the tray and picks it up by the handles, carrying it to his bedroom. I follow him and laugh when I get into the room right before he opens the door to let some fresh air in. "It smells like sex." He shakes his head. "And latex."

He walks out and puts the tray on the small table in front of the couch. I sit down and look up at him. "Milk or half and half?"

"Milk," he says, and I make him a cup of coffee and then make my own, taking a sip and moaning.

He sits next to me and puts my plate down in front of me. "I hope you like meat and veggies," he says, and I nod my head, grabbing the plate and sitting back on the couch, curling my legs to the side. I put my plate back down and walk back into the bedroom, grabbing one of the throw blankets at the foot of the bed. He's just looking at me when I get back and put the cover over my legs and then take my plate. "You ready?"

"Were you waiting for me?" I ask, shocked as he nods his head. I can't with this man. He is so much more than I thought he was. Besides being fucking funny, he is so considerate. "Eat," I tell him, and he smirks, cutting a piece of his own omelet, and I taste mine. "This is so good."

"Thank you," he says. "I made them both the same, just mine is bigger since I need more strength."

I throw my head back and laugh. "I fucked you as

many times as you fucked me." I look up and start to count the number of times we had sex. "Okay, maybe you got a couple more rounds than I did, but …"

He laughs, looking over at me. "I like seeing you in my clothes."

I look down as I chew my third bite. "It was the only thing I could find," I tell him. "By the way, who hangs T-shirts?" I ask, and I don't wait for him to answer me. "Psychopaths, that's who."

His laughter fills the whole yard, and I can't stop looking at him. He finishes his plate and leans back on the couch. I put my plate down on the table when I've had enough, leaving just a little piece. Grabbing my coffee, I lean back as he tosses the blanket off my legs and grabs one of them to lay across his legs. "Did you sleep well?" he asks, his hand slowly rubbing my leg up and down.

"I did." I put my elbow on the back of the couch and rest my head on my hand. "I mean, when you let me sleep."

He smirks and looks over at me. "You kept shoving your ass in my cock," he says. "Besides, I didn't hear you complain when you woke up with my mouth on you."

It's my turn to laugh. "You can wake me like that every morning," I say and then stop myself when I am about to add of my life. My heart hammers in my chest, and I try to make light of what is happening here, but I'm not sure I can. He's hands down the best sex I've ever had in my life.

"Well, if you had slept for ten more minutes, I would have," he says and looks over at me.

Rising, I move over to him and straddle his lap. I look down into his brown eyes, and the joke I wanted to say before is gone. Now the only thing I can think to say is, "Hi." I put my forehead on his while my hands go to the scruff on his cheeks.

"Hi," he says with a smile. His hand cups my face, and his thumb rubs my bottom lip. "I woke up this morning." He leans in and gently kisses my lips. "And I thought I was dreaming."

"What?" I ask, confused.

"You lying in my bed beside me," he says, smiling, his voice going even lower. "I thought it was a dream." I swallow the lump in my throat. "You, me, naked." His hands now grab my ass. "I thought it was a fucking dream."

"If it helps …" I kiss his lips softly. "I felt you all over me when I woke up this morning. My nipples are raw."

"That's what you get," he says, "for dangling them in my face." The shirt goes up. "While riding me."

"This thing," I say, not sure what to call us, "between us. It's so easy." I blink away all the emotions that want to rush out. "I never spend the night." I take a deep breath. "Yet with you, I'm not ready to leave."

"Then stay," he says. "Stay with me." He turns his head, and his tongue comes out to trail along my bottom lip. "Stay with me."

I try to come up with a quirky answer. I try to come up with a sassy answer, but all the words are swimming in my head, and the only word that I can come up with is, "Okay."

He puts his arm around my waist and stands, my legs automatically wrapping around his hips. He takes me inside, where he fucks me slowly until I beg him to do it harder. The rest of the day is us lounging around, moving from his couch where we have sex on, to him eating me out on his counter, to us having sex in the hot tub. When the sun goes down, he makes me dinner again, and the food gets cold when I thank him for doing another fucking romantic thing for me.

When I finally fall asleep that night, it's in his arms, and I fight off heaviness in my heart. Things are too perfect, and life can't be this perfect. Then I feel his lips on my neck as he says, "Good night, gorgeous."

TWENTY-EIGHT

MILLER

I GRAB THE bag from my closet and walk over to toss it on my bed. "You always wear that face when you take out that bag," Layla says from the middle of my bed, where she sits wearing one of my T-shirts. Her legs cross under her, and her wet hair hangs loose. It's been three weeks since she first came home with me for the weekend. Since that first night, she's spent every single night with me when I'm home. We haven't actually spoken about it, and I'm itching to talk about it. But I don't want to mess up the good thing we have. "It's not going to be long this time." She laughs. "It's for four days." She takes her hair and ties it on top of her head. "Last time, it was seven."

"I hate leaving," I tell her, tossing my things into the bag and then going into the closet to grab a couple of pairs of jeans and a few sweaters.

She rises, scooting over to me on her knees. "But just

think of the phone sex that we have." She moves the bag away and kneels in front of me on the bed, her head falling back so I can kiss her lips. I keep waiting for the day when it's not like the first time with her. I keep waiting for the day that I don't want her every single time I look at her. I keep waiting for the day when my heart doesn't beat faster with her beside me. I even check Google, and they haven't given me anything. She's at every home game now, and she waits by my car or just drives straight here and waits for me when there aren't games, and I'm home. I cook for her, and we just hang out with each other. I feel like I know everything about her, but I have this gut feeling she is keeping something from me. I don't know what it is, and I'm just waiting until it's the right time to ask her. "Plus, it gives my vagina some time to recoup."

I throw my head back and laugh. "You could just admit that you miss me when I go away." I lean down and kiss her lips.

"Oh, here we go," she says, laughing. "I told you the last time I missed you."

"No." I shake my head and walk away from her, going to grab some boxers. "You said you missed my cock."

"Well, obviously, your cock is on you." She laughs. "So in the end, I missed you, too." I pack my bag and put it off to the side.

"What time do you have to be at the airport?" she asks me as I walk over to my side of the bed.

"Nine," I tell her, slipping my shorts off, and my cock springs free. It's always ready when she's around. I slide into bed, and she takes off her T-shirt, throwing it beside her bed. She meets me in the middle of the bed, kissing my chest.

"What are your plans for the week?" I ask.

"I have dinner with Candace tomorrow," she tells me. "Where we are going to watch our men play hockey." I laugh. "Then I have lunch with Grandma Nancy the day after."

"Last time you had lunch with her, she sent me a singing e-card about my dick," I tell her, and she laughs. "It's not funny. I opened it in front of the guys, not knowing what it was."

"It's not my fault that you sexually satisfy her granddaughter, and she's proud of it," she says, kissing me. That night, I barely slept just like every other night before I leave. She gets up with me the next day at seven. We don't actually get out of bed until eight, and then I am rushing around the house, making sure I have everything. I kiss her goodbye at the door, not wanting to go.

When I get to the airport, I'm the last one to arrive right after Ralph, who mopes onto the plane. "I swear, you two are like love-sick puppies and make me want to gag," Manning says, fastening his seat belt.

"I'm not a love-sick puppy," I say to him. "I just didn't sleep last night."

"Yeah, which is how you look every single time we go away." Manning points out. "I'm disappointed in you." He points at me. "I expected better from you."

I laugh. "What the hell does that mean?" I ask him, buckling my own seat belt.

"It means you weren't supposed to fall in love with her so fast," Manning says, shaking his head, and my hands drop to my waist.

"I'm not in love with her," I say, chuckling anxiously.

Ralph, on the other hand, throws his head back and laughs louder than I've ever heard him laugh. "She's got you wrapped around her little pinky." I ignore both of them as they laugh, and the plane takes off. I close my eyes and drift off to sleep, only waking when the plane touches down. "Fuck, it's freezing," I say when we get off the plane in Ottawa.

We get onto the warm waiting bus, and I take my phone out to see that she already texted me.

Gorgeous: Six hours gone, a fuckton more to go.

I laugh and respond.

Me: Is this you telling me you miss me and not my cock?

Gorgeous: Ugh, so needy. Fine, I miss you.

I laugh and put my phone down and look over at Manning, who just glares at me. "Sick."

We get off the bus and walk into the hotel, grabbing our room keys. "Are we having a team dinner?" I ask both of them as we walk to the elevator to go up to our rooms.

"We meet down in the lobby in thirty," someone says.

The three of us nod and walk into the elevator since all of us are getting off on the same floor. I scan my key to the door walking in, tossing my bag on my bed. I take my phone out to FaceTime Layla, who answers right away.

"Well, hello there," she says, smiling, and I see she's wearing a sweater and sitting on her couch. "Did you just get in?"

"Yeah," I say. "We are meeting for dinner in twenty minutes."

"Oh, that sounds like fun." She smiles at me.

"You're gorgeous," I say to her. Her smile gets even bigger, and Manning's words play over and over in my head. You love her. "So," I say, "let's talk about the fact you miss me."

She throws her head back and laughs. "I knew that was going to come back and bite me in the ass," she huffs out. "Fine, you want to hear it?"

"I want to hear it," I tell her. "If you want to tell me."

"Ugh, you are so annoying sometimes." She rolls her eyes. "I miss you," she says softly, "which is as irritating to you as it is to me."

"Why is it irritating?" I ask, laughing at her now.

"It's irritating because it makes me feel needy," she says. "And I'm an independent woman." I see her face get angry. "It's silly. You are only going to be gone for four days. Jesus, it's not like you are going off to war."

"Gorgeous." I say her nickname softly, and she groans.

"No," she says, shaking her head. "Don't with that voice."

"What voice?" I ask, shocked.

"The voice that goes low right before you lean over and kiss the ever-loving shit out of me." She throws her hands in the air. "It might be my favorite," she says, and now I roll my lips. "After the one where you talk with your teeth together because then I know you're going to give it to me good."

I try not to laugh. "First thing, I always give it to you good."

"I agree with that." She smirks now.

"Second, I don't have different voices," I tell her, and she laughs.

"You so do," she says. "There is the one that is normal. Like now," she says. "Then the second that goes down soft when I do or say something that you really really like." She puts up her second finger. "Then the third is when I get under your skin and fight with you. You snap, and there is that vein right there." She points at her forehead. "That bulges out right before you snap." She gives me a sly smile. "That one I love, too, because the last time you used that one, I had your fingertips bruised onto my hips for five days." She winks at me.

"Well, if I was home right now …" I watch her. "I would definitely be the third one."

"Really?" she says, and I see her eyes get cloudy. We are no strangers to sexting or phone sex. "What would you do to me?"

"Take your pants off," I tell her, and she just looks at me.

"They were off the minute you texted me that you landed," she tells me, and I put my head back and laugh.

"If you keep talking like that," I say. "I might think you really like me."

She throws her head back with a groan, and I laugh now as she gets frustrated. She puts the phone down and takes off her sweater, showing me that she is fully naked. "If you aren't going to help me, I am going to have to take things into my own hands."

"Don't you dare," I tell her, and she glares at me. "Now, lie down and spread your legs."

She doesn't argue with me, and in five minutes, we are both coming. "Now I have to go to dinner." I tuck myself back into my pants and walk to the bathroom to clean up.

"I'm going to go soak in a tub," she says, getting up and walking back to her bathroom naked. "I'll send you pictures."

I shake my head when I hear a knock on the door. "Later, Adams." She disconnects as I walk over to the door and find Manning and Ralph waiting for me.

"You get your fix in?" Manning says, looking up from his phone. I laugh at him, and we walk out to eat.

The game against Ottawa is rough, and we lose three to one. We get on the bus right after the game and make our way to Montreal for a game the next day. I listen to Layla's show the next day, and even though I know she is going to rip me to shreds for the way I played, it still stings a bit. But she was right. My head was not in the game. I wish I could say it was better against Montreal, but I would be lying. Thankfully, I'm on the plane the next day while her show is on. I land, and I don't bother texting her, opting to go straight to her house.

I park my car in her driveway seeing her car and another car I don't recognize. When I spoke to her this morning, she sounded a bit off, but I didn't say anything.

I was going to text her when I got off the plane, but instead, I decided to surprise her here. Plus, I missed her. I get out of the car and walk up to her door, ringing the doorbell.

I turn to look around to look back at the car that is there, trying to figure out who it belongs to. The lock turns, and I look back with a smile on my face, expecting to see her. "He-" I stop speaking when I see a guy opening her door. "Oh." He is standing there in jeans and a white button-down shirt. His blond hair is perfectly cut and to the side. I know this guy, but I can't place him right now.

"Can I help you?" he asks, holding the door as my heart hammers in my chest. I must take too long to answer him. "Um, hello? Can I help you?"

My hand comes up, and I point at him. "Who are you?" I ask. My mind spins around and around with so many questions and thoughts. The only thing I keep asking myself is where is Layla.

"Who am I?" he asks, pointing at himself. My heart is picking up so much speed and is racing so fast I hear it in my ears as it echoes.

"Who the fuck are you?" I don't know what I'm expecting, but I do know that I'm definitely not expecting the words that come out of his mouth, crushing me. "I'm the husband."

TWENTY-NINE

Layla

I WASH MY hands in the sink and look in the mirror. This day has gone from happy that I was going to see Miller to fucking miserable because Richard decided it would be a good time to come to town and annoy the shit out of me. I've been ignoring his phone calls for the past five months, and this afternoon, there he was on my stoop as soon as I got home. Acting as if we are the best of friends, which we are not.

Walking out of the bathroom, I hear the front door close, and I wonder, or actually, I hope that he took the hint to fuck off. When I walk into the family room, I see him coming back into the house. I look at him, and my insides cringe, thinking of him. "I thought you left?" I tell him, folding my arms over my chest.

"I thought we were going to dinner." He smiles at me, and I roll my eyes. That smile that all the ladies fall for, including me back in the day.

"I believe I said fuck no," I tell him and then look at him, confused as to why he was at the front door, and then he came back in.

"Why were you at the front door?" I ask. I hear a car door close, and then the sound of the engine starting, and it sounds as if it's in my driveway. That can't be. Who else would come here?

"I think your boyfriend was here," he says. My heart sinks to my stomach, and my legs shake as I run toward the door.

Opening the door, I run to his car as he takes off. "Miller!" I yell his name as the car speeds away.

"Oh my God." I put my hand on my stomach. "Oh my God," I say over and over to myself. Running back into the house, I put my shoes on and grab my keys. "You need to be gone when I get back." I run around the room, trying to find my purse.

"Now," he says, putting his hands in his pockets, "is this any way to treat your husband?"

"Ex. Husband." I point out. "Ex-fucking-husband." I'm so angry that he's here. I'm angry that he got to Miller first, and I'm angrier that I wasn't the one who told him. That he found out from Richard.

"You know we are meant to be together," he says, and I look around to see if I can throw anything at him. I can't believe that I fell for his bullshit. I close my eyes, wishing today away. Wishing it was yesterday, and I'd forced myself to tell Miller the truth.

"You got what you came for," I tell him, pointing at the papers in the manila envelope. "Now you can go back to the hole you climbed out of."

"I was hoping we could talk," he says, and I just laugh. "I've changed, Layla." His voice goes soft, and I look at him, shocked that he would start this again. Shocked? Yes. But I don't know why I should be surprised.

"That's good to hear," I say. "I'm sure your wife is going to be happy to hear that."

"We aren't together anymore," he says, and I shrug. "I never got over you."

"That's too bad," I say. "Now close the door on the way out," I say, ignoring him when he calls my name. I run to my car and dial Miller at the same time. "Pick up, pick up, pick up," I plead with the universe, but the call goes straight to voice mail.

"Miller, please," I say, ignoring the tears that are now coming down. "I can explain," I tell him, and I wipe the tear away from my cheek. "Please," I say in a whispered plea. I make my way over to his house, calling him every minute. It goes straight to voice mail, and his voice mail's now full of all my messages. I speed there, my heart hammering in my chest, and I pull up right as he's taking his bag out of his trunk. He looks back at me, and I know that face, I've seen that face. It's been my face not too long ago. His eyes shielded without emotion, and I can only imagine how hurt he must be.

I put the car in park and jump out, calling his name. "Miller," I say, running to him as he ignores me and walks into his house. "Please, I can explain."

"Not interested," he says, his voice sounding defeated.

"Please, you have to give me a chance to explain," I say to his back, and it kills me that we have to do this here in the middle of his driveway. It kills me that I am not doing it while holding his hand as I wanted.

"A chance to explain?" He laughs bitterly, dropping his bag. "A chance to explain? You've got to be kidding me." He stops walking and turns around to face me.

In my whole life, I've only ever regretted one thing. Now standing here in front of him, seeing the hurt and pain on his face, I regret doing this to him. I want to go to him, and I want to hold his face while I tell him my side of the story. I want to tell him everything.

"I don't think I need you to explain anything to me. I pretty much got the whole story. Your husband sort of explained everything that needs to be explained," he says, his voice tight. I want to go to him. I want to sit him down and tell him the secret that I've been keeping from him. The secret that I never told anyone. The secret that I was so afraid to tell him, yet I knew that if we continued, I would have no choice.

"He's my ex-husband," I tell him, making sure he at least knows that. That whatever comes from this conversation, he'll know I'm not an adulterer. "And it was a long time ago."

"Do you think that makes it better?" he snaps, and the tears that I forced myself not to shed in front of him come now. I can't even try to stop them as they pour down my face. "You lied to me." The four words cut me off at the legs. "I told you from day one that I hated lies."

"I never lied to you," I say softly.

He laughs now. "All this time, you had trust issues with me. You doubted me all the time." He looks at me, shaking his head. "You made me jump through fucking hoops to make sure you could trust me. What a fucking idiot I was," he says. "Because all this time, I was the one who should have had you jumping through hoops. I was the one who should not have trusted you." He points at himself. "All this time, I wanted to show you how worthy I was of you, but in the end"—he looks me straight in the eyes—"you aren't worth it." He picks up his bag, his words cutting me to the core of my heart.

"Get the fuck out of here," he says, turning his back to me and walking into the house.

My hands shake, and I jump when the front door slams shut, leaving me in the middle of his driveway. I turn to walk back to my car, and the whole time, my legs shake and threaten to give out as soon as I reach my car door.

His words hit me over and over again. "You aren't worth it." I pull out of his driveway in a daze, the tears pouring down my face. I don't even feel them anymore.

When I pull up in my driveway, I see that his car is gone. I walk in, feeling like I just got hit by a Mack truck. My whole body aches, and I take my phone, texting Brian about tomorrow. I tell him that I have a fever and that I don't think I will be able to work. He answers right away that he will get someone to take my place and tells me to go to the doctor.

I open the door of my house and look around, seeing that he left all the lights on. I turn off the lights and drag myself to my bedroom. I curl up into a ball in the middle of my bed, and I close my eyes.

All I can see is the hurt on his face. All I can hear are the words he said. All I can do is pray that this is a nightmare and that tomorrow when I wake up, it'll be in his arms. But sleep doesn't come and take me. Instead, I get undressed and then slip on my sweats and his shirt. I climb back into bed, my body shivering, my teeth clattering.

I finally sob out loud for him. I cry for the man who chased me for the past four years. I cry for the man who made me smile more than anyone in my whole like. I cry for the lost tomorrows.

I cry for the man who I fell in love with but never got a chance to tell him.

THIRTY

MILLER

"GET THE FUCK out of here," I hiss at her. My heart shatters in my chest, the pain more than I've ever felt in my life. I want to hurt her as much as she hurt me. I want to roar out at anyone who gets in my way. My hands shake with the nerves that run through me.

I'm the husband. The three words that ended it all. Three totally different words than what I was going to tell her this weekend. I stood there, stunned. My heart beats so hard in my chest, and my mouth is dry. My head's spinning, not sure I understood. This man is her husband. The woman who I've fallen in love with is married.

I slam the door behind me, my back collapsing on it. Seeing her there looking more beautiful than she has ever before. The tears streaming down her face while she said he was her ex-husband. My stomach lurches at the thought of her married to someone. The lone tear escaping from my eyes. I listen as the car door shuts, and I listen to her drive away. Driving away from me, away from us.

Walking straight to the liquor cabinet, I grab the bottle of scotch. Unscrewing the cap, I don't even bother with a glass. I take three long gulps. The burning of my throat spreads to my chest and then to my stomach. I put the bottle down and close my eyes, but it just makes it that much worse. All I can see is her face, her beautiful fucking face with tears running down the same cheeks I kissed four days ago. The same cheek I rub with my thumb when she sits next to me, and I want to touch her.

I open my eyes again, and this time, I drink another three gulps. The burning is much less this time than the last. Grabbing the bottle, I make my way over to the window and walk outside. The sound of the pool fills the yard. I look up at the sky, wondering how this day started so good but ended up the worst day of my life.

Closing my eyes again doesn't help because all I can do is play the last month over and over again. The quiet nights with just the two of us. The nights spent out laughing at everything and nothing. Her face when she sleeps. Her face when she is happy. I drink more of the scotch, trying to erase all the memories. Trying to erase her from my heart.

Walking back inside, I don't even bother going to my bedroom, knowing it'll be worse in the place where it still smells like her. Instead, I sit on the couch with the lights off. In the darkness, I drink until my eyes can't stay open. I look down at the almost empty bottle and try getting up to get another one. But I fall back onto the couch, and the bottle slips out of my hand and crashes to the floor. I hear the shatter, but all I can do is lie down on my back. My hand's on my chest, resting over my pounding heart, and I wonder how it can beat when it's broken. "Why?" I ask the white ceiling that is now spinning. "Why?" No one answers me as my eyes slide shut.

Nothing helps when my eyes close in a drunken stupor, and nothing helps when I hear her laughter in my head. Nothing helps when I hear her moan my name. Nothing helps when I hear her sob out as if she is right next to me. My eyes shoot open to find I'm still in the darkness. I'm still in my own living hell.

I roll to my side, and as soon as my feet hit the floor, I hear the sound of crunching glass. "Fuck." I get up, not sure if I can actually walk. I stumble on the way to the closet that holds the vacuum, and only when I can't pull it out do I give up. Instead, I go over to grab another bottle of scotch, and this time, I walk on the other side of the couch. My phone beeps from my pocket, and I take it out and see I have missed calls. My eyes only focus on the word *gorgeous*.

My finger rolls over the name, and I open it and block her number. My stomach roils, and I think I'm going to be sick. I close off the phone and then open it again only to see the picture of us staring at the camera laughing. The pain in my heart is so strong that I look down to see if I have blood seeping out of my chest.

I do another thing I shouldn't, especially with a whole bottle of scotch in my system. I look through my pictures. Most of them of her. Most of them taken without her knowing. Most of them with her smiling at something. Then I look at the one I took four days ago. Her in my bed, her hair on the pillow like a fan as she looks over at me with sleep in her eyes. It was then I almost told her that I loved her. It was then it finally dawned on me that I love this woman with everything I have.

"She doesn't love you," I say to myself.

Putting my head back, I open the other bottle of scotch and take a swig. Swig after swig, the night haunts me. Every single time my eyes close, it's my own living hell. I try to force my eyes open, but nothing helps.

When I finally open my eyes the next day, the sun is streaming into the house. My mouth is dry, and my tongue feels like a cotton swab, not allowing me to swallow. I get up, and now the pounding in my head has me hissing. I walk over to the kitchen to grab a glass of water and two painkillers. I look over at the clock and see it's almost fucking noon. I also see the vacuum in the middle of the hallway.

I walk over to the spare bedroom, starting the shower and undressing. I get in and put my hands on the wall, letting the water cascade around me. I wonder if she feels hurt. I wonder if she is laughing at me. The poor fucking idiot who she strung along like a love-sick puppy.

Turning off the shower, I walk to my bedroom with the towel around my waist, ignoring the bed that she fixed before she left. I also ignore the note that I know she left on the bed. It was something she started doing so I could read it when I got home. I slip on my basketball shorts and walk back into the kitchen, grabbing two more painkillers. My head pounds like a jackhammer is inside it. I start the coffee, walking to the door where I dumped my bag. I slip on my sneakers, then walk back to the vacuum, and I clean up the shattered bottle.

The sound of the little pieces of glass clanking into the vacuum cleaner makes my headache even worse. The doorbell rings as soon as I shut off the vacuum, and I look over, waiting to see if the bell rings again.

When it does, I walk back over to the front door. My heart speeds up in my chest, wondering if it's her, but I know she wouldn't come back here. Not after the way I spoke with her yesterday. Not after throwing her words in her face. I unlock the door, and I stand here now shocked when I see her standing there. Her eyes are red from crying, or maybe she didn't sleep last night. Her hair is piled on her head, the big sweater she is wearing looks like it's swallowing her.

"Hi," she says, and I see that she is wringing her hands together. "I know that you don't want to see me," she says, and I almost slam the door in her face. "I just." Her voice hitches. "I'd like for you to give me five minutes of your time, and then you never have to talk to me again." She swallows now, and my stomach sinks.

"You have five minutes." I move out of the way and give her room to come inside.

"Thank you," she says softly and comes in and waits for me to walk into the house. She acts like she hasn't been in this house before. I see that she looks down, and from the side of my eyes, I can see her wiping a tear away.

She stops walking when she sees the half empty bottle of scotch and then looks over at me. "You drank?"

"Is that what you came over here to talk to me about? My drinking." I fold my arms over my chest.

"No," she says, looking back down again as if she's afraid of me. As though she can't stomach to look at me. "Can I sit down?" she asks, and I see that her hands are shaking now when she isn't holding them together.

"Did you drive here?" I ask, suddenly worried that she could have gotten hurt. But then I remember it doesn't matter. It isn't my problem. "Forget it. I don't care," I say, and I see her nod her head and swallow.

"I guess we can talk here," I say to her, looking at the couch, and she walks over and sits down. Usually, she would sit with her feet curled under her. Usually, I would sit beside her with my arm over her legs.

But now she sits almost on the edge of the couch with her hands in her lap. I sit down on the other couch, facing her. "Before I start, I want to say I'm sorry that you found out that way."

"What are you exactly sorry for?" I ask her. "Is it because I found out?" I glare at her, and she shakes her head.

"I shouldn't have come," she says, getting up now.

"You owe me the truth," I tell her, saying words that hurt me more than her. "After today, we never have to talk to each other."

THIRTY-ONE

Layla

I SHOULDN'T HAVE come here, my inner voice is screaming at me. *Why would you do this to yourself?*

I shake my head. It's not about me; it's about Miller. It's about him right now. I sit on the edge of the couch that I used to sit on right next to him. The same couch he made love to me on five days ago, the same couch that we binge-watched TV shows together. The same couch where I lay on his chest and fell asleep. I look around the house, feeling like a stranger, which is weird because, for the past month, I spent more time here than at my actual house. The half-empty bottle of scotch on the counter means he drank last night. That what I did pushed him to do things he doesn't do. That he wanted to wash away the hurt I brought onto him with alcohol.

I spent the whole night in bed, my body shivering. I just couldn't get the chill out of my body. I also spent the whole night silently crying. I didn't expect him to open the door, so I was shocked. Just seeing him made me feel just a touch better, knowing I could see him if only for five minutes. "I am sorry that I wasn't the one who told you." I answer his question and see the redness in his eyes. I want to ask him if he's hurting like I am. I want to ask him if he missed me as much as I missed him. I want to ask him if his heart hurts as much as mine does. I want to ask him to hold me. I want to ask him to give me one more kiss that I can savor. One more kiss to remember him by. One more touch, one more kiss, one more night, one more chance. I want to beg him to forgive me, but that is the selfish part of me. That part is not thinking about his pain or making his pain a priority. The whole night I put myself in his shoes, the whole night I imagined finding out he was married. I would be just as shattered as he was. I look at him sitting there, and it hurts, even more, knowing how it feels to be in his arms, knowing how much he completes me.

"So you still aren't sorry you lied to me," he says. "Because by you not telling me, you lied to me." I listen to the way his voice is tight and hurt.

I take a deep breath and start the speech that I practiced in the car on the way here. Over and over again, I tried to do it without the tears coming. "I was nineteen when I met Richard," I tell him, and I see that he just looks at me. "He was twenty-two and in town for a golfing event."

"Wait a second," he says, holding up his hand. "Was that Richard Chambers?" I nod. "The number two seated golfer in the whole world."

"That would be him," I say, taking a deep breath. "Obviously, he wasn't number two when we met." I have never told anyone this story, not even Grandma Nancy. It was for me and only me. My mistake that made me so cautious with my heart. The mistake that caused me to keep everyone at bay. The mistake that I never allowed myself to live, really.

"We met when my college newspaper sent me to cover the golf game. I was in charge of asking a couple of them questions. I asked him some basic golf questions, and he laughed at me when I had no idea what a par or a birdie was. He asked me out that night, and we dated for two years." I swallow. "In secret, of course. He was an up-and-coming golfer. His manager had this whole persona he was creating. He was a charmer, and he was friendly to everyone. He had to keep his single lifestyle going to get the girls running. We got married in secret also. His manager was the only one there and actually got me to sign an NDA about it." I laugh now, blinking away the tears. "God, it was so stupid. But I thought I loved him, and I thought he loved me. We would go out together often, but never once did he hold my hand, never with his arm around me, and when we did go out, the girls would flock all over him." I don't have to tell him like they were with him.

"His game was the best it had ever been, and he was riding the wave. His endorsements were coming in hand over fist. When he won his first-ever big title, I was standing there while he celebrated with a random girl who walked up to him while he was walking off the course. He let her fawn all over him. She wrapped her arms around his neck, and he held her around her waist. If you asked anyone, they would have thought they were a couple." My hands start to shake. "I told him it bothered me. He made it seem like I was asking to sacrifice his game by admitting we were married. On our wedding anniversary, I found a reservation that he made at this posh hotel. I showed up, thinking I was surprising him. I did my hair and makeup and made sure to wear his favorite dress. Only to walk in with him and the same girl who he celebrated with." I wipe the tear away.

"He tried to tell me it meant nothing. He tried to say it was the first time and that I was making a big deal about nothing. I called Grandma Nancy that day, and she came to get me." I look up for the first time to see him, and he just looks at me. I can't tell if he cares or not, but I want him to know it all. No matter what happens, I want him to know the little piece of me no one else knows. "She gave zero fucks about the NDA I signed and got a lawyer who hired a private investigator, and we found out that he had sixteen women scattered all across America who he would meet up with while he was 'on tour.'" I swallow now, wishing I had water. "Grandma wouldn't cave and made sure he paid through the ass. He dragged his feet during the divorce because he thought I would take him back when I just wanted to be done with him. Every five years, he has to pay me a portion of what he makes, which is why he showed up. He hand delivers the check."

"He's the reason you could afford the twenty-five

thousand?" he asks me, his jaw tight.

"Yes," I answer, and I see him fist his hand.

"That's why you didn't like women coming up to me?" he asks me. "So I had to pay for his mistakes." He laughs out. "Why didn't you just tell me?"

"Tell you what?" I look at him. "Tell you that I'm divorced. The night you spoke to me about getting married, my heart literally sank in my chest. How could I tell you that I was divorced when you would only get married once. Meanwhile, here I was, married and divorced. I couldn't muster up the courage, at least not then." I look at down at my hands. "But I was going to."

"Yeah, I can imagine when." His voice comes out harshly. "I mean, it's not like we had the time or anything."

"I guess you're right," I say, getting up. My body starts to get a chill, and I know that if I don't leave now, he'll be witness to the complete breakdown that I'm going to have. "Thank you for giving me a chance to explain." I turn around and start to walk out.

"Thank you," he says, his voice soft, and I turn around. "For showing me what type of man I want to be." He stares at me, and the tears form in my eyes so much I can't see. I nod at him and start to walk out.

"I'm sorry," he says, and I stop in my tracks, letting the tears fall before I turn around. "For what I said yesterday about you not being worth it." Whatever is left of my heart is now shattered. It's broken and shot to shit. I look at him and know that I will never love a man like I love him. I know that after everything is said and done, he is going to be the love that got away.

"I hope you find someone," I say the words, trying not to let my voice tremble. "I hope you find the love you deserve." I don't say anything else. I take one more look at him and walk out of the house. The door slamming behind me is symbolic to the relationship ending. To my heart shutting down, my body shutting down.

I practically run to my car, getting in, and I somehow hope that he comes running after me. I sit in the driver's seat and count to ten to see if maybe he'll forgive me. Seeing if maybe, just maybe I am worthy of his love. But the door stays shut. I have to give him what he wants, and he's made it clear he doesn't want me.

"Goodbye, Miller," I say to him and pull out of his driveway. I look back through the rearview mirror one last time, but all it does is show me that I'm driving farther and farther away from him.

THIRTY-TWO

MILLER

THE DOOR CLOSES behind her, and for the second time, I let her go. My heart screams to go after her, my head telling me that she doesn't want me. If she wanted you, she wouldn't have walked out. I get up, making myself coffee, my head spinning with her story. The pain that she was in while she told me her story killed me. Each word was like a kick in the stomach. Her hands shook so hard in her lap that I'm worried she'll get into an accident. Shaking my head, I walk over to my bedroom and grab a T-shirt, and then I walk out of the house. I have to make sure she makes it home okay.

I get into my car and make my way over to her house. My mind replays everything in my head. She married another man. I can't wrap my head around it. I can't imagine her married to that man. A man who treated her like that, who didn't cherish her. Who wasn't proud to have her standing beside him. I pull up on her street and see her park her car. She gets out with her head down and her shoulders shaking. She stops right next to her car, and I see that she almost falls. But she catches herself and holds the wall on her way in.

I watch as she closes the door behind her, and then I leave. My mind numbs as I get back home and walk into the house. I walk to the fridge, opening it and then closing it. Walking back to my bedroom, I stop in the doorway, and if I close my eyes, I can still smell her. I walk over to the bed and grab the note she left on there. I sit on the bed, unfolding the white paper and seeing her handwriting.

Miller,

Welcome home, and just so you know, I missed you. And your little friend, too.

P.S. It's not that little.

I laugh and then cry, tears coming down my face as I open the drawer beside the bed that holds all her other notes. I softly close the drawer and then lie back on the bed, but I can't stay in here. I feel her all around me. I get up, grabbing her pillow, and walk out to the spare bedroom. I kick off my shoes and fall onto the bed.

"I love you," I say out loud to the walls, hugging her pillow in my arms. My chest aches as I close my eyes and see her stumbling out of her car. I wonder if she's okay. I wonder if she ate something. I wonder if it hurts her as much as it's hurting me.

The night is the worst when I reach out for her, thinking she's there only to come up empty-handed. When I walk into the arena the next day, Ralph takes one look at me, and I just shake my head. He nods at me, and I want to know if he spoke to her. I want to ask him if she's okay. But I don't. I sit on the bench and look ahead as people get dressed to go on the ice.

He waits for us to be alone before he looks over at me. "You didn't have to come in today." His voice is soft.

"What else was I supposed to do? Stay in my fucking house that I want to burn down?" I look at him. "Is she okay?"

He shakes his head. "Candace went over there last night," he tells me. "I know how you feel." He should. Last year, Candace took off on him only to come back, and he refused to let go of her.

I grab a bottle of water from the table in the middle of the room. I take a sip. "Yeah, well, it was too good to be true." I taste the bitterness in my words as I get up. "Better sooner than later."

"You going to be okay?" he asks, and I take a sip of the water. The truthful answer is no. I don't think I will ever be okay. "I'm here if you need anything," he says, getting up and grabbing his helmet.

"Thanks," I tell him, and all I do is sit here. I watch people come and go, and I don't move. I get up only after Ralph comes back into the room. Sweat pours down his face, and he just looks at me.

"Have you been sitting there the whole time?" he asks, and only then do I stand.

"Yeah, I'm going to head out," I tell him. "See you tomorrow."

"You still coming?" he asks, shocked now.

"It's the team Christmas party," I tell him. "Of course, I'm coming." I don't tell him that I won't stay long, or that I was going to attend with Layla on my arm.

"Okay, I'll see you then," he says, and I make my way home. I shower in the spare bedroom and even sleep in the bed.

The next day, I force myself to get up and get ready. I slip on my black suit jacket and look at myself in the mirror. The team Christmas party is the place where we let loose and just have a great time with each other. It's always a blast, and I was looking forward to attending it with Layla. I shake my head. Grabbing my phone, I put it in my inside pocket and make my way over to the arena. I arrive at the same time as Ralph and Candace.

"Hey," I say, pressing the button to lock the car door. "Look at you two." I smile at them. "Parents gone wild."

Candace smiles at me. "It took a lot to get my ass out of sweats tonight," she jokes.

"Who is watching Princess Ari?" I ask. They both look down, and my heart sinks.

"Auntie Layla needed some cheering up, so …" she says, looking at me and then down again. I see that she wants to say something, but instead, she blinks away the tears. "Miller," she says my name, and I shake my head. I try not to be affected by the fact that she needed cheering up. I try not to think of her at all. But every single time I force myself not to think of her, the only thing I can think about is her stumbling. Fuck, I should have gone to her. I shake my head. She doesn't want me.

"It's fine," I tell him, putting my hands in my pockets

and ignoring the pain in my chest. "It'll be fine. Now let's get in there," I say, pulling open the door and seeing a winter wonderland theme. "It looks like Frosty the snowman barfed all over the place," I say, laughing, and I look around. "I'll catch you later," I say, walking away from them. I don't want them to look at me with pity. I walk over and see some of the rookies with girls. I nod at them and walk away but then am called back by one of the girls.

"Hey, can we get a quick picture?" one of them asks, and I want to say no. But I smile and nod my head, putting my hands in my pockets and trying to stand as far away from her as I can. She thanks me, and I just walk away, running into Manning.

"Hey," he says. "Where's Layla?" I look down at the floor and then up again. "Oh, shit."

He slaps me on the shoulder. "I'm so sorry, man. I didn't know. But …" I'm sure he wants to ask when this happened, and I just shake my head.

"It's all good. It is what it is," I tell him, trying to ignore the pain from my chest. Fuck, this is going to be harder than I thought. This whole getting over her is going to be rough. "How do you do it?"

"Do what?" he asks, looking around.

"How did you stop loving her?" I motion with my head to his wife.

"The question you should be asking me," he says, "is when did I realize I was in love with her. The answer to that is never." He shakes his head. "I don't think I ever loved her. Liked her, sure, I'll give her that. But love?"

He shakes his head. "Never." I look at the floor and then up again. "Shit, she's coming this way."

"There you are, sweetheart," she says sweetly and slips her arm in his. "I was looking for you."

"Where the hell do you think I'm going to go?" he says and tries to get away from her.

"I'll see you guys later," I say and make my way around, saying hello to everyone I need to say hello to. We sit down and eat, and as soon as the plates are cleared, I make my way out.

Being here is more than I can handle. I make my way home and stop in the middle of the driveway when I see two cars parked there, and I walk into the house and stop when I hear the soft Christmas music. "Shit," I say, walking into the great room.

"Hey," the interior decorator, Judy, says, "we are almost finished here." I look around and see that they transformed the great room into a Christmas wonderland. The tree stand in the corner almost touches the ten-foot ceilings. There are little trees everywhere with lights on them. The fireplace has a garland handing on it with an "Our First Christmas" frame that I told her to put up. Three white socks hang on the fireplace with fake candles flickering around.

I was going to surprise Layla with the tree when we got home tonight. I was also going to ask her to spend Christmas with me and meet my family.

"That's fine," I say, swallowing down the lump in my throat. "Take all the time you need. Close up when you leave," I say, heading back to my bedroom and slipping out of my suit. My phone falls out of my pocket, and I look down to see Layla staring back at me. I pick up the phone and rub my finger across the screen.

I take one more look at it and then erase it, replacing my screen saver with the team logo. "It'll be better tomorrow," I tell myself. "It'll be all better tomorrow."

After I slip quietly out of my bedroom, I enter the spare bedroom again. Tomorrow, I'll go back to my old life. I lie on the bed, and I have this feeling of emptiness all around me. I feel lost. I feel empty. I feel pain. I feel numb. I feel all of it, and I know that all it will take is one look at her, and my world will be full again.

Closing my eyes, I turn on my side and hug her pillow. "One more night," I say to the darkness. "One more night." I close my eyes and get lost in all the memories of her.

THIRTY-THREE

Layla

"MERRY CHRISTMAS," I say when Grandma Nancy opens the door. She claps her hands, and the bells that she is wearing around her wrist make noise. "Oh my," I say, seeing the reindeer headband she is wearing. "It's all Christmas up in here."

"Come in." She pulls me in by the wrist. "What are all those presents?" She points at my hand.

"It's Christmas, silly," I tell her, going over to her tree and placing them under it. She's had this tree since I was a little girl. The colored lights always made me feel like it was home. Some of the ornaments hanging are the ones I made in school. "Did you lose more weight?" she asks me after I shrug off my jacket. I look down at my outfit of jeans and a bulky sweater, hoping that it would have hidden the fact that I did lose some more weight.

"I've been super busy," I lie to her. It's been almost a month since I last saw Miller face-to-face and had my heart broken. I keep hoping that every day will be better, and I have to be the one to admit it's not getting any easier. In fact, it's getting harder. Of course, it doesn't help that he is having the season of his life, and I have to talk about him daily. I watch the games alone, curled up on my couch. I fall asleep to images of him only to wake with my pillow soaked with tears.

"You have to make time for yourself," she says and just looks at me, and I nod.

"What time is this party?" I ask, changing the subject. Every single year, I join her and her friends. The whole seniors' home gather in the main dining room with all their families. Everyone brings a dish, so it's a potluck. Last year, we had over two hundred people, yet we had food for four hundred.

"I'm just putting the finishing touches on the brownies," she says, walking to the kitchen.

"Grandma," I tell her.

"Not those types of brownies," she says. "I don't share those brownies with anyone." She winks at me.

I watch her put her homemade chocolate frosting on with red sprinkles. "Now, let's get to the party." She points over at the five aluminum platters on the table. "Can you bring those?"

"Sure," I say and then pick it up. We walk down the hallway and come to the common dining room that is also a game room and where they watch movies. It's now transformed with tables all along the wall for the food, and then round tables are set up all around with chairs. The middle of the room is left open for the dancing that is surely going to come. I follow Grandma to the table, and she points at the other table, so I walk over and put down the trays. I look around, seeing that the whole place looks so festive.

"Every year, I just get more blown away." I hear my grandmother say and watch her look around the room. "I have to scope out who is going to be getting a special Christmas present." She smiles at a couple of the guys who are around her. "Oh, I see a good one under the mistletoe." I look at the direction she is looking at.

"There is no mistletoe," I tell her, folding my arms over my chest.

She pulls one out of her pocket. "When life hands you lemons, you make lemonade." She winks at me and walks away. I see her catch the guy who looks like a deer in the headlights, and then she just lays one on him. "Merry Christmas," she tells him, then comes back over to me. "That should get his motors going."

I shake my head, and five minutes later, the room is filled with people. We get in line to grab our meal, and I wish I could say I felt festive, but I don't. I grab the turkey and stuffing and a biscuit, following Grandma over to a table. We sit with her friends as they tell stories about how everything has changed. I eat until I'm stuffed and get up to go get some pie. When I get back to the table, the music starts to play, and I see her friends getting up to go bust a move.

"Are you having a good time?" Grandma asks, sitting back in her chair.

"You know I always have a good time with you," I

say, smiling.

"Have you spoken to Miller?" she asks me, and I shake my head and blink away the tears that have struggled to stay inside all day. "Have you tried to call him?"

"No," I say the truth. "Grandma, he blocked me."

"You don't know that for sure," she tells me, and I look at her. "Okay, fine, I don't know how those things work, but you can't go on like this." She puts her elbows on the table now. "You didn't even take your divorce this bad."

I shrug. "I think it's time for a change," I tell her, and she just looks at me. "My contract is almost up, and I was thinking …" I say, looking out at the dance floor that is full of people with their families celebrating. Kids dressed in their best clothing, running around chasing each other with balloons. Sons dancing with their mothers, and fathers dancing with their daughters. "I'm going to talk to someone about transferring." She doesn't say anything to me.

"Running away isn't going to change anything," she tells me, and now a tear does come out of my eye.

"It's been a month, Grandma, and my chest still hurts when I think about him. It's been a month that I wake up in tears. I just need a fresh start. I need to not say his name every single day. I need to not have to watch him on the television and have my heart break because I can't talk to him or see him." I look down at my pie, grabbing a napkin. "It's just too much for me."

"You think that if you move away, it's going to be better?" she asks me. "You love him, baby girl. That love won't go away."

"I know," I admit. "But it might make it a little easier. Maybe."

"Well, wherever you go, I go," she says, and I look at her, shocked. "You didn't think I'd let you move away from me."

"Your life is here," I tell her, looking around.

She shrugs. "If we are being honest …" She looks around. "It's slim pickings these days."

I laugh now for the first time in a long time. "Why haven't you gone to him?"

I shake my head. "You didn't see the hurt in his eyes or the way he looked at me. Whatever he felt for me, it was gone the minute he found out I not only lied to him but I was also divorced.." I swallow. "He's going to make a great husband," I tell her, the words almost not coming out. "I have to give him the chance to get to that."

"Why don't you give yourself one more chance?" she says to me. "Why don't you go and fight for him?"

My heart goes to my throat. "What if he doesn't want me?" I shake my head. "I don't think I can survive it twice."

"Baby girl," she says. "The best love is the one fought for."

"That's what Google says," I tell her, laughing at the little joke that reminds me of Miller.

"May I have this dance?" The man who Grandma kissed before comes over and holds out his hand for her.

"If you play your cards right," she says, putting her hand in his, "you can get more than a dance." He smirks at her, and I just watch her spend the night dancing. I smile at the kids who bump into me and smile at the parents when they kiss their kids goodbye.

I get up finally and walk over to kiss my grandmother. "I'll call you tomorrow," I tell her, and she hugs me.

"Don't give up," she says, kissing my cheek. I walk back to her apartment to grab my jacket and make my way home. I unlock the door and shrug my jacket off. I undress, slipping into my jogging pants and a large shirt. I grab my cover and cover myself on the couch. I just lie here watching the white lights on my tree twinkle.

I didn't want to put up a tree, but Granma Nancy came over while I was at work and transformed my house. I grab my phone, and my heart speeds up.

"Here goes nothing," I tell the universe, pulling up Miller's name.

Me: Merry Christmas, Miller.

THIRTY-FOUR

MILLER

GORGEOUS: MERRY CHRISTMAS, *Miller*.

It's been two days since I got that text. Seven days and I was tempted every single day to text her back. But I just couldn't; my heart was telling me that I had to see her to say what I needed to say.

"What are you doing in here?" my father asks, walking into the game room. My parents arrived this morning. The rest of my family is coming in tomorrow morning for the festivities leading up to the winter classic game. The whole town has spent the month preparing for this. I still don't get how they are going to have ice for us to skate on in Dallas, but they said it's going to happen. We will finally be able to skate on the ice tomorrow.

"Just thinking," I say, and he sits in front of me. This whole month has flown by, one day into the next, yet I felt stuck. I spent Christmas with my parents at their house since it was easy for everyone. I made an excuse to bail out early, landing on the twenty-fourth and leaving the twenty-fifth at night. I spent Christmas night lying on my couch watching the lights on the tree, wondering if she was all by herself or if she was out with friends or maybe even with Grandma Nancy.

"Well, the way you are looking at that phone, it looks like bad news," he says, sitting in front of me. "What's up with you?" I look up at him. "Your mother says something is wrong with you, and I told her she was wrong." He puts his foot on top of his other leg. "Seeing you now, I think she might be right."

"I think I fucked up, Dad," I tell him, and he just looks at me, waiting. "I …" I start to say and rub my hands over my face. "I don't even know where to start, to be honest."

"They say starting at the beginning is the best." My mother walks in, carrying a tray with coffee on it.

"I thought you might need something to drink," she says and goes over to sit down next to my father.

"You were right," my father says, kissing her head and putting an arm around her shoulder. "Now out with it," he says to me, and I tell them the story. From meeting her four years ago to chasing her. To the date with Grandma Nancy that had my mother laughing so hard she was crying to the ex-husband opening the door.

"So you just let her leave?" my mother asks, wiping the corner of her eyes with a tissue. "You just let the love of your life leave without going after her?"

"Idiot," my father says. "What is wrong with you?"

"She lied to me." I try to tell them my side.

"She was afraid to tell you the truth. She came here with her heart on her sleeve, and you let her leave," my mother says, shaking her head. "And it's been a month?" she shrieks. "A month."

I put my hands on the top of my head. "I know, Mom. I just don't know what to tell her."

"I would start with I've been an idiot," my father cuts in, and my mother nods.

"And my parents raised me to be better than this," my mother adds.

I stand, frustrated because they are right, but then scared that when I finally do go to her, she'll tell me that she doesn't feel the same way. That it was a one-way street, and I was the only one who felt it. "What if," I start to say, and my mother holds up her hands.

"What if I didn't say yes to your father all those years ago? What if you don't tell her how you feel and regret it for the rest of your life? What if she's the one?" my mother asks, and I don't answer her because I can't. "Son, you have one life to live. Don't you want to live it with a love that's so big it fills your soul?"

She doesn't say anything after that, and neither does my father. They just sit there and change the subject. The next day is crazy, getting on the ice with my family arriving, and then having a team meeting. I go through the motions and smile when I need to smile. The whole time, I'm thinking of Layla, and my heart feels tight in my chest. My house is full to the brim with my sisters and brothers and all their kids. It's something I've always loved yet now feels void. New Year's Eve comes, and my family opts out of the team party to stay home. They kiss me goodbye when I leave and tell me they will see me tomorrow.

The whole team is staying at the hotel tonight. I walk into the hotel, and there is movement everywhere. People are everywhere, and when I check in, I try to make it out of the lobby before someone sees me.

Three hours later, I'm slipping on a suit jacket and making my way downstairs. The ballroom is decorated in the team colors, and there are hats all around the room. The music is already pumping, and the kids are running around free. I spot a couple of people I know and say hello, then walk over to the bar where I order a water.

"Hey." I hear from beside me, and see that it's Becca.

"Hey, yourself," I say, leaning in and kissing her cheek. "You look nice."

"Do I?" she says, looking down at her black dress. "It's a big night."

"It's a big week," I say to her.

"You ready for tomorrow?" she asks, and I nod my head.

"As ready as I'll ever be," I tell her, and she smiles.

"Perfect," she says, grabbing a glass of champagne from a passing waiter. "Now if you will excuse me, I see Nico." She smirks at me. "I love ruffling his feathers."

I shake my head. Becca is known to be cutthroat, and she doesn't care whose balls she has to squeeze in order to get the best contract for her player. It's why she's got the best client list around.

I watch her walk away and then see Manning coming

my way. "You look like you're in a great mood." I laugh when he glares.

He looks around to make sure we are alone. "She booked a room for our son to sleep in by himself." He shakes his head. "The kid is seven." He orders a water, and the two of us stand here watching the room get fuller as the minutes go by. "We should mingle," he says, and I nod, pushing away from the bar and stopping when I see four of the rookies together.

"Are you boys staying out of trouble?" I ask them, and they just smirk at me. I remember what it's like to be them. They are thinking about the game tomorrow, but they are also thinking about banging most of the girls here. Looking around, I see so many girls all of a sudden when a blonde comes over our way.

"Oh, shit." I hear Patrick say, then he looks at me. "I'm so sorry."

I don't have time to ask him what he means by that because the girl is right beside me. "Miller, this is my sister, Kimberly," he says to me. "She is your biggest fan."

I smile at the girl in front of me, and her face lights up. "I am," she says to me. "I mean, my brother is good and all, but he's not the best."

"Kimberly," Patrick says. "I'm right here."

I laugh now and hold out my hand. "It's nice to meet you, Kimberly."

"I should get a picture," Patrick says. "Do you mind?"

"No, of course not," I say, but I really do mind. Suddenly, I want to get out of here, but she puts her hand around my waist, and I don't move. I pose for the picture, and then she turns to look at me after.

"Thank you so much for the picture," she says. "You are having a great year."

"It's been great so far," I say. "Now, let's hope we can beat Nashville tomorrow."

"I have no doubt you will," she says. "I'm sorry about my little brother," she says, and I laugh.

"He thought by telling you that you were my favorite, it would embarrass me." She laughs now. "I bet him fifty dollars that I would ask you to dance." I look at her. "I actually bet them all fifty bucks." She points back at her brother and his four friends.

I laugh now. "You did what?"

She shrugs. "I wasn't going to let them tease me without egging them on. I know this is totally awkward, and I'm sorry, but would you dance with me? Even if it's for half a song." I take a deep breath. "It's two hundred dollars."

"Sure," I say, walking to the dance floor. I put my hand around her waist and look over at the guys with their mouth hanging open. "You boys better pay the lady." They all groan, and I chuckle.

I feel eyes looking at me as I turn around on the dance floor and listen to Kimberly tell me about her work. My eyes fly up, and I see her just looking at me. My heart fills my whole chest as I take her in. My feet don't move now as I stand mesmerized by her. She is more beautiful than she is in my dreams. She looks like she lost weight, and I wonder if she's been sick. Her gold sparkly skirt hugs her hips. The white long-sleeve shirt is tucked into the skirt. She lifts her hand to say hello to me and smiles at me, but the smile doesn't reach her eyes.

"Are you okay?" Kimberly's voice makes me look down at her. *Oh my God*, I think to myself, *she must think I'm here with her*. I look up and see her walking to Candace as she smiles at her and hugs her. I see her going to Ralph and giving him a hug also, and I want to run over to her and take her in my arms. I want to ask her how she has been doing. I want to tell her that I have thought about her every single day. I want to tell her that it doesn't fucking matter that she was married. I want to tell her all that, and I want all of that with her. "Um, Miller." Kimberly laughs now uncomfortably. My eyes fly back to Kimberly. "Do you have to go?"

"Um," I say and then look back up when I hear Nico beside me.

"Hey, Miller, can I borrow you for a minute?" he says, and I just smile at Kimberly.

"Okay, but first, I have to do something," I tell him, and he shakes his head.

"I need you, Ralph, and Manning for a photo op," Nico says, looking around and spotting Manning and Ralph, who nod at him when he motions with his hand. I look around the room and see her mingling and saying hello to everyone. Her purse is in one hand while she shakes with the other hand. Her hair is longer than I remember. She must feel me watching her because she turns back around, and for a split second, our eyes meet again. I wonder if she can see how much I miss her. I wonder if she knows that I spent all of Christmas Day thinking about her. I spent the past month building up the courage to go to her, hoping she didn't slam the door in my face.

"What do you need?" Manning says, and I turn my head, hoping that this goes fast so I can get to her. My hands itch to touch her if just for a second. My heart yearns to just be next to her.

"We need to get a couple of shots of the four of us," Nico says. "Let's go over there." He points at the photo station setup.

I don't know how long I spend there posing for pictures. The girls have us changing places and then switching around, and I am about to snap when she finally says, "I think I got it."

Without listening to anything else, I just walk to the dance floor and look around the room for her. I turn in a circle as I look for her everywhere. I finally spot Candace walking back into the venue and run to her. "Where is Layla?" I ask. She looks down and looks back up again, and I can see the tears in her eyes.

"She's gone," she says, and my stomach sinks. "I just walked her out." Her voice is low. "She had a headache." I nod at her, and I know she wants to say more, but she doesn't.

"Okay." I turn around and make my way out of the room. Walking out of the building, I hope that maybe the universe will work in my favor for once, but it won't be tonight.

I walk back into the hotel and make my way up to my room. There are people everywhere, and thankfully no one stops me. Taking the card out of my pocket, I hold it up to the lock, and the door opens. I walk over and sit on the bed in the dark room. The only light coming inside is from the open curtains.

I put my head back and get up, shrugging off my jacket when I hear the sound of people yelling and counting down. Then the sound of fireworks going off out of my window. I walk over and look outside. "Happy New Year, gorgeous," I say to the sky.

My phone pings in my pocket, and my heart speeds up thinking it could be her, but it's just from my parents saying Happy New Year.

I open my Instagram to post when I see her picture. She is right next to Grandma Nancy. Her eyes look wet from crying, and the tip of her nose is red. I wonder how old this picture is. I look down and see it was posted twenty-seven seconds ago. I also see that it's from Grandma Nancy's account. I started following her the day after our "date." I also see there are more photos, and when I swipe right, I have to sit down. It's another selfie, but this time, she is looking at the camera with her thumb under her eye, wiping a tear as she tries to smile. I notice it's the same shirt she was wearing tonight. I can't stop staring at the picture. I can't stop thinking of how she looked tonight. My chest tightens even more when I see the caption.

New Year… New Beginnings

THIRTY-FIVE

Layla

I WALK OVER to the outfit I wore last night. The outfit I picked out especially for the night. I was going to bite the bullet and go to him. I bend over, grabbing the dress and the top, and throw it in my walk-in closet in the corner.

I picked out the outfit and did my hair. My stomach was in my throat as I made my way there. My hands shook when I walked into the ballroom. My eyes found him right away, and my heart broke when I saw him dancing with someone else. I lifted my hands when he looked at me and smiled. In the end, I want him to be happy, and if she makes him happy, then I have to accept it.

I left within ten minutes. Candace saw my face and knew I needed to get out of there. She ushered me into a cab, and I went to Grandma's house. She opened the door for me, her smile dropping off her face when I tried to block my sob with my hand. I toasted the New Year with her and made a decision that it was time for me to leave. When I got home, the emptiness screamed out, and I knew deep in my heart that I couldn't stay there.

Grabbing my jeans, I slide them on and huff out when I see they are a bit loose. I walk over to the bag in the corner and take out the Dallas jersey that the radio station gave me for today. My job is to interview the players' families and get the inside scoop on how they prepared for the day.

I'm already dreading it. I grab my press badge and slip on my heeled boots.

When I arrive, I park where they told me to park and look around to see if I see Candace or Ari anywhere. They scan my badge, and I put my phone in my back pocket, where my ID is with my credit card.

"Hey," I say when I get to the radio station booth that is set up there. They are on the air right now, and Tony waves at me and then says my name on air.

"Okay, where do I go for this?" I ask the woman who is holding the clipboard, and she looks and finds my name.

"You are going to go through that tunnel there." She points at the white tunnel. "Families have been told and are already there." I grab the mic from her. "Press record on here." She shows me how it works, and I walk away, amazed at how they transformed the football field into a hockey rink. People are going crazy behind the scenes to make sure it's perfect. I look up in the stands and seeing that fans have started to trickle in.

I walk into the tunnel and spot Candace, who is with Ari. Ari claps her hands the second she sees me. She is dressed in a Dallas jersey with her dad's name on the back, and Candace has two green bows in her hair. "Are you excited?" I say, grabbing Ari from her and kissing her. "You are the prettiest little girl," I say to her, and she points at Candace, calling her mama.

I pick the microphone to my mouth. "What did your dad do to get ready?" I ask her, and she just says dada. "Okay, Auntie Layla has to get her work done so she can enjoy the game."

"How are you feeling?" Candace asks, and I shrug.

"Shitty," I tell her the truth. "Okay, I see some family members." I hand Ari back to her. "I'll catch up with you later," I say, turning around and seeing a family I've never seen before.

"Hi, guys," I say, smiling, "I'm with the radio station, and if you don't mind, can I ask you some questions?" They are all wearing Dallas jerseys, but I can't see the name on the back.

"Sure," the woman says.

"How excited are you guys to be here?" I ask, and she smiles.

"So excited. We never thought you could have ice outside in Dallas," the woman says.

"You and me both," I say, laughing. "It's Dallas."

"Right," I say. "How different is this to when you brought them to their games when they were younger?"

Her eyes light up. "He hated hockey," she says.

"I'm sorry, who is your son?" I ask her at the same

time I see him walking toward us.

"Hey, guys," he says and then bends to kiss the woman on the cheek. "Mom, Dad," he says and then looks at me. "Layla." He says my name, and I just blink because the words are stuck in my throat. "Guys, this is Layla."

"It's nice to meet you," the woman says, and I look at her and smile.

"Thank you guys for answering my questions," I say, trying to get away from him as fast as I can. "Good luck today," I tell him, and my heart is beating so hard and so loud that I think I'm having a heart attack. This has to be it. I turn and walk out of the tunnel and enter a random tunnel. Putting my hands on my knees, I try to get my breathing back to normal. "I can't do this," I say to myself. I walk as fast as I can to the tent and hand her back the microphone. "Sorry, I'm not feeling well." I turn toward my car, running most of the way. The faster I get away from them, the better I will feel.

Only once I get home do I breathe out a sigh of relief. I walk to the couch and turn the television on, seeing the players taking the ice. I lie down as the tears roll down my face. The camera goes from player to player, and I close my eyes when they stay on Miller. His face ready for the game.

They drop the puck, and one minute in, Nashville makes a sloppy pass that gets intercepted by Miller, who takes it and scores one-handed. He throws up his leg and yells out. While Manning and Ralph skate to him and celebrate with him. He skates to the bench as he goes down the line.

He is on fire for the whole game, and I will go on record saying that this is his best game ever. He finished it with three goals and two assists. They skate to the middle of the ice and hold up their sticks for the crowd. They skate off, and I watch them call Manning for the third star, Ralph for the second, and I smile as I look at the television, my heart aching in my chest, as Miller skates out to accept his first star. Turning off the television, I make my way back to my bed, lying down and staring at the white wall. The tears come freely now. "Tomorrow," I say to myself. "You are not going to cry."

I hear a soft knock and turn toward the doorway, wondering whether that's what it was when it sounds again. I slip out of bed and wrap a sweater around myself. Another knock comes at the door, and I turn on the light and unlock the door.

I stand here now with my mouth hanging open. Miller is there with his hands holding my doorframe. He looks like he just stepped out of the shower. His suit fits him perfectly, and I see he's not wearing the suit jacket.

"Miller," I whisper his name, and I wonder if I'm dreaming. "What are you doing here?" I ask him.

"Did you love me?" he asks, and I look at him. "In the time we were together, did you love me?" I shake my head and see the defeated look in his eyes. "That's all I needed to know," he says, turning to walk away.

"You asked me if I loved you," I say, my voice louder, and I close the sweater, feeling the cold go through my body. He stands there in front of me. The man who owns my heart, the man who I will do anything for, the man who I let go so he can have his perfect life.

"Yeah," he says, putting his hands in his pockets, and I see his tears now.

"Well, the answer to that is no," I tell him. "I didn't love," I say, putting my arms around my stomach. "I love you."

"What?" he whispers.

"I love you, Miller. Everything about you, from the way you do the sweetest things for me to making sure I'm always okay. To just holding my hand and showing you how a woman needs to be treated. Showing me that it's okay to open your heart," I say, not even caring that I'm crying or that in two point three seconds, I'm going to be a blubbering mess. "I love you so much it hurts to see you. I love you so much that I let you go. I set you free so you can find that woman who has not been divorced and who is pure."

"What the fuck?" he says out. "A woman who is pure?"

"Yeah!" I shout out. "One who hasn't been tainted by divorce. That can be yours and yours alone!"

"I don't give a flying fuck if you were divorced a thousand times," he says, running his hands through his hair. "I care that you lied to me."

"Why do you even care now?" I say, angry that we have to hash this out. Angry that he is here and instead of being swept away by him, I'm feeling more pain than I did before. "It's been a month now. You blocked me." I point at myself. "You moved on. Just let me be," I say, grabbing the door for support. "In a month, I'll be gone, and we never have to see each other again."

"What?" he says. "You're leaving?" He puts his hand to his chest. "You can't leave. Did you not get my text?"

"No," I say, shaking my head.

It's his turn to talk. "I love you so much that my chest hurts," he starts telling me. "I love you so much that I don't sleep in my bed." I open my mouth. "I love you so much that I kept trying to think of ways to make it up to you. I kept trying to come up with ways to get you back. I thought that I would do it the next day, but I kept thinking that if you wanted me, you would have come to me."

"I came to you!" I shout, wiping a tear away. "I came to you." I walk out now. "You let me go."

"If you give me a chance," he says. "I'll never let you go again." His voice breaks at the end.

I put my hand in front of my mouth and sob out. He takes two steps to me, and I'm enveloped in his arms. His arms wrap around my waist as he picks me up, and my legs and arms automatically wrap around him. I bury my face in his neck, smelling him in. "What took you so long?" I ask him quietly.

"Fucking Google," he says, and I throw my head back, and I laugh but only for a minute because his lips find mine.

THIRTY-SIX

Miller

My tongue slips into her mouth, and I forget about everything. My heart soars in my chest, and I pull back from her mouth and just hold her in my arms. She lays her head on my shoulder and buries her face in my neck.

Walking into the dark house, I go straight to her bedroom. "I missed you." I hear her whisper when I sit on the bed. For the whole day, I was strung up, snapping at everyone—my parents, my siblings, journalists, the equipment manager, just about anyone who tried to approach me. Then I walked out and saw her laughing with my parents, and all I wanted was to hold her by my side and tell them that this was her. This was the woman who I was in love with. But she ran off, somehow disgusted by me, and all I could think about is that the last time she saw me, I was with another woman.

"I missed you so much," I say to her, and I suddenly

want the lights on. I want to see her. I lean forward and turn on the lamp beside her bed, illuminating the room in a soft yellow. "We have to talk," I tell her, enough with the silence between us.

She is about to climb off my lap, but I tighten my hold around her. She looks into my eyes, and I can't help but lean in just to touch her lips. Her hand comes up to rub the scruff on my face. "Hi," she whispers, leaning in again just to touch my lips with hers. "You're here," she says, and I see a tear forming in the corner of her eye. She kisses me again. "I'm not dreaming."

"You're not dreaming, gorgeous," I say. She hangs her head and buries her face in my chest. My hands find her face and pick it up so she looks at me. The tears rolling down her cheeks kill me. "No more tears."

"I never wanted to keep it from you," she says softly. "I just …" She shrugs. "I didn't want you to judge me."

"For starters, I don't give a flying fuck that you were married. I actually should send him a fruit basket or something." Her eyebrows close together. "If he wasn't such an asshole, I wouldn't be here with you."

"I mean, if you put it like that, we should send him flowers, too." She tries to joke and sniffles.

"The second part, I forgot about you being married five minutes after you left my house." I push her hair behind her ear. "I followed you home," I tell her, and she opens her eyes. "I should have come after you. I should have parked the car and got out and had the balls to talk to you." I swallow the lump in my throat. "But I was scared you'd tell me you didn't love me. I was afraid

I was the only one who felt this. I was afraid that after everything was said and done, you didn't want me like that."

"I know it's too late," she says, "but I was going to tell you that weekend. I couldn't continue like that. It was just too heavy on my heart, and you needed to know the truth."

"Just so you know," I say, "I loved you then. The time away from you, it killed me slowly inside. Not to come home to you. Not to speak to you. I used to listen to you every single day. I would close my eyes and pretend you were beside me. I was a shell of a man. I spent Christmas with you on my mind. I drove by here when I got back from my parents', and the lights were off, so I thought you were out."

"I spent it with Grandma, but then I came home and cried." She smiles shyly. "I cried a lot this month. I would go to bed and wake up sobbing. It was too hard. Watching you on television every night and then talking about you as if you were a stranger, as if my heart wasn't broken. I just couldn't do it anymore. I was going to ask to be transferred tomorrow."

The thought that she would have just left without me knowing is like a kick in the balls.

"I was so stupid." I kiss her lips. "Tonight after the game, I skated off the ice, and I went looking for you. I almost ran down a couple of reporters, and then I found some lady who works with the radio station, and she said you left because you weren't feeling well. I played the whole game so you could be proud of me. I played, hoping you would see me, and when I got off, all I wanted was you. I wanted to hug you and kiss you. I needed you by my side." I look down. "I never moved on." I repeat the words that she threw in my face. "I was dancing with Patrick's sister. When I saw you walk in, my heart … it just started beating. You were so beautiful I had no words, and then you smiled and walked away, and I was just stuck. All I could think was I had to get to you, but then you were gone."

"I went there to try to win you back," she tells me, and my breath hitches in my chest. "I was going to tell you that I love you and hoped that you loved me, too. But then I just … I …" She brings her hand up and rubs away a tear with the back of her thumb. "I wanted you to be happy, so if she made you happy, I had to accept it."

"You," I tell her. "You are my happy. You are my everything. You." I kiss her lips. "I'm sorry," I say softly. "I'm so sorry that I wasted this whole month."

"I'm not," she says, and she smiles. "I don't think I would have known how much I love you had this not happened. I knew that what I was feeling was love. I knew that I was teetering on uncharted territory. We just clicked so easily, and it wasn't even a struggle. It just came so naturally that I thought it was all in my head, and then I didn't have you, and I knew." She puts her hands on my chest. "I knew that you …" She smiles as two tears roll down her cheeks. "Had wormed your way into my heart." She laughs and shakes her head. "I know it's crazy to even say. It's only been a little while, and well …"

I grab her face in my hands. "I get it. I know now that you are a piece of me. I know that I want to be with you all the time. I want you to be there when I get home, and I want to wake up with you next to me. I want to hold your hand and take you out. I want them to know that there is no me without you."

"Make love to me," she says. I peel her sweater off her and toss it aside. Her tank top is a little bit loose on her.

I just stare at her, and she hugs her waist. "I know I lost a bit of weight."

"Nothing that a few carbs and a little love can't cure." I smile at her and then look up. "I don't have a condom." I want to kick my own ass right now.

"I haven't been with anyone," she says and then looks down. I can imagine what's going through her mind.

I put my finger under her chin and raise her head until she is looking in my eyes. "There has been no one." I see her breathe a sigh of relief. "Are you on the pill?" I ask, and I suddenly realize I don't give a shit if she gets pregnant.

"I am," she says, and I slide her tank top off, tossing it over to where her sweater is. She pulls my shirt apart, and I see a button fly. "I missed you," she says. Wrapping her arms around my shoulders, she squeezes our bare chests together. My lips crash onto hers as I spin us, placing her down on her back. Her legs open for me, and I sit back to grab her shorts and peel them over her hips when she arches her back.

She lies there in front of me naked, and my mouth

waters. "Every single day, I would go to bed thinking of your face. Every day, I would fall asleep to my memories of holding you. Of you saying my name." I unbutton my pants, pulling them down as she just watches me.

I lean forward now with my cock in my hand, rubbing it up and down her slit, and I ever so slowly slide into her. We both moan when I'm all the way in her, and her legs tighten around my waist. My mouth goes to her as I make love to her. Soft, slow, and savoring every fucking moment. "I love you." I breathe out when she lets go of my lips and kisses my neck. "I love you," I repeat over and over again, pounding into her faster now, harder now.

"More." She arches her back and begs me for more, and I give it to her. I give her everything.

"Mine," I say as I slam into her. "Fucking mine," I say right before we both jump off the ledge.

THIRTY-SEVEN

Layla

WHEN I WAKE, I'm surrounded in warmth and then feel a hand on my breast. Opening my eyes, I smile when I realize I'm cocooned in his arms. *It's not a dream.* Throughout the whole night, I kept waking up just to make sure he was still here and that I didn't dream he came back.

Seeing him at the door was one thing, but hearing the words that came out of his mouth and having him say he loved me was so much more than I could ever imagine. He told me he loved me over and over again all night long.

"Morning," I say, turning in his arms. I hook my leg over his hip, leaving me open and right on top of his cock. "Hmm, and what a good morning it is," I say, sliding down. He moans and rolls onto his back. His hands grasp my hips as I ride him, then move up to my tits where he cups them and rolls my nipples. I look down, seeing all the bite marks along with the little red dots from his beard. My hands rest on his chest while I move up and down. He waits for me to come before he flips me over like a rag doll. My legs and arms wrap around him, wanting to be even closer. My muscles scream as I moan out again, and he buries himself deep in me coming again.

He collapses on top of me and then turns us to the side to take his weight off me. "Morning," he says, kissing my neck, and I cuddle into his chest. My stomach growls, and he laughs. "Well, I guess that means we should get up and head over to my house. My parents are expecting me."

I try to relax the thumping of my heart as he slowly peels himself off me. He gets up, and I follow him into the bathroom. He stands by the sink with the warm water on as I start the shower and step in. "What should I wear?" I ask, putting my face up under the water spray. "Should I wear a dress or jeans?" I look over at him to see him leaning against the sink, looking at me.

"It doesn't matter what you wear. You look gorgeous in anything," he says with a smirk. I see his cock getting ready for another round, so I hold up my hand.

"We are not going to be late because we had another round." He laughs at me as I get out and wrap myself in a towel and rush out of the room. I step into the closet and look at all my options. "What color should I wear?"

"Pack a bag!" he shouts.

I slip on a black pair of jeans and pull on a soft pink long-sleeved cashmere sweater over my bra. The high neck covers any marks he could have left on me. I walk back into the bedroom and see him already dressed with his pants and shirt on. "Does this give off the 'I love your son please like me' vibes?" I turn around. "Or should I wear a longer sweater that covers more?"

He laughs now. "That looks fine." He starts to button his shirt and realizes four buttons are missing. "Did you pack a bag?"

"Yeah," I say. "When do you leave?" I ask him, hating it already.

"I leave for eight days next Wednesday, so pack for a week," he tells me, and I just nod at him. If he had told me this before, I would have glared at him and told him that he was not the boss of me. I mean, he is still not the boss of me, but now, I don't even care, to be honest. I just want to be with him.

He eyes my bag when I walk out of the closet carrying it. "I said eight days," he says as he grabs the bag from me.

"I plan to be naked for most of those days, so I only need a couple of things." I shrug, and he comes over and kisses me.

"I like the whole naked idea," he says. Grabbing my hand, we start to walk out of the house, and I stop.

"I should take my car," I say. "I have to work on Monday."

"I have five cars," he tells me. "You can take one of mine."

"That makes no sense." We just stare at each other because we're at an impasse.

"We are going to be late, and you know my parents are not going to believe that we are late because we got into a fight. Especially after I haven't seen you in a month." I open my mouth to argue with him. "You do have that glow about you." I put my hands to my cheeks. "You look gorgeous. Now let's go before I take you back inside, and we're really, really late." He opens the car door for me, and I walk to him, tilting my head up and waiting for him to kiss me. He kisses my lips, and I get into his car and watch him walk around the car. I look out the window as we make our way to his house. The butterflies in my stomach are uncontrollable at this point.

"I legit think I'm going to vomit," I say, putting a hand to my stomach as soon as he pulls up to his house and parks in the garage. He leans over to kiss me softly and then gets out of the car, walking around and opening my door. When he holds his hand out, I grab it to get out of the car. "I'm not kidding," I say as he practically pulls me to the front door.

"Gorgeous." He cups my face in his hands. "They are going to love you. How can they not?" he says, opening the door.

Closing my eyes, I breathe through my nose and can smell the food cooking already. I stop walking. "I didn't get her flowers or a cake."

"What?" he asks, and I can hear talking coming from the kitchen.

"I'm showing up empty-handed," I say, starting to panic. "Who does that? It's like rule book 101."

"Says who?" he asks, folding his arms over his chest.

"Google," I tell him, and he throws his head back and laughs so loud I hear the talking in the kitchen stop. "Great, now I can't escape."

"Where the hell were you going to go?" he asks me, and before I can answer, I hear a woman's voice.

"Oh, you're here," she says. I look over and see a woman wearing jeans and a sweater with an apron over it. "The food is almost ready." She walks to us. "Sweetheart!" she shouts over her shoulder. "Layla and Miller are here." She stops in front of me, and I want to tell her I'm sorry about taking off on her yesterday. I also want to tell her that I'm sorry I didn't tell her who I was. God, could there have been a more awkward time than right now? The only thing I can do is smile at her.

"Mom," Miller says, putting his arm around me, most likely to keep me from bolting. "This is Layla. Layla, this is my mom, Sara." I'm about to answer her when I hear another voice.

"Oh, good, honey." Turning my head, I'm shocked to hear my grandmother's voice as she rushes over to hug me. "You are here." She then turns to Miller and winks at him. "Well, well, well, we meet again." She kisses his cheek. "I was just telling your parents about our first date."

My mouth opens as I see Miller's father looking at his son. "You ran away from her." He points at him, and I just stand here.

"What's going on right now?" I ask, hoping someone answers me.

"Miller thought it would be a good idea for us to have breakfast together," Grandma Nancy says with a huge smile.

The oven beeps just then, making Sara turn to look at his dad. "The casserole is ready," she says. "Sweetheart, let's get the table set." With a smile, he follows her into the kitchen.

"I have to say I'm a bit disappointed in you, Miller," Grandma says, turning to follow his parents. "I thought after a whole month of not seeing each other that she would have trouble walking today. Or even limping." She shakes her head.

"I'll have you know she was." With a shriek, I slap a hand over his mouth before he says something I don't want my grandmother or his parents to hear. She throws her head back and laughs out loud as she walks to the kitchen.

"I can't believe you invited my grandmother over," I tell him, and he just shrugs.

"I figured you would be nervous as it is, so having someone else on your side wouldn't hurt," he says, and I just shake my head.

"Have I told you that I love you?" I ask him, and he bends to kiss me.

"I want to go change," he says, pulling me with him into his bedroom. He puts the bag in the closet, and I walk over and toss my purse on the chair. Looking around, I see scraps of paper on his side table. Upon closer inspection, they are the notes I left him each time I left. I sit on the bed and open the first one.

"You kept them?" I look at him when he walks out of his closet, wearing jeans and a shirt.

"It was my last lifeline to you," he says, sitting down on the bed next to me and wrapping his arms around me. "I would read them at night."

I wipe the tear away from my eye and look at him. "I love you," I say softly, and he leans in and kisses my lips softly.

"Knock, knock, knock," his father says, sticking his head in the room.

"The food is on the table," he says, looking at us. "Nancy just put her special brownies in the oven."

I jump up at the same time that Miller jumps up. "Um," I start to say.

"They smell very earthy," he says, and I run out of the room to the kitchen.

Sara and Nancy stand there, laughing at something. "Oh, good, you guys are finally ready," Grandma says. "I just put the brownies in."

"Oh, no, no, no, no, no," I say, shaking my head and walking to the oven. "Grandma," I say to her. "How could you bring this here?"

"Why wouldn't I bring them here? I took an Uber," she says. "Plus, it's to help you relax."

"I am not eating these," I say, pointing at the oven and then turn to see Sara just looking at me while Miller and his father join us.

"Um, Miller." I say his name to get his attention. "Would you perhaps, I don't know, Uber eats us some cupcakes or something?" I look at him wide-eyed, and he just nods.

"Wait," Sara says. "Why can't we eat the brownies?"

I look at Miller. "I told you this was going to be bad," I tell him, and I blink away tears. He rushes over to me and puts his arm around me. "This is."

"I don't see what the fuss is all about," Grandma says.

"Those are her special space cakes," Sara says. "And I, for one, was excited for that."

"I love your son," I say. "Like a lot." She just smiles at me, and Grandma Nancy puts her hands together in front of her mouth. "But I've been divorced, and I know it's like I'm tainted. But I really do love him, and if I could go back …" I wipe away the lone tear that's escaped from my eye.

It's Sara's turn now to throw her head back and laugh. "Honey, you aren't tainted just because you got divorced." She comes to me now. "No one is tainted. It just means they have to search a bit harder to find their missing lid." I arch an eyebrow. "Every pot has a lid. Some are too big, and some are too small, but then you find the right one." She pulls me in and whispers, "Thank you for loving him as you do." I look at Miller. "And for giving love one more chance."

EPILOGUE ONE

MILLER

Six months later

"I CAN'T BELIEVE it's almost time for the season to start," I say from the middle of the sunbed. The soft white curtains dance around us from the warm breeze. I'm lying in the middle, wearing my shorts as Layla lies beside me in her bikini. Her legs are intertwined with mine, and she has her arm lying across my stomach.

"I don't know if I want to go back," she groans as we watch the soft waves hit the white sand. We've been in Turks and Caicos for over three weeks, just the two of us. I rented us a private villa right on the beach away from everyone else. "Are you excited about the new season?" she asks as her finger draws figure eights on my chest.

"I think if we get better, we might even make a play for the cup next year," I tell her. We finished fifth in our division and were knocked out in the second round by St.

Louis, who went on to win the cup.

"I think so, too," she says, looking up at me now. Her face looks sun-kissed. "Want to go into the water with me?" she asks me, sitting up, and I just shake my head. She gets off the bed and walks down to the water. My hand reaches behind me under the pillow, grabbing the red box that was placed there by our butler after lunch.

Rising, I walk to the shore, admiring the sunset on the horizon. She turns around and smiles at me as she walks out of the ocean. "Was the water nice?" I ask, holding a towel open for her.

"It would have been better if you came in with me." She tilts her head up so I can kiss her. In the six months we've been together, the only time we've been apart is when I'm on the road. She moved all her stuff into my place a month ago when she finally sold her house. "Love you," she says after I kiss her. It's crazy how in love with her I am. It's even crazier that I got her to fall in love with me.

"I love you," I tell her, the red box in my shorts getting heavier and heavier. "You know that, right?" She looks at me with a strange look on her face. "I mean, I hope you do."

"Umm …" she says. "I kinda have a feeling." She laughs. "I think. Is that a trick question?"

"Do me a favor," I say, handing her my phone. "Ask Google if I love you."

"What?" She laughs. "How in the hell is Google going to know that answer?"

"Just would you do it," I urge her, my palm getting

sweaty. I wanted to propose to her as soon as the sun started setting because there were candles that spelled out "marry me."

"Fine," she says. "Does Miller love his girlfriend?"

"Read what it says," I tell her, hoping like fuck this worked.

"It says Miller Adams fell head over heels in love with his girlfriend, Layla Paterson, over four years ago. But he had to get his head out of his ass to prove to her that she was the one for him." She laughs now, looking at me, and I just watch her. She goes back to reading. "Layla Paterson once paid twenty-five thousand dollars to go on a date with Miller. It was on that date that Miller knew she might be the one." She looks at me. "Is that so?" She shakes her head and goes back to reading. "Miller had to practically beg Layla to move in with him, and when she did, he knew there was only one thing left to do." I get down on one knee now, but she doesn't stop reading. "On a warm day in the middle of Turks and Caicos, Miller got down on one ..." She stops reading and looks at me. "Oh my God."

"Layla Paterson," I say, "will you marry me?" I open the red box to show her the four-carat square diamond with the infinity band of diamonds. "Will you be my wife and love me forever?" She puts the back of her hand to her mouth and looks over my shoulder at the Marry Me sign now lit up bright. "Make me the luckiest man around and be my wife."

She nods her head at me as she sobs out. "Yes," she says, launching herself at me. Kissing her lips, I rise and swing her around in a circle.

"I knew Google was always right," I tell her, and she throws her head back and laughs.

EPILOGUE TWO

Layla

Six months later

"OH MY GOD, what is that smell?" I say, coming into our bedroom. Miller's lying in the middle of the bed dressed in shorts and a shirt that look wet.

"That would be me." He lifts his head. "I didn't shower after practice."

I scrunch up my face and lean against the doorframe. "Why the hell not?" I ask. "And why would you lie on our bed?"

"I was exhausted," he says, sitting up. "Come sit with me."

"No." I shake my head. "You smell like cheese. If you make me throw up"—I point at him—"I'm going to hit you." I'm almost at my twelve-week mark. Almost at the point when we can tell people although a couple of people have guessed it since I don't drink wine anymore.

Grandma Nancy felt it in her bones. Apparently, it also didn't help that I threw up on her shoes.

It happened by accident when I forgot to take a pill and then doubled up the next day. I knew there was a chance, and well, wild horses couldn't keep him out of me, especially since he'd just gotten back from a four-day road trip. When my period didn't come, I just thought it was a mistake, but the seven pregnancy tests I took told me otherwise. I was scared he would say he wasn't ready, but instead, he insisted I marry him that weekend, which was beyond ridiculous since it was Thursday. Yet he flew his parents in on Friday, and on Sunday afternoon in the middle of the backyard, I married him. I look up at the picture hanging in the middle of the room. Us on our wedding day, walking down the aisle after we said I do. The camera had caught me laughing while he was kissing my ring. It was beautiful. He was beautiful. Our life was beautiful.

"Now, can you please go and take a shower?"

"Will you come with me?" he asks, and I peel my shirt off. "That's my girl."

"Actually, it's the hormones in me that will not let me say no," I tell him over my shoulder. "Who knew getting knocked up would make me even hornier?"

"According to Google, it's the estrogen and progesterone in you," he says, and I turn the water on.

"Whatever it is," I say, "I need you now." I pull up his shirt. "First, I'm going to soap you up and get that smell off you, and then it's on," I tell him. He laughs, picking me up and placing me in the shower.

He washes while he teases me, and I can't hold back. I put my foot on the bench and play with myself while he watches. I'm about to come when he picks me up and slides me down his cock. My head goes back, and in a matter of seconds, I'm coming all over him.

He gets out of the shower before I do, leaving me to wash my hair. Once I turn off the water and dry myself off, I walk into my walk-in closet. Hanging my towel, I slide on a pair of panties, then step into his closet and grab one of his T-shirts.

"What did you want to eat for supper?" I ask him as I walk out of the closet and shake my wet hair out of the towel.

"Oh my God," Miller says. "Oh my God," he says again as he looks at something on his phone. Then his eyes come up to mine. He shakes his head, and then he dials someone. "Manning, it's me. Call me. Come here if you need to."

"What in the hell is going on?" I ask him. He turns his phone and gives it to me, and I gasp as I scroll through the picture with the caption.

Dallas captain is hot on the ice but apparently not hot enough to keep his wife satisfied. The captain's wife is seen here getting hot and heavy with an unnamed man in what looks to be someone's car. From the looks of it, she left him looking mighty happy.

www.ingramcontent.com/pod-product-compliance
Lightning Source LLC
Chambersburg PA
CBHW072044190726
48294CB00005B/1405